CONSIDER ME GONE

Time Shadows Book 1

JANE THORNLEY

1

That afternoon, the air hung with such humidity in the streets of New Orleans that Romy felt coated in syrup. Praline heat, she thought as she steadied her breathing—sticky and seductive.

The scent of brown sugar wafted from the open windows of the candy shops while rum cocktails flowed in the bars. Everything in the French Quarter simmered and boiled until it distilled into something rich, intoxicating, and far too addictive for a single taste.

"Is she real, Mommy?" Romy heard a little girl ask. From the corner of her eye, she could just see blond curls and big plastic sunglasses.

"She's a real person, Susie, just not a real angel," the mother said from somewhere to the right. "She's only pretending to be made of stone like those angel statues we saw on the big cemetery tour."

"Like playing make-believe?" the little girl asked.

"Yes, but for money, sweetheart. She's what is called a 'performance artist.' Some people do that when they can't get other kinds of work."

Irritation stabbed Romy just to the left of one fake wing. Well, what did she expect? It's not like the truth read any better: a doctoral student dressed like a kneeling angel trying to lure a ghost. No, she corrected, not a ghost, but a past life event. And in order to recreate exactly the right conditions, she had to stay focused.

People thought she was crazy kneeling as still as death in the summer heat. Surely she had to be mad to pose in these conditions? Traffic noises and conversation wrestled with her concentration. The heat leeched her energy. She'd knelt for nearly an hour with no results until weariness weighed her down and a headache loomed at the edges of her temples.

I'm drunk on this place, she thought. A sober person would have left town at the first sign of trouble. A sober person would never watch her career shatter into a thousand pieces, or push her body to extremes day and night. A sober person would never kneel perfectly still in the burning heat waiting to connect with a man who had been dead for centuries.

But she could not stop herself. She needed answers.

Maybe the migraine threatening like far-off thunder destroyed her concentration? Maybe she wasn't trying hard enough. Or maybe she was trying too hard.

Coins clinked in the little bowl at Romy's feet, but the moment she dipped her head in thanks, the headache detonated.

Startled by the sudden pain, she instinctively pressed her hands against her forehead and waited for the throb to pass. As she counted the seconds, the child's chatter receded along with the honking horns and traffic noises of the French Quarter.

She opened her eyes on a street immersed in a watery light that smeared her vision. Everything became foggy and indistinct. She blinked, stunned. Instead of exhaust fumes, she inhaled the pungent odor of dung. A horse whinnied nearby. Waves washed ashore from somewhere behind her, though she had been standing nowhere near the river.

She had crossed into the past at last. Her heart quickened and she readied herself for the encounter.

A man's voice speaking French rose out of the background. "Answer me, damn it! Are you a spy, is that it? Speak, why don't you?"

Dark hair plastered over a bruised forehead above a jaw clenched in pain. Blood soaked the linen of his shirt and she read agony in his eyes.

She tried to speak but couldn't. A roar of foreign thoughts and emotions whipped through her, none of them hers.

"Why have you done this?" he asked. "Why? Speak!"

Speak? She longed to scream her throat raw, to kick out at the world for the unfairness of everything. She knew that with a desperate certainty but couldn't fix on the reason why. Something in this long-ago lifetime had been lost and something remained in danger still.

"I am a soldier," she whispered at last, though neither the words nor the voice were hers. "A soldier does what must be done. Love and war should never mix, no?" Her voice rasped. "Is that not the soldier's creed? For once, it is the woman who is the warrior and the man the pawn."

She heard the pounding of hooves thundering down the path. They came! She had to escape. Hitching up her skirts, she turned to run, but as she did, the world around her burst into noise and motion and she felt herself falling forward. A hand shot out to catch her. Shrugging it away, she stumbled blindly on.

Only when she tripped over her gown and pitched into a skid across the pavement did reality hit. She had catapulted into the present as suddenly as she had fallen into the past.

"Mommy! Look, the Frozen Angel's fallen!" a child cried.

The Frozen Angel's fallen?

"Susie, hold Mommy's bag. Miss, are you all right? We were watching you and you started to run."

Romy blinked up into the concerned face of the woman—thirtyish with a cap of highlighted gold hair.

"You called out in another language. French, I think. I couldn't understand a word," the woman said. "You need a doctor."

"No!" Romy pushed herself up from the ground and gazed around her. "I mean, thank you, but please don't worry. I'm fine, really. Just a bit dizzy." Where had she been? She shook her head, trying to dislodge wisps of powerful emotion she didn't recognize. She gazed around at the busy street, overcome by a sense of terrible loss. "If they hang him, it will be my fault," she mumbled.

"Who?" The woman's face registered fresh alarm.

Romy paused, staring at the woman. "The man."

"What man? You called out for someone. Is that who you mean?" The woman's hand remained on Romy's arm.

"Did I say a name?"

The woman nodded. "Antonio."

"Antonio," Romy said with a nod. "His name is Antonio."

"Your boyfriend?"

"No." She didn't have a boyfriend and she didn't know anybody named Antonio. "You'll get covered in white," Romy said, trying to restore normalcy to this ridiculous situation. "From my greasepaint." She pointed to the woman's hand.

The lady glanced down at the smudge of white on her palms. "Oh, it'll wash off. Are you sure you don't want a doctor?"

For the first time, Romy noticed the woman's T-shirt, the camera, the shopping bag from one of the souvenir shops—a tourist, then. "No, really. Thanks for your help. Now, if you'll excuse me."

But the woman wouldn't leave. "Susie and I must have watched you for, like, ten minutes, and you didn't even blink," she said. "A lot of people just kept right on walking, you know, but Susie wanted to stop and watch. There's got to be an easier way to make a living, if you know what I mean."

The little girl, no more than six years old, stood nearby, gazing up at Romy with an expression of utter wonder. She pointed to the feathered wings Romy wore strapped to her back. "A pretend angel," she whispered. "Can you fly?"

Romy stifled a laugh. "No, I can't, sweetie. Believe me, if I could, I would have long ago." Like on the day her world began to fall apart.

"Stone angels, real or pretend, can't fly, Susie," her mother said.

"Bet you could if you tried," Susie insisted, following along beside her mother as Romy made her way back to her upended milk crate pedestal. "Wanna try now?"

"Hush," the mother said.

Romy smiled. Pressing her fingers to her forehead, she forced her head to clear. Now she felt drained and empty, almost bereft. The two other times she had experienced the phenomenon, it had been the same—exhausting, baffling, frightening.

Around her, the faces of the watching crowd registered a mix of concern and curiosity. Most had dispersed, probably disappointed that the amazing Frozen Angel—the performance artist who could make like a statue for nearly an hour—had confirmed her humanity in such a pathetic way. Romy sighed. Yes, she was a mere mortal and today especially she felt the weight of years bearing down.

She watched the last of her audience trail away, heading for their chicory coffees and beignets along Decatur Street. How many customers had she attracted this time—twenty, twenty-five, thirty?

Peering into the imitation marble dish she used as a till, she took a mental count of the contents—maybe twenty-five dollars, much less than usual, but she had gained in other ways. At least she now had a name. Antonio.

"Are you sure you'll be okay?" the woman asked again, still hovering.

Romy nodded. "I'm fine, really. I'm not used to the heat. Thanks, anyway."

Maybe the temperatures had impacted the force of this encounter. Either that or she could be losing her mind but, deep down, she didn't believe her sanity at issue. Frazzled, yes, more than a little lost, and sometimes desperate after everything that had happened, but definitely not crazy. Yet.

"I know I couldn't do what you do in these temperatures," the woman continued. "I almost hate to leave the air-conditioning to go outside. How do you Southerners stand it?"

"Actually, I'm from the North," Romy told her. "I've been here on a study visa for three years."

"Really?"

"Really." A pang of regret hit as she thought how her doctoral prospects had taken an even bigger tumble than her Frozen Angel but thinking of Adrian only intensified the pain. Some things were too hard to explain, even to herself.

She attempted to straighten her wings with a shrug. Those heavily feathered monstrosities, bought from a lady who made Mardi Gras floats, drooped over her shoulders on a broad elastic harness. After securing the fastenings, she stooped to pick up the crate and bowl, nesting one inside the other and covering both with the white canvas cloth. Now she could use her free hand to lift the long starched gown to keep from tripping.

Turning, she dropped a practiced bow to the woman and her daughter and prepared to make her way home. Pulling herself upright, she took a deep breath and walked down St. Philip Street with slow, measured steps, masking her fall with some semblance of dignity. She'd remain in character all the way home. Part theatrics, part good business, she fixed a glazed stare on the path ahead and walked as if with unseeing eyes.

People did a double take and moved from her path. In New Orleans, where dressing up was part of the culture, the sight of a stone angel walking the streets in her own solitary procession still had an unsettling effect. Old Mr. Benjamin, who took visitors for rides in his mule-drawn wagon, always crossed himself when he saw her coming. Cindy Murphy, who took the tourists for walking tours through the French Quarter, as did Romy twice a week, addressed her clients in hushed tones when the Frozen Angel walked by. At dusk, like now, when her costume took on a ghostly sheen, people scattered from her path.

Amazing to have such power through illusion. Respect, she decided as she crossed Royal Street. They respected what she represented—one of those strong, dignified guardians of forever that perched atop the cities of the dead. But today, as she walked home slightly weak and uncommonly weary, her angel stumbling, she felt the presence of another weighing her down. Whoever or whatever the identity of that woman who spoke to Antonio, the one who spoke through her, Romy sensed their fates were inextricably connected. They shared something with that man, something that could survive time itself, something that kept calling her back to the past.

A glimpse of her reflection in the shop windows showed a tipsy-looking angel with one wing askew. How fitting.

She took a deep breath and carried on, trying to fortify herself while blocking away the memory of an unknown man accusing her of treachery.

2

Dusk seeped an ultramarine into the sky over Governor Nicholls Street. Romy trudged up the steps to the tiny house she shared with her friend. A gray half-shotgun cottage tucked deep into the back of the French Quarter, it had a long, narrow shape, tall shuttered windows, and belonged to Joquita's aunt, who rented it to the two women for half the going rate.

Few such cottages that had survived Hurricane Katrina. Most of the others on the street had been reconstructed or demolished, which made seeing this one with its windows aglow even more welcoming. Living here was an honor Romy never took for granted.

She shoved open the door and stepped into the kitchen, calling out, "I'm getting too old for this!"

"Hell, girlfriend." Joquita swung around. "Would you honk twice before barreling in like that? You scare the bejesus out of me in that getup."

Joquita stood barefoot in the middle of their cramped galley kitchen wearing a red cotton shift and a pair of oven mitts, her large brown eyes wide. A lean, sinewy beauty with hair in cornrows and skin the color of polished walnut, she always took Romy's breath away.

Tonight, one hand grasped the aluminum tray of a steaming diet frozen dinner and the other held an open book. Joquita had been studying.

Romy pushed away a pang of regret at the thought of her own lost studies as she unfastened her wings and let them drop into a heap on the floor. "Are your nerves shot or something?"

"Maybe, but every time I see the Frozen Angel, something kicks in and my teeth start chattering," Jo said, watching her. "I guess that says something about your acting. Either that or your skill in the greasepaint division has reached new heights." She hesitated, peering into Romy's face. "You all right, girl?"

Romy rubbed her eyes and gazed at her friend, unable to contain herself a moment longer. "It happened again, only much stronger this time. It was like I was sucked into a time vortex, powerless to stop the trajectory, just falling, falling. I know I'm on to something here, Jo, I just know it!"

"Oh, hell."

"Hell—yes, it feels a bit like that. I mean, who am I when I go there, who am I speaking to? This time, I found myself in somebody else's head again while they used my lips to speak to this man. This time he accused me of treachery, treachery! I don't think I'm going crazy but I know it sure sounds that way."

"Sit." Joquita pointed toward a chair at their linoleum-topped table and slid into the place opposite. Romy collapsed on the seat and watched Joquita pop the plastic cover from the dinner tray and shove it toward her. Sometimes the five-year difference in their age seemed enormous. At thirty, Romy felt old.

"Here, you need this more than I do: glazed chicken and rice, food of Diana, Goddess of the Hunt."

Romy wrinkled her nose as she gazed down at the packaged food. "Is the goddess still trying to squeeze into a size-six toga?"

"Very funny. Ha ha. Eat."

"No thanks. I think I'll finish off the rest of Aunt Loo's gumbo and leave the toga fodder to you." But she made no move to the fridge. All she had the energy to do was sit, hands in her lap, and stare at the gray-and-pink flecks in the tabletop. "Why aren't you asking me for details?"

"I'm waiting until you recover, girl. Look at you, you're all done in. Why do you keep doing this Frozen Angel shit, anyway? That piddly amount of money can't make up for what working two jobs is doing to your body."

"Even a little money helps right now but you know I'm not doing the angel freeze for that." It had started as a lark, a kind of bet with her thesis adviser, and had quickly evolved into something extraordinary. And dangerous.

"Oh, right, I forgot: you have a gift for playing dead for fifteen-minute stretches." Jo made a play of slapping her forehead.

Romy laughed. "It's not that, either—not all of it, anyway. I only care about the phenomena, you know that. I have to figure out what's going on and get some answers. Consider it research, if you must."

"So, instead of finishing your thesis, which I remind you is proper research, you can play dress-up and hunt for ghosts every night?"

"You think I'm crazy."

"I think you're stressed. Isn't that what the doctor said?"

Romy shook her head. "Dr. Wilkins hasn't a clue about this stuff and you know it. What medical practitioner can diagnose what doesn't show up as a tumor or a rash? If it's not physical, it doesn't exist. The truth is that I'm seeing things, experiencing genuine encounters with the past. What student of history can let something that significant pass?"

"One who wants to stay sane. Or how about one who wants to get back into her doctoral program and finish her damn thesis?"

"Look, Jo, today, for the first time, I felt and saw everything through another woman's eyes, a woman who lived at least two hundred and fifty years ago. I really experienced her existence for a split moment in time, including her feelings and emotions, understand? This is raw, living history. This is past life relived. And I saw him again, too, that man in the vision, and he's becoming more focused each time. Again, he was accusing me of something and it's as if I know I've done something terribly wrong but I don't know what or how. I swear, this is not my imagination but something much bigger."

Joquita stared at her, shaking her head. "You haven't been yourself since this shit started, girl. You've got to get a grip. These hallucinations—"

"Not hallucinations," Romy insisted. "It's like I'm gazing straight into the past."

Crossing her arms, Jo frowned. "Let's just agree on something, okay? We're historians. Our approach is logical. We don't do ghosts. We don't 'gaze into the past' except through our imaginations. It's not possible."

Romy held up a hand. "And as historians, we form hypotheses and gather information to either prove or disprove our theories, don't we? Just because we can't yet explain what's happening, doesn't mean we should dismiss it out of hand."

Did that make sense? She paused, sorting it through. Yes, it did make sense and formed the gist of the argument she'd used with Dr. Adrian Countway, ex–thesis adviser, maybe the man of her dreams, and the one person who held her future in her hands. Adrian.

Joquita propped her elbows on the table. "All my life, my aunt has talked on and on about ghosts and spirits and I've always managed to stay uninvolved. I even consider it a badge of honor to stay grounded growing up in my aunt's household. Now my own roommate is getting into it, too. I detest this paranormal shit."

"The term 'paranormal' only applies to what we have yet to understand. Maybe sometime in the future, we'll prove that splicing present to the past is simply a matter of physics." Romy sat back, liking the sound of that. She almost sounded as if she knew what she was talking about.

"Fine, but until the next Einstein pops out with a tidy explanation, let's just agree that we don't have a clue why you're having these spells and go from there. I'm worried about you, okay?"

"I'm worried about me, too."

"Good enough, so we agree on something. Two intelligent, educated women should be able to figure out what's happening with or without physics. Why don't you tell me what occurred today while I nuke the gumbo."

"I'll get it."

"No way. Stay put, girlfriend. I don't want you dragging your sorry white butt around this kitchen covered in greasepaint. I'll feed you, you talk to me, and then you can shower that crap off."

"Spoken like a true scholar."

Joquita laughed, their easy friendship back in sync. Ever since Romy had met Jo on campus during their first year at Louisiana State Grad School, they had been friends. Romy believed their obvious differences—a white Canadian close friends with a black American—only intensified the bond.

In ways, they both felt marginalized, even persecuted, by their historical connections, if not by present circumstances. Romy came from poor Acadian stock and Jo proudly traced her lineage right back to slavery. Their ancestors had both struggled for existence right there in old New Orleans.

And they were both orphans raised by relatives and had made the study of history their life's focus. To be a historian, to spend her life pursuing the past, which Romy often found more absorbing than the present, was all she had ever wanted. Jo, too.

"Rom?" Romy looked up into Jo's worried gaze. "You're gone again," her friend said. "You were about to tell me what happened today, the guy from the past?"

"Right." Romy began summarizing her recent experience. "This time I tried to pick out the details of his clothing in a way I never had before. I saw the lace on his sleeves, noticed his hair, could even smell scents that were definitely not of modern Decatur Street—somewhere near the river, I think. I was not here, Jo. I was in another age speaking in someone else's voice, feeling someone else's emotions. In fact, now that I think about it, I felt as though I were eavesdropping on another woman's life and thoughts."

Jo ladled the soup into a blue ceramic bowl and popped it into the microwave, shaking her head the entire time. "Weird. Describe clothes, give me details."

"I could only see him from the waist up but he seemed wounded." For a moment, fresh grief threatened to swamp her, and once again, nothing about this grief felt familiar. Swallowing hard, she continued. "He had wonderful, intelligent eyes."

"Cripes, you sound like an audition for a soap opera. Describe clothes, not eyes. I'm looking for historical identification. Skip the mealy words."

Romy shook her head. "That's just it. This emotion, these feelings I have toward him, don't come from me but from the woman whose body I occupy when I have these encounters. It's like I carry a residue of emotion back into the present with me."

Jo swore under her breath. "Are you saying that this ghost woman is influencing you in the here and now?"

Romy shivered. "That's exactly what I'm saying. This is why I have to keep on with this. I must find out not only the identity of the man but the woman, too, because both are messing with my current life."

"Hell. Tell me what this dream ghost was wearing."

"He's not a ghost." Or was he? She shook her head, more at herself than Jo. "The lace of his jabot looked to be of good quality and so did his shirt—linen, fine weave, you know? I had the impression of blue silk but I don't recall actually seeing any. Everything was dirty, torn and...bloody."

"Seventeenth or eighteenth century?"

"Eighteenth." The conviction in her voice surprised her. "Maybe around the mid-1700s."

"How do you know that?" Joquita asked as she slipped the bowl of steaming gumbo from the microwave.

The rich peppery brew tickled Romy's nostrils. She picked up a spoon. "I just do." She glanced up at her friend and winced. "Well, that's the way things work since this phenomena began. It's like I know things I shouldn't or couldn't. And it's getting stronger. Not very scientific, I realize, but I don't think science will help with this one."

Joquita frowned, her dark eyes troubled. "So you say. What else can you tell me about this guy?"

"He's not a 'guy,' Jo. He's...I don't know—someone important, someone special."

"And you just know that how?"

Romy shrugged.

Jo sighed. "Okay, then, I'll cede to the fact he's special—has to be if he's making guest appearances in this century—but would you please stop referring to him in the present tense? He doesn't exist in this world, Rom, understand that. The look that comes over your face when you talk about this...this, um, apparition, creeps me out."

Romy swallowed a mouthful of the best damn gumbo in the South, a declaration by a cook no one dared challenge, at least not in this lifetime.

While she acknowledged the many flavors piquing her senses, her friend returned to her seat and began jabbing away at the frozen dinner. The model-thin Joquita, of all people, did not need diet fodder.

"The apparition," Romy said after a moment, "is named Antonio."

Joquita nearly dropped her fork. "It has a name?"

Romy nodded. "Apparently. I just remembered how the woman who peeled me up off the pavement told me I'd been calling out to 'Antonio.'"

"Banderas?"

"Be serious."

"I'm trying but everything about this situation makes me want to be totally irreverent. Okay, okay, so his name's Antonio. He could be Mexican but most likely Spanish."

"Exactly." Romy closed her eyes, remembering. "Only he was speaking French, high archaic French, with a Spanish accent. Educated. Not of this century."

"That's Romy Landry with the minor in linguistics speaking, I presume?"

Romy grinned. "Do I know my dead accents or what? The lady told me I was speaking in a foreign language, too, probably French."

"Well." Joquita stared at her. "That's something, I guess, though I don't have a clue what."

"It *is* something." Romy felt a surge of hope. "Now I can start searching the records, see what I can find out." Here, at least, was a specific task.

"Not I, *we*," Joquita said. "Think I'm going to let you have all this fun on your own? All we have to do is find out whether a Spanish nobleman with Antonio as a first name—providing he is a nobleman as fine linen rags do not a nobleman make—lived anywhere in, let's say, um, a one-hundred-square radius of New Orleans. Providing these visions you're having even center on New Orleans and not Spain or Mexico or a dozen other ports where the French and Spanish languages mingled, that is. Oh, and we have at least a two-hundred-year time span, too, give or take a decade or two, and all minus a surname and without much concrete fact to go on."

Romy made a face. "What's your point?"

Jo stabbed the air with her fork. "I'm saying it will be a walk in the proverbial park. We might want to start researching around the time of the Spanish occupation of New Orleans, let's say mid-1700s. There might be a few Antonios running around during that period, one notable one in particular."

The obvious one had occurred to Romy, too. "Antonio de Ulloa, first Spanish governor of the Louisiana colony."

"Who arrived in 1766 and was chased out of town not long afterward," Jo added. "Could that guy possibly be your ghost?"

"We don't know if this is a ghost, remember? In some ways it doesn't feel like a ghost. I feel like I've been given a lead role in a period film without my knowledge. It's like I'm *inside* a ghost, living history like a tourist in time."

"Sounds reasonable. Time tourists could be a thing."

"Look, let's just narrow down the times of my experiences a little more. Oh, and find out who he thinks he's talking to. Obviously, I'm not Romy Landry when I'm seeing this man."

"That's comforting."

"So," Romy continued, gathering momentum, "our research should begin mid-eighteenth-century New Orleans."

Joquita, a calculating look flickering across her face, studied Romy for a moment before saying: "Why not ask the foremost authority on the period, your very own thesis adviser, Dr. Adrian Countway?"

The name gave Romy's heart a jolt. "Ex–thesis adviser."

"Every time I say his name, you look like you swallowed shoe leather. Okay, so spill it: what really happened between you two, anyway?"

"I told you."

Jo shook her head. "You did not. You said you found him sexy and intellectually stimulating but that he didn't return the interest so you decided to apply for another thesis adviser, as if that makes sense. So what if you want to jump his bones? You don't leave your studies because of something like that. You're both adults. Get over it already."

"I can't," she whispered.

"What do you mean? The sensible woman would find herself someone else, another man who appreciates the attractive, brilliant woman she is, and then jump into bed as often as needed to scratch that itch."

Romy threw up her hands. "But I never claimed to be sensible."

"My point is: get on with life. Broken hearts can be mended easier than doctoral degrees. No man is worth giving all this up."

Romy groaned. "You're so damned pragmatic but it's not that simple. I fell for him hard, really hard, and totally lost my self-control like some oversexed freshman." She sighed, staring down at the table. "Now I can't even bear to be in the same room with him. It's so humiliating."

Jo shrugged. "So he rejected you. Get over it. There's other fish in the river, as they say in the Big Easy. No one as committed to her goals as you are should walk away from a doctorate months away from achieving a degree. I'm sure if you went to see him, he'd take you back in a minute. You were his star student."

Romy squeezed her eyes shut. "I haven't seen him since. I just sent him a text."

Jo cursed. "You sent him a text! Are you serious? At least you could have picked up the phone. Look," she said, leaning forward, "I don't usually give advice—"

"More than once or twice an hour."

"—but you should go see him in person at least. The doctor made a point of speaking to me in the library the other day. I've taken a few classes from him but his reason for talking to me had to do with you, no matter how much he pretended otherwise."

Romy gaze locked on Jo's. "What did he say?"

"He wanted to know how you were, that's all. He seemed baffled and genuinely worried as hell. Maybe you owe him a proper explanation."

Romy felt as though she'd swallowed a concrete block. "I'm working up the courage to do exactly that. Now change the subject, please, so I can enjoy the rest of this gumbo."

Jo lifted her arms in exasperation and picked up a fork to stab at a piece of chicken. "All right, but the topic is only temporarily off the table."

"Fair enough." Romy sighed with relief and picked up her spoon.

"All I know is that this whole ghost business is making my toes curl. Look, I said I'd help you with the research part but this is sounding more and more like supernatural shit to me. That's way out of my league and yours. It's time you took this baby to another kind of expert, since you refuse to bring a historian into the picture."

Romy, caught as she was in the middle of the last spoonful of gumbo, nearly sputtered. "Not Aunt Loo. As much as I admire your aunt, I always feel like genuflecting or something every time I'm around her. Do you know she actually admonished me for not keeping the cottage tidy that day she dropped by to pick up the rent?"

Joquita grinned. "Girl, you're just lucky she didn't box your ears. Still, this ghost business is right up her alley. She lives for shit like this. She says she 'knows more about the paranormal than anybody in Nawlins and, in this city, that's never been disputed. I would never make this suggestion lightly, girlfriend—I feel like I'm feeding you to the dragon—but you need help and Aunt Loo's the one who can give it. What are you doing tonight?"

Romy shook her head. "Working, I'm relieved to say. I promised I'd take Cindy's tour group tonight. She's got relatives in from Arizona visiting but a flock of tech conventioneers are booked for tonight's tour. I couldn't possibly let her down."

Joquita grinned and shook her finger at Romy. "Stay of execution only. I'll try to arrange things for tomorrow night, if Auntie isn't set to close some deal to sell St. Louis Cathedral or something. You'd better knock off tomorrow night's Frozen Angel thing in the meantime, at least until your battery recharges."

"Friday night's are my best times, you know that."

"You're working way too many long hours," Jo commented through a mouthful as she scraped up the last of her glazed chicken and carried the tray to the garbage container. "Even without the makeup and your natural pallor, you look all done in. You've got to cut back."

"Can't. I'll have to finish my thesis next term, once they assign another thesis adviser, and that means another year of tuition. Now that I've forfeited my scholarship, I need money more than ever."

"Shit. Just listen to those words roll off your tongue, woman: 'now that I've forfeited my scholarship.' You have more problems than money right now."

"Look, I'm working on it, okay? In the meantime, I'll forgo the angel performance just this once and see your aunt." Without thinking, she crossed herself. "May the saints preserve my soul."

Jo laughed. "Romy, Aunt Loo does things differently but don't you go insulting her with by showing up with garlic around your neck and making on like she's a voodoo queen, you hear?"

"I hear."

"Sure enough, you do. I'm warning you for your own good. Auntie's a busy woman, though. Hope she can squeeze you in. The last I heard she was entertaining a crowd of diplomatic folk who came to the mansion for a spiritual consultation. I think she sold one of them an estate around here."

Romy grimaced. "She's phenomenal, more than a little intimidating."

"So, good luck with her. Now, I'm going to the library. Two-thirds into writing my thesis and counting!" She swung into a little dance across the kitchen.

"At least one of us will finish their thesis on time."

Joquita stopped in her tracks and crossed her arms. "My head is crammed with all these treatises on slavery. I tell you, there are days I just want to walk into the streets and scream at every white person I see, with certain exceptions, of course. You I prefer to scream at for other reasons. In the interest of variety, you give me plenty of choices. Never mind. As soon as I finish this chapter, maybe I'll see what I can find out about your tattered Spaniard."

"Thanks, Jo. You're fabulous. I'll make it up to you, I promise."

"You bet your white ass you will. Just wait until I think of something fitting. In the meantime, you're endlessly beholden to me and don't forget it."

"I won't, but will you come with me to your aunt's tomorrow night in case she tries to turn me into a toad?"

"Don't push it, girlfriend. No way I'm sticking around when she gets into her mumbo-jumbo mode. If you croak, it's your problem. Besides," she added with a grin, "I've got a hot date, something you could do with once in a while."

3

Romy ran her fingers through her still-damp hair, trying to squeeze her curls dry as she walked down the sidewalk.

Overhead, flickering gas lanterns fought the electric glow of shop windows while the sound of clopping hooves echoed in the street. Everywhere she looked, the aggressive present bullied the past in this city. For everyone but her, that is.

For her, the past often expanded inside her heart with such intensity that she temporarily lost sight of the present. For most of her life, she had seen the past as an overlay, a vision of another time superimposed over modern sights and sounds. She'd always dismissed it as a hyperactive imagination. Until recently.

Now it was as if something inhabited her mind like a separate entity, swamping her with someone else's emotions, someone else's life. Navigating the crowd that evening, she could almost feel a presence ghosting her footsteps.

I am drowning in the past, she thought. *I am dying in someone else's life.*

Would Adrian believe her enough to help?

Shivering in the heat, she tried to focus on the upcoming meeting. Whatever happened, she could not seem crazy. Free from greasepaint and the white plaster-like substance smeared in her hair, at least she looked human again. Only the just-showered freshness would never last.

Already the muggy air pressed against her body with a hot, sticky embrace that caused her skirt to cling to her legs like a lover's touch. As if, she laughed to herself. Her last lover had been years ago and now the only man she wanted wasn't interested.

Tonight she had chosen a black print shift, chic in that it hung with a simple grace from her shoulders, practical because it was still loose enough to catch a random breeze, and attractive because she knew its plain lines revealed her figure without being vulgar.

She knew she was reasonably attractive with her brown curls and brown eyes—not gorgeous like Jo but passable. Really, she needed all the confidence she could get. A glance at her reflection in a shop window confirmed that she looked pulled-together and composed, though her insides were in turmoil.

She checked her watch: 7:15—less than half an hour to reach Adrian's door, ring his bell, and say what had to be said before scrambling off to meet Cindy's tour group at eight. She'd go for brief.

More time might lead to more words and more words might lead to more embarrassment. Get this over with was her mission. Either he'd help or he wouldn't, end of story. One way or the other, she had to get on with her life.

Practicing sentences in her head, she paused in the door of a gift shop and gazed over at the two-story building across the street.

Leave it to Dr. Adrian Countway to own one of the choicest pieces of French Quarter real estate. Located in the center of Royal Street, the house had been built just after the fire of 1794, with all the rounded pediments, tall windows, and ornate wrought-iron balconies common to Creole-Spanish architecture.

Joquita's aunt, a prominent real estate agent, had located it for him after the professor had decided to sell his Baton Rouge apartment for someplace "deep in the throb of history," as he described it. He leased the street-level shop to an upscale clothing boutique while taking the upper floors as his own.

The balcony's wrought iron traced an intricate silhouette against the tall lighted windows. Romy stared. So, he was home, not visiting family in

Boston. No excuses left. Now she'd have to do something she should have done weeks ago.

How long since that fateful day—three weeks, a month? She stepped off the curb and gave the thin fabric clinging to her legs a tug while she walked. Would he be able to hear her throbbing heart?

Moments later, she had climbed the stairs and forced herself to ring the bell, listening with amusement as the device tinkled the opening strains to *"When the Saints Go Marching In."*

She knew without ever having been inside that his new flat would be decorated like his office—a jumble of artifacts and antiques gleaned from his travels and interests. If he ever managed to find a decorator to suit him, it would have to be someone with a curator's eye combined with a joke-shop wit.

Above all else, she reminded herself, she must remain in control. Whoever or whatever from the past impacted her life must remain safely tucked away during this interview or all would be lost. He already thought her mad.

The door swung open. "Romy?" He stood there with his wire-rimmed glasses magnifying those marvelous gray-green eyes and his expression echoing surprise. A halo of warm, moist scent surrounded him with hints of clove and bay rum aftershave, his dark hair curling damply around his ears.

Her heart tilted as she inhaled deeply, breathing out with a little gust. For an instant, she thought she might do something ridiculous and swoon.

"Dr. Countway," she said, finding her voice. "I've just dropped by to deliver a fifteen-minute explanation for my recent behavior. Can you spare the time?"

"A whole fifteen minutes?" He glanced at his watch. "Does this mean you don't believe the three-sentence text you sent was enough?"

"I—"

"Allow me. I know it by heart: 'I apologize for any confusion this note may cause but on no account must you attempt to contact me. I will not answer your calls or speak to you if you approach me on the street. Consider me gone.'"

She couldn't believe she wrote such nonsense, and in a text, no less. "My word choice wasn't up to my usual standards. May I come in?"

She didn't stutter, mangle her words, or otherwise make an idiot of herself. Yet. That was something. Even so, if he looked closely enough, he'd see her trembling and, as always, he was looking very closely.

He cleared his throat. "Of course, my apologies if I seem rude. I don't have much time, either, as it turns out. I'm meeting someone for dinner so fifteen minutes should just about do it. Come in."

The chill in his voice hurt but what else could she expect? Adrian could be so stiff and formal when annoyed. Taking a deep breath, she stepped across the threshold.

From the beginning, she thought she could control herself, would never behave like one of those foolish freshmen who threw themselves at attractive professors. Sex and power was too strong a brew for many young women to resist. Yet, at thirty years old, she expected to be both old enough and smart enough to navigate her way around that quicksand.

But she had been so wrong. A crush, for heaven's sake! And a crush of such intensity she had lived in fear of making a fool of herself by exposing some lovelorn gaze during tutorials or doing something worse.

In the end, worse won. She'd made a pass at him, right in his office, right before his display of rare African fertility carvings and right in the middle of a heated discussion on eighteenth-century sexual politics.

His shocked expression as he held her at arm's length told her everything she needed to know: she'd crossed the line; she'd breeched the code of ethics between professor and student; she'd put both of them in an untenable position. How could she stay after that?

On impulse, she texted him and exited her studies, her thesis, and maybe even her career. Spinning with confusion, she had no explanation for any of her actions.

Until now.

"How's your book coming?" she asked, studying a montage of eighteenth-century printers' blocks on the wall.

A scan of the rest of the room took in a baby grand piano placed before the tall windows, a wall-mounted mahogany bookcase stuffed with artifacts, and a Flemish hunting tapestry behind a moss-colored leather couch. Two comfy-looking leather chairs were angled together beside a small pedestal table in the middle of the room.

Here was the home of a man with an insatiable appetite for the rare and arcane, a man who collected artifacts as if they were touchstones to the past, a man who excited her in multiple ways, both physically and intellectually. A man she could not have.

"Excellent, thank you, but I doubt you came by to check on my 'publish or perish' woes." His voice maintained the cool veneer of a man with his defenses firmly in place. "I trust this small talk won't gobble up too much of your allotted fifteen minutes. Please take a seat."

"Every minute's budgeted for."

He nodded, a smile playing on his lips as she sunk into one of the club chairs.

"I see you've moved some of your statues from the office to here," she said, pointing to the Cameroon carving of a pregnant female deity perched on the piano. "I'm sure Moonapula appreciates the view."

"I'm trying to acclimatize Moona to city life as gently as possible while still preserving her queenly pride of place," he said, taking the chair beside hers. "I'm having a proper stand made so she doesn't have to suffer the indignity of vibrating every time I play the piano."

Finding herself fidgeting with her purse straps, she laid the bag at her feet and folded her hands in her lap. "Vibrations are very good for pregnant women, I understand. Where's her mate?" She glanced around for the three-foot-tall statue of the companion god, Ulla. She spied him tucked behind a stack of books, his erect phallus discreetly shielded from view. Now she didn't even try to suppress her grin. "No pride of place for him, I see."

The wry smile that crossed his face always took her breath away. "He's also waiting for a proper stand so he can stand up properly, so to speak. In the meantime, I simply can't risk having his appendage amputated by the workmen I still have hanging about. The other day, I came home to find a baseball cap hanging from Ulla's crowning asset."

"Oh, the indignity!"

"Horrible. For the sake of the fertility gods everywhere, I tucked him out of sight." Then his smile disappeared. "Is it true you're still doing statue performances off Decatur Street?"

Ah, the sudden about-face. "Frozen Angel. Yes."

"Why, for heaven's sake?"

"Because I've had the most interesting experiences while frozen like a cemetery angel and I don't care how bizarre that sounds. My experiences are part of my explanation for my recent behavior, by the way."

"You don't owe me an explanation," he said, his voice softening. Was he even aware of how seductive that tone could be? Silk running across bare skin, a tongue tracing a wet trail down the back of her neck.

An instant of dimly remembered memory slipped and slid at the back of her brain—wet tongues, deep kisses—but she had never experienced anything so heated in all her waking life. She shivered, trying to catch Adrian's words.

"It's perfectly understandable when two people work in close proximity and share so much together for attraction to combust, but—"

"Stop. Please." Was he about to say that it wasn't possible for a tenured professor to enter into a relationship with a student without jeopardizing his career? That he was secretly engaged to some European professor or some fashion model with floor-to-ceiling legs, or, the worst possible scenario, that he didn't find her attractive? Did she need to hear any of that? "Do you believe in past life regression, Dr. Countway?" she blurted.

He sighed in annoyance. "Call me Adrian, for God's sake. I haven't been Dr. Countway to you for months, and to answer your question, in the absence of proof, no."

"Proof being something concrete, you mean?" she asked. "Like, um, a video filmed during some past life event? No, wait—we all know videos can be faked, so that wouldn't work. Tell me, Professor, how do you prove the existence of a personal experience? Never mind," she added with a wave of her hand. "We both know it can't be done to academic standards because it depends on trust in the person describing the phenomenon."

He shot her a look of disbelief. "Are you implying that you're experiencing past lives?"

"I'm saying I'm being affected by past lives, yes. For weeks, it's been as if I'm being possessed by another personality, a woman who lived in eighteenth-century New Orleans, a Frenchwoman. I've literally not been myself." It sounded lame even to her.

"So, this woman caused you to want to kiss me, is that it?" Now she read amusement along with the skepticism.

Her cheeks flushed. "Of course. You don't think I'd lunge at you like that otherwise, do you? Had you seen any signs that I'm a lunging kind of woman before that?"

"Well." He hesitated. "No overt signs of lunging, no."

"Seriously, the truth is that another woman's emotions are affecting me and confusing my own. It's embarrassing, humiliating, and I haven't handled it well so far."

"You are serious."

"I am. Something is happening to me, something that can't be explained by fact alone," she added. "I'm frightened and...well, I could certainly use your help."

"Of course I'll do anything to help, you must know that," he said, his expression solemn, puzzled, and concerned all at once. She had the overwhelming urge to finger one of those tiny damp curls frolicking at his shirt collar. "How can I help? Anything I can do. Have you seen a psychiatrist?"

Damn, just when she allowed herself a flare of hope. "I'm talking about the paranormal, Dr.—I mean, Adrian. Medicine won't help me here."

Then with a historian's attention to sequence and detail, she described everything that had happened to her, right up to the possible identification of Antonio de Ulloa and the woman he accused of treachery. By the time she had finished, she had used up all but five of her allotted fifteen minutes.

And Adrian looked stunned. "I hardly know what to say." From his miserable expression, she knew he didn't, or couldn't, believe her. "And this woman's identity?"

"Maybe a prostitute or a French colonist, it's hard to tell. I haven't heard her speak much and, when I have, she's been extremely distraught."

"An Acadian?"

"I don't think so. She seems too well-educated for a peasant farm girl." She could just imagine his derision if she should conveniently manifest into her topic of study.

Leaning forward, his hands clasped loosely between his knees, his words were every inch the academic. "Romy, this all sounds highly unlikely. For one thing, Ulloa was a very private and principled man. He had very little interaction with the locals during his two-year stay in New Orleans—a Spaniard out of his element trying unsuccessfully to stay out of hot water with the French."

"I know that."

"On top of everything else," he continued, "he was a writer with a writer's tendency toward the reclusive and also a devote Catholic as well as a newly married man. To think he may have had some kind of a relationship with a prostitute is just—"

"Highly unlikely, as you said."

"Exactly."

"Even though he was presumably a healthy man with the same inclinations as other men, regardless of religion or marital status?"

He looked uncomfortable. "Well, of course, he may have entertained a woman of ill repute, seeing as every second house in New Orleans was a brothel. The point is, there's no evidence of him behaving in that manner."

Ill repute. How like him to slip into that kind of old-fashioned terminology. Romy smiled. "I suspect he might even entertain a woman of 'ill repute' despite his marriage vows. Wouldn't be the first time a man had done that, would it? Bet he wouldn't want to advertise it, either."

A flash of annoyance crossed his face. Adrian Countway approved of principle and integrity, championing any historic personage who held up against the odds—his kind of hero.

It was one of the things that endeared him to her, that old-fashioned upstanding nature coupled with a powerful personal magnetism and a sexuality of which he barely seemed aware. That his one and only fiancée fell for another man a decade ago completed the picture. Rumor was that he still held the torch. "In his case, there's nothing to prove he behaved in that manner."

"Looks as though we're falling back into our same old argument, Adrian. You insist on evidence whereas I explore speculation."

"A historian's speculation needs to be grounded on some identifiable proof, Romy, as I've so often said. From all accounts, Ulloa was a disciplined man, a naval officer as well as a scientist of the first order. He would understand the perils of fraternizing with a people who detested him. Furthermore, mention of another woman has never emerged in his writings or in any of the accounts."

"The fire of 1788 eliminated most of the city's records. I assume Antonio, a reputation-conscious officer of the King of Spain, not to mention a married man, wasn't about to admit to being involved with a local woman in his correspondence, anyway. His public persona would be focused on his accomplishments, not his nature."

That wry smile again. "I see this affliction you've described hasn't deadened your debating skills."

"I said I was being possessed, not lobotomized."

Adrian only nodded as if accepting her irritation. "We're not going to agree here, either, are we?"

"Look, Adrian, you know the real human story goes far beyond documents and accounts. It exists within the very souls of the people."

"I've never disagreed with you on that point, but unless those souls talk, how can you prove anything? We historians can't believe in past life regressions, possession or, God preserve us, ghost sightings."

"Souls do talk, damn it, and by historians, I presume you mean you?"

"I am a historian, Romy, and so are you. I know you have an extraordinary sensitivity toward the past, coupled with a heightened imagination, but do you seriously expect me to believe that you have been encountering Antonio de Ulloa y de la Torre-Giralt, a man who died in 1795?"

"Frankly, I'd hoped you'd trust my judgment enough to do just that."

"Do you realize how one of the symptoms of mental distress is not knowing one is—"

"Crazy?" she offered.

"Distressed, I was about to say. You'd been studying too hard, slaving over that thesis, marking papers for me, and working part-time besides. I blame myself for pushing you too hard." His face had flushed the color of a Mississippi sunset.

"Let's get one thing straight, Professor: I pushed myself hard," she said, getting to her feet. She winced as the damp leather peeled away from her bare legs. "I don't let you or anybody else do it to me." Damn him.

"Wait, I'm sorry." He held up his hands as if to ward off a blow. "I guess I sounded like a patriarchal—"

"And condescending."

"And condescending—"

"Prick," Romy finished for him.

His mouth quirked. "Ouch. Blame male conditioning, despite my efforts to blast away the bloody stuff. That doesn't change the fact that I'm worried about you. I believe you're experiencing a form of mental collapse. Please, Romy, see a psychiatrist."

"No thanks. Time to go. Thank you, anyway." The old weariness tunneled down on her like a freight train at high speed. Anger alone kept her momentum going.

"At least consider it. There are so many conditions that could have similar symptoms to those you describe," he continued.

"Like disassociation, schizophrenia, split personalities?"

"I'm no expert, but yes, actually."

"I know this much: what I'm experiencing is none of those things." Why had she thought he might believe her? "I'll be going now."

He sighed, and looked at her with that steady, searching gaze of his that made her want to run headlong into his arms, the arms that never opened in invitation.

"Romy, wait. Please. You have such a stunning mind, so much potential, I—I hold you in the highest regard, but now I'm afraid that stress, or whatever the nature of your current affliction, is plummeting you right into crisis. You need help."

"I know that, Dr. Countway," she said, moving toward the door. "I could use yours, as a matter of fact, just not the kind you're offering. Keep your list of handy psychoanalysts."

"Isn't your student visa expiring soon? Won't you need my assistance to remain in the country or are you planning to return to Nova Scotia?"

He touched her arm but she shook him away. "I'll figure that one out when the time comes."

"Please, Romy," he begged her. "I can help you if you return to the department. At least tell me you'll consider coming back once you've recovered, after you've had a rest, I mean."

She turned to face him. "That's not such a good idea under the circumstances, is it?"

He hesitated, seeming hurt, distressed. "No, perhaps not," he said softly.

"So, again, consider me gone," she said, striding out the door.

4

Why had she put herself through that? Visiting Adrian had solved nothing, yet she still could not, would not, put that man out of her mind. It's as if he'd been fused right to her heart, which kept throbbing with a timeless intensity.

And now she was going to be late. Only a few minutes left to reach her destination.

Picking up pace, she trotted down the street, heading toward the river, weariness weighing down her limbs. Maybe Jo was right: either cut back on her hours or collapse in a heap.

With a little luck, this tour group would be a subdued lot and she could breeze through the highlights route and be home in bed before ten-thirty. Wow, she lived such an exciting life: one minute acting like a graveyard angel and the next longing for bed. So much for a misspent youth.

Approaching the Jackson Brewery building minutes later, she fingered her grandmother's gold cross hanging at her throat. She'd inherited it from a mother she could barely remember. Uncle Gerard, who had raised her, once claimed the cross might protect Romy against the vampires he was convinced populated the streets of New Orleans. He was probably joking but she thought about it every time she touched the old cross nevertheless.

The technology conventioneers would be waiting at the Greyhound tour depot. The small round building located between the river and the railway tracks served as a common meeting place for local tour groups.

Tonight she scanned the clusters of waiting tourists for a likely looking crew and spied FlashTeck: Delivering Tomorrow Today logos plastered on the sides of red canvas bags. There were eight of them, all men, each sporting the distinctive bright blue button of the French Quarter Highlights Walking Tour.

"Hi, there," she greeted the group. "I'm Romy Landry, your tour guide, that is if you're my group for tonight's Highlights of the Vieux Carré tour."

"Vieux Carré?" a big man with short red hair and glasses asked, leaning over to breathe happy hour fumes in her direction.

For a moment, his lime green striped T-shirt appeared in her vision like a jolt of neon. "It'd be worth a tour to the garbage dump just to be in your company, sweetheart, but we booked for the French Quarter, see?"

"'Vieux Carré' is French for 'old quarter,'" Romy explained, plastering a smile on her face that she hoped wouldn't slip before the evening was done. "Sorry for the confusion."

"Speak English for us, then, honey. We're all Americans here," the man told her, bleary blue eyes looking her over with the scrutiny of a used car buyer.

Romy suppressed her temper. Nothing annoyed her more than a rude adult who didn't have a clue about his own country. Only dignity kept her smiling, that and the need for tips. A woman had to be practical as well as principled.

"Oh, don't mind Stan," another man said, elbowing the big guy out of the way. "He's just been hitting the bars a little too early tonight. Makes him cranky."

Several degrees younger than Stan, this guy had an engaging smile and a fresh-shaven face that, combined with his polo shirt, gave him a '50s-era vibe. He extended his hand. "I'm Dave from Milwaukee, the eastern sales manager for FlashTeck. My team and I are charged up for tonight's tour, aren't we, guys?"

The men, mostly dressed in shorts and T-shirts, nodded their assent.

"I've heard this is a great way to get a feel for the French Quarter," Dave said. "Are you from around here, Romy?"

She smiled, liking him immediately. "No, but I'm sort of distantly related to the folks in New Orleans, being from Nova Scotia and of Acadian descent. Have you heard of Longfellow's poem *Evangeline?*"

Dave nodded. "Something about a girl and some guy being separated or something? Lots of tears and wailing?"

Romy laughed and recited a few lines. *"And with the ebb of that tide the ships sailed out of the harbor, Leaving behind them the dead on the shore, and the village in ruins.'"*

"Yeah, that sounds like the one." Dave grinned.

"Longfellow based the poem on a real historical event that occurred in 1755 when the French-speaking Acadians were banished from Nova Scotia —then called New Scotland—for refusing to swear allegiance to British rule."

"Kind of like what we Americans did when we declared independence," one of the others said.

"Yes, kind of," Romy agreed. "Only the Acadians didn't fight. They just asked to be left in peace. Since tensions were still high between the French and English in the colonies at the time, the British couldn't allow it. In the end, some of us migrated to parts of Louisiana and today 'Cajun' refers to the Acadian culture in this state."

"So, you're Cajun?" Dave asked, obviously intrigued.

"No, the Acadians who settled here, those who brought their culture to mix with the other settlers, are the true Cajuns. I consider myself a Canadian Acadian." And one who might be expulsed the moment her visa expired, she thought.

"Okay, okay," grumbled Stan. "Let's get on with the show."

Romy nodded. "Come on, then. I'll tell you more as we head toward Jackson Square. That's where we'll begin our tour tonight. All set?"

The men nodded. "Just give us a minute, though," Dave said. "My wife, Amy, just popped into the shops to do some shopping, so maybe we can pick her up along the way?"

"Sure thing," Romy said, glad to know there'd be another female to suffuse the testosterone brewing in the group. At the same time she hoped that Amy wouldn't fiddle away too much precious time.

As it turned out, the group had to wait at least fifteen minutes before the woman emerged with her booty. At the sight of the short redhead overloaded with bags, a few of the men gamely offered to carry her parcels.

Stan, Romy noticed, was not among the gallant of the FlashTeck team. He hung back from the group, hands shoved into his short pockets, looking uninterested in everything she said while his eyes strayed to her chest repeatedly. Had she not been on the job, she would have leveled him with a steely gaze and maybe a curt word.

"Aren't the guys great?" Amy said, trying to fall into step beside Romy as the group made its way down Decatur Street.

With a penchant for platform-soled shoes, Amy clopped beside Romy as she chatted away. "Dave didn't want to take me at first but I said, 'Hey, you can't go to New Orleans without me!' Like, we only just had our honeymoon. Besides, I've always wanted to come here so how could I miss the opportunity? While Dave runs his booth, I hit the shops. It's been great."

Romy nodded, trying to impart a little information between Amy's streaming monologue and Stan's ogling. She stopped two blocks from Jackson Square and pointed to an ornate steel roundel embedded into the walls of one turn-of-the-century building.

"Do you see that? It's called an earthquake bolt and you'll notice plenty of them on our tour. Nervous architects purchased them from persuasive salesmen following the great San Francisco earthquake of 1906. They were believed to fortify the structures against shake-ups."

Stan suddenly sidled up to Romy shoulder. "So forget all this architecture crap. Tell us something interesting."

Romy smiled her most charming smile. "And what would interest you, Stan?" How many beers to drink in a thirty-minute span? How to belch at public functions? "Ask away."

"How about what are you doing later tonight?" Stan said with a feral grin, looking toward the other men for an audience.

Yeah, right. She turned her back on him and carried on down the street. "How about an overview of the city's history instead? Do you know that New Orleans is reportedly the most haunted city in North America?"

"Yeah, I've heard that. Spooky!" Amy said.

"I'll point out several buildings known for ghost sightings tonight. This city has a turbulent history going back nearly three centuries, so there's no surprise that restless spirits prowl these streets."

Was Antonio one of those? she wondered. Was she seeing ghosts?

"Hey, what's that up there?" Dave asked, pointing to the next building over where spikes of iron encircled the top of a column.

Romy looked up at the ornate but equally forbidding ironwork. "Oh, I present you with *chevaux de frise* and *garde de frise*, both French terms meaning 'to guard.' Homeowners afraid of the slavery uprisings put them around their houses to keep out possible burglars. Some versions, like along the wall up there, are made of bits of broken glass."

Stan leaned over and whispered, "You got one of those guard things protecting you, too, Frenchie?"

How she wished she would just let herself go and say something to get this lug off her back. Disgusted as much with herself as him, she turned her back on her offender and led the group into Jackson Square.

This was going to be one long night.

Following her articulate, vivacious tale of the square's history, Romy led her little clutch of conventioneers deeper into the streets of the French Quarter.

She kept her talk detailed enough to inform but not overwhelm her listeners. Still, there was no way she'd scrimp, no matter what. A good story deserved an equally good telling, regardless of her audience's attention span.

Besides, one never knew who might be listening. She liked to imagine the past as an eavesdropper. Sometimes she could almost sense the spirits listening in on every word. With that kind of scrutiny, even if only imagined, she always gave every tour her absolute best.

She touched on stories behind the city's most famous characters—the pirates and governors, prostitutes and grand ladies—who swept through three hundred years of New Orleans history and left little behind but a few sketchy facts.

No haunted house passed without mention or famous locale without her touching on the story behind it.

Sometimes she had no idea where her tales came from but out they came with such compelling detail that the source seemed unimportant.

Luckily, the city's wrought-iron balconies and cobbled streets worked their own magic. Even the occasional passing car and honking horn seemed to fade into the background as "Nawlins" made the storyteller's job so easy.

Tonight, when a hush seemed to descend the streets of the French Quarter, Romy could depend on the stage to set itself.

By ten o'clock, even Stan had stopped listing toward the bars and Amy no longer paused before every shop window. Romy finally had the Flash-Teck team exactly where she wanted them: exhausted.

"You mean, the Ursuline nuns really got those young girls ready for the New Orleans bachelors like some kind of meat market?" Drew from Boston asked.

The little group, weary but enthralled, had gathered outside the gatehouse of the former Convent of Saint Ursula as the evening deepened around them and the gas-light lanterns flickered along the streets.

"Well, yes, a manner of speaking. Actually, it wasn't as simple as that." Romy suppressed an unexplained tremor. Certain places around the city intensified her sense of foreboding, as if history itself breathed down her neck. The Ursula Convent had always been one.

She glanced over her shoulder at its French Colonial architecture, at the dormers perched on the steeply pitched roof, feeling a strange familiarity with one of the few local edifices she had never actually stepped inside. For whatever reason, she had never been able to bring herself to cross that threshold.

Just for a moment, from somewhere just at the edge of her senses, she thought she heard a faint tap-tapping sound of a stick on stone. The sound clawed at her spine. Gazing over her shoulder toward the street, as expected, she saw nothing.

Turning her attention back to the group, she forced a smile. *Mind on business, girl.* "Remember how I said New Orleans didn't have many marriageable women on hand by the day's standards?" All but Stan's eyes studied the structure. The bastard's interest continued to focus on her boobs. "Well, in 1745, New Orleans was a French colony—an outpost, really, just on the edge of civilization. Adventurers, outcasts, and entrepreneurial French noblemen populated its streets."

"So?" Stan mumbled.

"So, New Orleans had become the place of exile for France's unsavory citizens as well as a magnet for the day's version of entrepreneurs. There were slaves, pirates, explorers, and people from many parts of the world," she continued.

"Not a good place for women," Amy remarked.

"Not ladies, no. What women survived in those conditions were hardly the sort the King of France wanted to breed new citizens. So, in order to keep those lusty Frenchmen from marrying the indigenous peoples or—heaven forbid—the peasant Cajun French or even slaves, he sent the sisters of Saint Ursula along to educate a more suitable gene pool. In their care, young middle-class virgins were shipped over—"

"You mean, white virgins," Stan said with a grin.

"Well, yes, white virgins." *Why does that matter, you insufferable pig?* But Romy pressed on. "As I was saying, many of these girls had no idea what they were getting into because—"

"Or what was going to be getting into them!" Stan guffawed.

"Oh, be quiet, Stan," Dave snapped. "We want to hear her, not you. Go on, Romy."

Romy pressed one finger into the bridge of her nose where a headache began to brew like a far-off storm—migraine again. Damn. For a moment, she lost her train of thought. "Anyway," she began, rallying, "these girls were called 'the casket girls' because each one was given a casket-shaped box filled with linen with which to start their new life, or so the story goes. They were raised here, inside these walls, educated to be proper wives and mothers until their marriage day."

"Wow," Amy murmured. "Imagine that. What kind of marriage advice could a bunch of nuns give?"

Romy sighed as she drew them away toward Chartres Street. Mention sex, and she had everybody's ear, delve too deeply into history and most took a mental detour. Luckily the tour was almost over.

"Maybe the sisters taught them how to keep their eyes closed and do it for king and country?" Dave said, falling into step beside Romy as Amy flanked her opposite side.

Romy nodded. "My guess is that the nuns instructed the convent daughters to be good wives and mothers but left out all the practical details."

"Virgins 'educated' by virgins," Amy remarked, her expression faraway. "How practical is that?"

"They weren't all virgins," Romy replied. "At least one of them knew a great deal more about life, as Mother Marie well knew." Romy stumbled, stunned at what she'd just said.

"What? Who's Mother Marie?" Amy turned to Romy, her eyes wide. "And that's, like, the opposite of what you just said."

Romy faltered, scanning her memory for something to explain her words. "I don't even know why I said that. A brain blip, I guess."

"Hot little French numbers probably don't need anybody to tell them how to get it on, anyway," Stan said, wedging himself between Dave and Romy. "That kind of knowledge comes naturally to Frenchies."

Obviously Stan had flunked Gender Sensitivity 101 as well as Cultural Enlightenment and Basic Intelligence for Beginners. But with a migraine threatening, she needed to stay cool more than ever. Surely she could survive this jerk awhile longer.

Bourbon Street came next but by then commentary would be kept to a minimum. Like most of the tour guides, she delivered her groups here at the end of the tour so her peeps could indulge in the perpetual festivity that percolated the street.

Romy still managed to point out the best jazz houses, identify a few key buildings, and recommend bars and eateries. Finally she brought them to the corner of Bourbon and St. Peter Streets. With the surrounding noise, it would be a miracle if anyone heard a thing she said.

"And now the moment you've all been waiting for," she called, turning to face them. "Bourbon Street, where a little bit of Mardi Gras is alive and well every day of the year. I'm going to deliver you to one of the city's famous watering holes where you can explore the Quarter on your own afterward. How does that sound?"

"Fantabulous," one of the FlashTeck dudes called out. "Bring it on!"

"And that's exactly what I'll do. Follow me."

Pat O'Brien's was the closest, so that would be the destination of choice. She'd do as she always did: settle them in with a drink in a glass as high as an apartment building.

Her reward would come shortly afterward when she'd slip off home to bed with her pockets jingling with tips.

5

Romy ushered the group through the stone archway into Pat O'Brien's courtyard establishment. She loved the place as much because of the historical ambience as the flaming fountain or party atmosphere.

Though the building was built in 1791 and had originally been the site of a Spanish home, little was known about the occupants. Still, there was just something about the balconies overlooking the courtyard that plucked at some long ago memory she could not grasp.

Meanwhile, her peeps tended to love the twelve-inch souvenir glasses of mixed alcohol that she had arranged by way of drink vouchers. Most visitors stayed on for more, of course.

"Hi, Lucas," she greeted the doorman. "How about a few good tables for my friends here?"

Lucas, tonight's gatekeeper host, was a tall, good-looking black guy who Jo had briefly dated and whom Romy had come to know from regular tour visits. If she hadn't been so smitten with Adrian, she might have fallen for him herself. He worked at the drinkery part-time as a way to fund his business management studies. His enjoyment for people seemed to come as natural to him as breathing.

"Sure thing, Romy," he said with a wink. "Any group of yours is a group of mine. I'll find you some good spots. Got a big group clearing out now. How y'all doing, anyway?" he called over his shoulder as he beckoned the troupe along. "Enjoying Nawlins, folks?"

Stan called out, "I'd enjoy it more if I could find myself a date for the night. Got any real women in this city? I was expecting hot little numbers in a place like this."

"Oh, be quiet, Stan," one of the FlashTeck guys called out. "You wouldn't know what to do with a hot number if you tripped over her."

The others guffawed as Amy linked arms with Romy and rolled her eyes. "He's just getting over an ugly divorce," she whispered. "The first couple of times I met him he wasn't like this."

"Really?" Romy said. As if she cared. All she wanted to do was to get home to bed, not hear the sorry tale of a relationship gone bad. She had one of her own, minus the relationship part. Nine-fifteen. Twenty minutes away from mission accomplished.

They followed Lucas onto the lush patio. True to his word, he sat them deep in the garden courtyard a few yards away from the fountain's multi-colored fire-and-light display. "Here you go folks—a prime spot for the light show."

"Wow, look at that: fire and rain," Dave said appreciatively.

As they took their seats across three tables, Lucas leaned over to whisper into Romy's ear. "See you've got a live one there. If he gives you a hard time, I'll boot him out on his ear."

"Thanks, Lucas, but I can handle him," Romy whispered back. "I didn't take kickboxing for nothing, that is if I can still do my thing after months of no practice." As if she'd had time to do more than study, work and breathe in months.

Lucas backed away, laughing, hands up in surrender. "I wouldn't tackle you, girl."

Romy laughed, too. As if she'd ever use her kickboxing for anything other than exercise. What a ludicrous thought. Her smile died when she gazed across the room and saw Adrian Countway enter the courtyard with a woman on his arm.

She forgot to breathe.

He strode midway across the space, scanning the courtyard for a table, as if determined to select his own seat rather than be directed by the host

—so like him. But who in hell was that woman, anyway? She looked familiar but Romy couldn't place her.

Adrian Countway with a woman? Well, why not? Why wouldn't an attractive single man be with a date? But thinking logically couldn't stop the sense of being punched in the heart.

It was as if someone had tipped a cauldron of boiling emotions down her throat. This wasn't jealousy, this was rage. Or maybe lust or guilt—a brew too powerful and unexpected to bear.

How dare he! She fought an overwhelming urge to run over to him and slap his face, beg for forgiveness, demand an explanation, all at once. But for now, Adrian seemed to be looking in every direction but hers.

Bewildered, she struggled for control while her bile rose and her body trembled. Thank God he hadn't seen her yet. Where could she hide? A headache pounded her cranium with the force of a head-on collision. Escape, she needed to escape before she did something unthinkable.

Keeping her head down, she plotted her route. She'd dash around the perimeter of the courtyard and up the stairs to the ladies' room. Only the crowd jammed the corridors and she had to push her way through the crush. Still, she only managed to take the first three steps to the second level before Stan caught up to her.

"Hey, Frenchie, wanna dance?" he said right behind her.

Startled, Romy turned and looked straight into his eyes. With one hand gripping a glass of beer, he reached for her with his other and began tugging her back down the stairs.

"*Allez-vous-en!*" she cried, tugging her hand away and running farther up the stairs. "*Laisse-moi tranquille!*"

"What the hell! You're not talking that French crap to me, are you?" he called after her. "Come on, baby, don't give me that. You know what you really want. Let me give it to you, American-style."

Blazing fury, she ran back down until she stood one step above him. In one quick thrust, she shoved him hard with both hands, and watched as he stumbled backward, arms flailing.

For a stunned instant she saw his glass fly into the air and smash onto the stone floor, registered his shocked expression as he clutched the railing.

This can't be happening. She couldn't have just done that.

Recovering his balance, Stan charged back up toward her, red-faced and calling out, "Damn little foreign bitch," in a stream of verbal shrapnel.

The crowd stopped. Everybody stared.

But Romy didn't run. She waited for the drunken lout to get close enough for her to smell his beery breath before delivering a swift kick where the idiot would feel it most.

The force sent him reeling backward and this time he would have hit the floor had Lucas not caught him on the way down. "Okay, buddy, you're outta here," he said, righting Stan and setting him on his feet.

"Me? That French bitch pushed me!"

Romy's gaze met Lucas's before she glanced over his shoulder long enough to see Adrian pressing through the crowd toward her, shocked amazement all over his damn handsome face.

She turned, taking the steps two at a time until she reached the long outer hallway to the washrooms. A thrill of power mixed with an adrenaline rush pushed her headache temporarily into the distance.

Damn, but that felt good! Bastard got what he deserved...but then a dizzying sensation seemed to be sucking her down.

"Romy, stop, please!" Adrian's voice.

By the time she reached the ladies' room, the headache had arrived with blinding intensity and, with it, a churning of nausea. She pushed her way through the vanity room toward the stalls muttering, "Sorry, sick," to everyone in her way. She reached a cubicle just in time.

Minutes later, she settled into a chair in the adjoining vanity room, trembling with weakness deep inside the eye of the headache's storm.

Time stalled inside the migraine's center. Propped in a chair, she dimly heard women come and go, heard the washroom door swing open again and again with every sound or sensation magnified inside a gray, sick haze.

One woman passed her a wet towel, another a glass of water. Many others asked if she'd be all right. Women understood headaches in the deepest sense and the waves of sympathy soothed her.

Eyes closed, she nodded her thanks and said she just needed to keep her eyes closed and not move. No, she didn't want a taxi, thanks.

Then, after what seemed like hours later, she heard a woman's voice penetrate her fog.

"You're Romy?"

She blinked up at the woman standing over her—a blonde wearing an eye-stabbing red dress.

"Aren't you the Frozen Angel lady Susie and I met today? I'd recognize you even without the greasepaint. Small world, isn't it?"

Romy tried to focus on the woman's face. Susie's mother, she realized in shock, was Adrian's date. She couldn't grapple with that just then. All she could do was stare as the woman's red shift morphed into a long black dress and back again. God help her, but maybe she really was going mad.

"Are you going to be all right?" the woman asked, her expression concerned. "I'm Veronica, by the way. I'm with Adrian Countway, and he asked me to see how you were. We were just about to go to a show but he insisted I check on you first. Look, supposing I give you cab fare so you can get yourself home?"

Romy stared into her steel blue eyes. "What are you wearing?" she mumbled.

The woman glanced down at her red dress and back to Romy. "What do you mean? Forget my clothes. You should go home or to a doctor or something. You had an episode earlier, too."

Shaking her head took too much effort. "Migraine. Can't move. Just need to be left...alone." And the ladies' room had become her refuge against whatever or whoever waited for her beyond those doors—Adrian, Stan, her tour group, the explanations for her embarrassing behavior. Besides, if she tried to walk now, she'd only topple over.

"I'll call you a cab."

"Don't. I mean, no thanks," Romy said, hearing how her voice turned harsh. "Please. Just turn off that one overhead light when you leave. I just need to be alone."

"You look like hell. If I were you, I'd get myself some help."

"*Laisse-moi tranquille*," Romy mumbled. "Leave me alone!"

"Suit yourself." After hovering awhile longer, Veronica left, switching off the lounge light on her way out.

Romy averted her face from the direction of the stalls where the punishing white fluorescence still blasted. Though she heard women mutter around her after that, no one seemed to notice her sitting in the dark.

THE MINUTES PASSED IN A FOGGY STRETCH. SHE MUST HAVE DOZED. When she bolted upright, her heart galloping, stillness had settled everywhere. She heard no sounds—no voices or music rumbled from downstairs. Could she have slept right past closing time? Now she'd have to find her way out of a locked, alarmed building.

Befuddled, she rose, taking a few tentative steps toward the door. Too dark, everything was far too dark. Outside, the corridor hung suspended over a lake of shadow where things croaked and cheeped and only a single sconce of burning rushes lit the way.

She blinked. Since when did O'Brien's use that little touch of dangerous authenticity? Where were the building's exit signs and the night lighting?

She glanced over the balcony, disorientated. New Orleans' ambient violet sky made luminous at night by a million lights had been replaced by stars spangling over a foreign world of ghostly trees and strange shapes. She shivered, despite the warmth. This was no New Orleans she knew.

Gripping the railing, she attempted to steady her mind. Not a dream, she realized. Once again, she had been spliced into the past. So how in hell could she splice herself back?

A woman's voice sounded nearby. *What takes him so long? Surely he has not forgotten our rendezvous?*

From what Romy could tell, she was totally alone, yet the voice was very close, too close. It took seconds before Romy realized that the voice was inside her head!

She stifled a scream. Someone was thinking in French inside her mind! With those thoughts came a rush of strange feelings, of powerful anxiety mixed with anticipation.

Tonight will be the night. I will do this thing at last.

Romy felt her heartbeat increase and her hands go clammy and slick. She tried to wipe her palms on her skirt but her arms refused to move.

I hear footsteps! He comes!

Footsteps sounded down the corridor and her body turned to the dark shape of an approaching figure. Romy's feet, disconnected from her will, moved down the corridor toward the man. A bizarre zap of electrified joy hit, a joy she could observe yet not quite embrace.

"At last, you have come," she whispered in French as she fell into the man's arms. "I feared you would not."

"I had to slip out unnoticed. I believe Señora Viscaya suspects, but, oh, Claire—"

Her lips found his before he could speak, her tongue plunging deep inside his mouth, eager to taste the hot, dangerous elixir of whiskey, smoke, and man.

She heard his sharp intake of breath, whether from the shock of her boldness or the force of his own desire, she could not tell.

He suddenly wrenched himself back to hold her at arm's length, searching her eyes. Torchlight flickered across his face. "How long I have waited for this. I—"

She pressed her hand to his lips before he could speak again. "As have I," she whispered. "Love has its own sanctity, yes? For once, we will let love rule. Let us not speak, let us do!"

"Claire, my sweet Claire," was all he said, but all she knew or cared about communicated in the way he returned her kiss, the way his questing hands now roamed across her body, the way his breath quickened, his heart pounded.

Claire. Romy clung to the name, experiencing everything, hearing Claire's every thought, sharing the same emotional and physical heat, all the while struggling to remain herself. It was like experiencing an X-rated movie in virtual reality.

As Claire's hands ran across the man's body, Romy tried taking mental notes of the man: lean frame, medium height, long dark hair half-hidden under a broad hat, thin beard—no goatee, maybe—a sharp interesting face. Those eyes! How could she forget them? It was Antonio! And could he kiss! For a moment desire swamped her along with Claire, all attempts at being a detached observer lost as she sank under a hot tide.

Claire's hand slipped down the man's thigh to massage the thick satin straining across the man's crotch. *Oh, he feels so wonderful!* Romy, awash in heat, agreed completely.

"My God, Claire," the man said with a gasp. "You do not behave as any convent girl I have known."

She fell to her knees with a laugh. "And how many convent girls have you truly known, sire?" she asked as she began to unbutton his breeches.

He leaned against the wall, bracing his legs to give her full access, his face flickering so many emotions—wonder, anticipation. "Pitifully few if this is what they teach you!"

❧

"Romy, what in God's name are you doing?" His voice choked outrage.

Romy looked up into the flushed face of Adrian Countway. She snatched her hand away in horror. The clear memory of Claire's actions confirmed her situation: she had been massaging Adrian's crotch just as Claire had been stroking Antonio's. Here. In a public place!

"It's not me," she said, scrambling to her feet. "It's her. You have to believe that!"

"Is it drugs or alcohol, Adrian?" a woman said with a grim laugh.

Romy swung around, gazing right into Veronica's face. All urge to explain herself evaporated. Pushing past the two of them, she fled, heading for the stairs.

"Wait! Romy, please!" Adrian called after her.

Romy reached the restaurant's main floor and dashed through the courtyard. The crowd had thinned to a few night owls hanging out by the bar. Faces blurred, voices fast-forwarded into a buzz. Nothing or nobody mattered.

Outside, peace briefly enveloped the sidewalk until she turned the corner and waded into the neon frolic of Bourbon Street. Laughter poured around her like cocktails over ice. A saxophone played a smoky riff from somewhere overhead while rock music threatened the sound barrier farther down the road.

An unknown male voice called out to her to show him her "titties" in exchange for a string of beads. Romy stepped over the cheap plastic necklace and kept running.

Stumbling to a walk, she glanced over her shoulder. No sign of Adrian or anyone else following. Straight down Bourbon was the quickest route home but she couldn't risk the catcalls and leers for the next two blocks.

Instead, she cut down Ursulines Avenue, intent on crossing Dauphine

Street and then right to her Governor Nicholls Street cottage, avoiding anyone who might be dogging her path.

Of course, Adrian knew where she lived and might get the fool notion to wait for her there. He'd urge her to seek medical attention and, after tonight, she'd hardly blame him.

Her heart finally slowed. What had just happened? She'd just had a past life experience not associated with her Frozen Angel performance and it had occurred with violence and excruciating consequences.

She needed help and soon. If not so late, she would have hopped a taxi to Louisa Dupré's residence and begged for assistance right on the spot—as if Louisa ran an emergency clinic for the paranormally challenged. *Get a grip.* She coughed out a laugh, thinking of how ludicrous all this had become. It couldn't be happening and yet it was.

She fought for calm. The danger had passed, in any case. She'd survive, maybe even leave town and change her name, take an education degree back in Nova Scotia, and forget all this.

My God, how far had she fallen? From stellar historian to some confused little mess wandering lost in two centuries?

This end of Ursulines Avenue had the quiet of a residential area. Most folks occupying the cottages and houses on either side had long ago tucked themselves into bed, their air conditioners whizzing in the humid air.

Romy paused under a tree, totally drained. For a moment, she listened to the soothing sound of the leaves rustling in the breeze high overhead, taking a moment to steady her thoughts.

Then footsteps punctuated the stillness. A glance over her shoulder confirmed that nothing or no one followed. She stared in disbelief down the darkened street as the eerie tapping sound manifested no more than yards away. It seemed to gain in volume, heading toward her in little angry thumps, yet nothing visible connected to the sound.

Heart hammering, she broke into a rapid walk. Both footsteps and the tapping intensified on her heels. Another glance over her shoulder and still nothing. Fear severed thought. She broke into a run.

Romy knew she'd never make it home—still too far with too many secluded spots along the way. Maybe she could scream, bang on someone's door, call out for help? Would anybody rouse themselves in time?

Whatever it was, it was gaining on her. She needed a busy thoroughfare, a restaurant, a bar. Maybe back to Bourbon Street?

Dauphine Street stretched ahead with more houses, many barricaded behind gates and protective grilles, many more still boarded up and abandoned. Even in the daylight this street could look like a ghost town fighting to be reborn.

If she turned left and ran as fast as she could, maybe, just maybe, she'd reach the beating heart of the French Quarter and those crowds she'd just escaped would protect her with their very realness.

No more than two house lengths away from the corner of Dauphine, she stumbled as pain seared her forehead. Doubling over, she gripped her skull, realizing with sickening certainty that this meant she'd be jettisoned into the past again, now, of all times. She tried to prevent the transition but it was useless: the headache pounded as the surrounding world changed.

Lowering her hands moments later, she found herself standing with her back pressed against the wall of some very dark place, perspiring heavily and terrified. She knew she was trapped back inside Claire's life and that their terrors had merged.

Someone pawed her in the dark, cruel hands squeezing her breasts, attempting to rip off her dress.

"Let go of me, you oaf!" Claire cried out in French. She could not make out his face, yet knew him all the same.

"Not this time, little Frenchie. This time you are mine! I said you pay, yes? Well, now you pay!" The man's voice came in broken French edged with Spanish.

She pushed him away, kicked at him, tried to claw at his eyes. He only held her by the wrists and laughed. Releasing one wrist quickly, he slapped her face with enough force to slam her head into the wall. "Do it easy or do it hard—you decide."

"You will be punished!" she sobbed. "He will hang you!"

"He will hang me in any event so I may as well have my fun."

Romy thought she recognized the man shoving Claire down into the rubbish pile—not his face because it stayed deeply shadowed, not the shape of his body or the inflection in his voice because those differed, too. No, she knew him by his soul. It hit her like a recognition of twisted darkness. Struggling beneath him she tried to kick out but her legs were pinned under his weight.

"What's this, Frenchie? Still playing games? Come on, you got me turned on now."

Now Stan's voice, Stan's breath. Had the past spliced with the present again? She seemed to be in some back alley, wedged between two garbage cans and a rickety door.

"Why are you doing this?" she managed to ask in her own voice; Claire and she were flipping back and forth.

"'Why are you doing this?'" he mocked, pitching a girlie falsetto. "You're finally getting friendly, that's all. Now you'll finish what you've started."

"Listen to me, something really strange is going on. The past and the present are influencing one another. I—" Romy began.

"Shut the fuck up. Time to put out. I'm only going to do what you've done before, see? I heard that you were rubbing some guy's dick back there. You'd do it for him but not me, eh? Now, I'm gonna take what you won't give," he whispered.

A brutal parody of a kiss followed, all alcohol and slime. She couldn't breathe. All she could do was struggle in mute disgust as the full impact of her predicament struck. Trapped in a dark alley with this drunken bastard, one minute in the past, the next in the present!

Fueled by rage, she thrust her knee into his groin, feeling the instant satisfaction of bone impacting flesh.

Grunting, he reeling backward and cursed. "You bitch! You lousy, good for nothing bitch!"

On her feet now, she tried squeezing past him for the open street but he grabbed her by the hair and flung her back against the wall. The side of her face hit the brick and nausea followed.

A woman cried out in French. But as she struggled with dizziness and tried to regain her feet, another man's voice called out. She heard his rage followed by a cry of male pain, the sound of which chased her all the way down into the blackness.

6

"What happened to you last night?" Romy hauled her head up from the pillow and stared at Joquita. "Jo?"

"Who else would be traipsing around your bedroom at eleven o'clock in the morning bearing gifts of coffee and beignets?" She dropped a bag on the bedside table and handed Romy an ice pack. "Hold that to your head. You look a mess. I asked what happened last night."

Romy groaned as she touched the ice to her cheek. What *had* happened last night? What she remembered was far too bizarre to be real.

Wincing, she propped herself against the headboard and tried to think. Half-remembered images rolled around her head like a badly edited nightmare spliced with an erotic dream gone bad. "Maybe I spent part of last night on an aphrodisiac laced with some hallucinogen?"

"Can you bottle that?" Jo studied her, her face a mask of worry.

"It's not funny. I don't even remember coming home."

"Do you see me laughing? That bruise on your face looks bad, girl. Did you have an accident? Run into one tourist too many?" Jo dragged over a chair. A moment later, hands braced on her knees, she was staring anxiously at her friend. "Go on, start from the beginning."

Romy leaned forward. "Wait a minute. I just need to think and try to sort things through."

"You need a doctor, too."

"No way. I don't want a stranger asking me questions I can't answer. These are just bruises. They'll heal." She gingerly touched her other cheek, saw the bandages on her arms. "Who did this?"

"You tell me. Somebody tended to you last night. So, do you remember? Another ghostly rendezvous or something?"

Romy stared down at the coverlet, her eyes tracing the pattern of fragile green vines twining amid bloodred roses. She pressed a fist into her temple. "I had a migraine, the worst of my life, and retreated to the ladies' room at O'Brien's to ride it out, only then…oh, hell, back up: that was after I pushed a man down the stairs."

"You what?"

"It gets worse. What I'm remembering just couldn't have happened—all these bizarre, disconnected visions from the past and the future mixed together. It's different from the Frozen Angel experiences. Last night was more like watching television where all the channels keep jumping around. I even blacked out entirely at times."

A picture of Adrian's shocked face flashed into her mind. Romy gazed back into her jumbled memories, aghast.

"You remembered something. Spit it out."

Romy shook her head. "I couldn't have done that," she moaned.

"Done what, damn it?"

"I suddenly found myself on my knees in front of Adrian Countway, trying to unzip his fly."

"You're getting the sex channel now?"

Romy groaned. "Will you be serious?"

"How can I? Didn't I just hear you say that you were about to deliver a blow job to the professor?"

"Oh, God." Romy buried her head in her hands. "Don't say it like that. It wasn't me, it was Claire. She met Antonio for a rendezvous, a very heated rendezvous, and while she was…well, while we were at it, suddenly Antonio was Adrian."

"Shit, girl. Don't tell me that."

"There were people standing by watching and there I was on my knees.

He was mortified, I was mortified. He stopped me before I could go further. I was just...appalled, devastated, embarrassed like you wouldn't believe. I got up and ran out of the building and then..." She struggled to sort through the fuzzy images of Bourbon Street and Ursulines Avenue flipping around inside her head. Was she remembering an attempted rape in two timelines?

"Go on."

She sat stunned for a few moments, not focusing on Joquita's words.

"Hello? Are you there, girl?" her friend demanded.

"No, yes. I mean, I'm here," Romy acknowledged, her fingers twisting the edge of the bedsheet. She pressed her hands to her face again. "I think someone tried to rape me. Well, both me and Claire separately at the same time. Oh, my God, am I going crazy?"

Joquita met her gaze with a look that said it all. "I'm no expert but it sure as hell seems that way, girlfriend."

Romy shuddered. "First, I'm being pursued by some unknown person, then suddenly I'm in Claire's body fighting another attacker in another time and place, and then I'm back in my own skin again being pawed by one of my customers. That would be Stan, the ignorant boor I pushed down the stairs, by the way. I lost minutes, hours—I don't know how long. I can't remember much of that, either." A sob caught in her throat. "What's happening to me? Am I psychotic?"

Jo jumped to her feet and began pacing. "Girl, I don't know what's happening to you but you're a mess, I know that much. Besides having supposed past life encounters, now you're getting roughed up by the tourists and maybe by ghosts, too? Don't try telling me this isn't one for the police. Forget the past shit for a minute. If some bastard tried to rape you last night, he needs to be charged. In fact, how do you know he didn't successfully rape you, considering that you blacked out?"

Romy sent her a pointed look. "I'd know that much."

"Okay, but this Stan moron still deserves to have his ass kicked."

Romy stared straight ahead. "But he...he did have his ass kicked."

Jo swung around, her voice rising to a pitch. "Now, what the hell does that mean?"

"Someone came to my rescue last night. Another man arrived, I'm sure of it. Everything's so muddled. I remember hearing two men's voices and grunting, the sounds of fighting, even while I was struggling to get to my feet. I couldn't see them in the darkness and then I blacked out again."

"You still need to report the assault," Jo insisted, staring at Romy with a determined gaze she knew too well. "It's the only concrete thing we have to go on. Go to the police."

"And say what? How will I explain how I even ended up in that alley with Stan in the first place? I don't know how I got there. The last thing I remember, I was running away from some invisible pursuer, hearing weird tapping noises and footsteps."

Jo frowned. "You tell them what you think you know, no matter how crazy it sounds."

"But what do I know? Nothing! I can't go to the police. I have far too much explaining of my own to do and I need those answers first."

"Then I'm calling Aunt Loo right now. She'll have some ideas about this stuff."

For once, Romy didn't protest. While Joquita punched the numbers into the phone, she climbed out of bed and made for the bathroom.

She was in the midst of splashing cold water on her face, wincing as the water hit her cheek, when Jo yelled in through the door. "I can't reach her. She's not answering her cell. Probably closing a big deal or something."

Romy leaned against the sink, staring at her bruised face. Louisa Dupré would likely be away earning her next million, selling office buildings or some antebellum estate outside of town. "That's okay," she called out. "I'll wait to see her tonight."

In the welcome light of day, the horror of last night receded. She could definitely wait. Then a sudden thought struck: Where was her purse? She hadn't seen it this morning.

Tossing aside the towel, she ran out of the bathroom and searched frantically under the bed, on the chairs. "It's gone! Damn it!"

Joquita, still pacing, looked over at her friend. "What's gone?"

"My purse, I lost my purse last night. I can't believe it."

"Considering your state of mind, you're lucky you didn't lose a whole lot more." Jo joined in the search, both women raking one end of the cottage to the other. "What did you have in it—credit cards, what?"

"No, nothing like that, only my lipstick, brush, a Swiss Army gizmo, and a little cash, very little cash—nothing worth stealing. I hadn't even collected my tips yet—oh, and my identification with my address and everything including my tour operator tag. That's the important thing."

"Okay, okay, calm down."

"I am calm."

"You are not. Just because you're not hyperventilating doesn't mean you're calm. You must have left it back at O'Brien's."

"Maybe," Romy whispered, suddenly overwhelmed, "but I think I had it with me after that because I remember clutching it to my chest at one point. It's probably back in that alley where Stan attacked me but I don't even know where that place is. Jo—" she turned to her friend "—if Stan's got my identification, he knows where I live."

Jo thrust the phone into her hand. "That does it: call the police," she said, enunciating every syllable.

"Right. I give up. The police, it is." Romy dialed the number, realizing she had no choice. After a moment, a Constable McCory introduced herself, but instead of explaining the whole messy tale, Romy only told the officer that she'd dropped her bag someplace in town last night but had no idea where. "I'm afraid someone will find my address," she ended.

By the time she hung up, Jo's arms were crossed. "How lame was that? They'll just stick that complaint right in with all the other hopeless cases because they have no information and no reason to think it's important enough to care."

"I know, I know. She told me how unlikely it was they'd find anything."

"Like I said."

Romy sank onto the edge of the bed and buried her face in her hands. "I'm not interested in nailing Stan, Jo, please get that part. I have too many other things to worry about right now. All I wanted was my bag back."

"Here, drink your coffee." Jo passed her the paper cup from the bag she'd brought. "We can always have the locks changed but my guess is this guy will catch his plane back home accompanied by a huge hangover and a pile of foggy memories. He won't come after you, the bastard. I'd like to go after him, though."

Romy nodded, sipping the coffee, allowing rational thought to gain a foothold in her frenzied brain. She was panicking, that's all, being foolish. As Jo said, he wouldn't come after her. "But I'll still have the ghosts to attend to."

"Yeah, and that's something we'll leave for Aunt Loo tonight. Will you hang together until then?"

"Of course. I'm not falling apart, just getting a bit frayed on the edges," Romy said, continuing to sip.

"Unraveled, more like it."

Romy gazed at her paper cup, hands trembling. "Oh, that's so good. Aren't you having any?"

"I had my two cups for today. Look, I don't want to leave you alone but I have a big test in twenty minutes followed by classes. Say you'll stay here and rest. I'll call between classes and make sure you're all right."

"I have no plans." And sadly, that was true. She, who always had a million things to do and prided herself in doing them efficiently, suddenly came up empty. No studies, no papers, no classes. "You go. Ace that test."

Jo smiled slowly. "Girl, you're breaking my heart. Seeing you like this is so damn wrong. Someone's got to pay for it, or some *thing* does. Those headaches seem to trigger the episodes. Why not see a doctor about those at least?"

"I've been, remember? I have prescriptions for meds that don't change a thing. You'd better get going."

"Yeah, I'd better. Here, take a beignet, too." Jo offered her the bag. "I bought a bunch. And good luck with Aunt Loo tonight."

"Sure you won't come with me?"

"No way. She'll be talking mumbo jumbo and always tries to drag me into it somehow. I'd rather edit in the library where it's safe."

7

Joquita's Aunt Louisa lived in the Garden District of New Orleans, the land of stately old homes, tree-lined boulevards, sweeping gardens, and plenty of money.

Romy believed that Louisa had chosen this area partly because it amused her to live so deep in enclaves of a traditionally white neighborhood, though that community, like others, had varied its color scheme over the years.

Aunt Loo had not been born into wealth, she had earned it.

As Romy passed through the wrought-iron gates and up the flagstone walkway of a twilight garden so lush and deeply planted it could be rainforest, she thought maybe Aunt Loo also needed something grand enough to suit her expansive style.

Louisa Dupré owned prime real estate all over New Orleans and could never live anywhere small or anywhere else. Where would she squeeze in the art collection, the antiques, the interesting people who often needed to stay under her roof for weeks at a time?

But Louisa was no hoarder. She shared, giving deeply and with generosity. Millions of her dollars went to help the people of New Orleans, first to recover from Katrina, and later to support her fellow citizens during the coronavirus. Helping New Orleans' poorest citizens seemed to be at least part of the reason for her wealth.

Romy felt unaccountably young around Aunt Loo. Though the woman couldn't be a day under fifty-five, she seemed much younger yet ageless at the same time. When you spent time with Aunt Loo, everything you believed about the universe shifted.

And what did Romy really know of the universe despite her six years of postgraduate education and her life experience? Far less than she had originally thought.

On the other hand, here was a woman who had become successful financially as well as spiritually, by all accounts, and thus had achieved some kind of balanced life. Now all Romy could do was pray she had the answers.

She walked up the stairs just as some electronic timer turned on the outdoor lighting. Her eyes remained fixed on the deep green door ahead, all the while wondering how she'd phrase her story this time. She hadn't done the greatest job explaining herself to Adrian, though she knew words hadn't been the biggest difficulty there.

Adrian. No. Don't think about him.

Her hand hadn't yet reached the buxom goddess knocker when a voice greeted her from behind the shrubbery. "No need to touch them knockers. If it's you, Romy, just take yourself in."

Romy peered over the railing and grinned at the sturdy woman wearing coveralls standing amid the bushes, Louisa's gardener-cum-groundskeeper. "Is that you, Rae Dawn?"

"It's me burnin' the midnight oil. She wants you to go right in through the kitchen and out into the patio. Been expecting you. I got the side gate blocked on account that I'm laying down flags for her new meditation garden. Lots of statues, bamboo, and another pool, is all I know. Can't go that way, is my point."

"Oh, right. Thanks."

Romy knew about the Katrina garden, the place where Aunt Loo beseeched all visitors not to mourn but to send love and light to the victims. It was right next to her corona garden, a space where visitors could send love and light to anyone afflicted with the virus. The patio, however, was neutral ground.

More statues and salvaged architectural bits greeted her eye. Every visit to this house was worth the price of admission, if Louisa ever chose to charge.

She was often designing some bold new scheme that would inevitably send a glossy magazine's editor scurrying out with a camera team upon its completion. Despite her many talents, it was still Louisa's reputation as a woman wise to the ways of the paranormal for which she was most famous in New Orleans.

Romy pushed open the door and paused, looking back at Rae Dawn. "By the way, have you seen Jo?" She couldn't help but hope her friend had changed her mind.

"Nope, not today."

Sighing, Romy shut the door behind her and stepped across the threshold of Louisa's 1846 mansion. Inside the house seemed hushed and still. Tiffany lamps glowed from the corners of the rooms, adding splashes of color that seemed to coordinate with the gardenia-scented air.

Along the marble hall heading toward the kitchen, tables were arranged in intriguing vignettes such as tiny water gardens filled with floating lilies and an inlaid buffet table staging vials stuffed with pitcher plants.

Pitcher plants? Romy paused. Yes, Louisa had filled vases with the rich maroon and lime green of carnivorous plants. The effect was weirdly beautiful, though Romy couldn't help but imagine Louisa running about feeding the plants gourmet stick bugs.

Passing through the spotless kitchen, Romy spied a tray of something draped with linen towels on the granite countertop, no doubt delicious tidbits made by either Louisa or her chef.

Anxiety hit anew. Supposing Louisa was expecting company? What if her meeting tonight had to be cut short when she so desperately needed counsel?

She wouldn't be expected to discuss something personal and embarrassing in front of strangers, would she? Swallowing hard, she stepped through the French doors onto the patio and caught her breath.

The night had settled in around the dusky garden, clotting inky shadows beneath the trees and fern-lined paths. Ahead, in the main patio room, a fire burned in the towering Gothic fireplace while tea lights glowed in glass pots marching along its carved mantel.

"I like an outdoor fire in the evenings, no matter how warm the night. Takes away the edge of damp, to my way of thinking," said a deep melodic female voice.

Romy blinked, realizing the voice came from behind a large wrought-iron chair, one of a cluster gathered before the fire. Only then did it occur to her that she might actually be the worthy guest for whom the food awaited in the kitchen.

How nice. She had never felt special enough to warrant particular attention before. She smiled. "Yes, it does. It warms the heart."

"Sometimes the soul needs warming first." Louisa had her back to Romy with her legs stretched on a small stool. The long thick hair had been loosed from her workday chignon and now hung in unruly waves to her shoulders.

"Well, come out, why don't you? Take a seat and pour yourself a julep. I can feel the anxiety wafting off you in waves."

"Is it that obvious?" Romy asked as her feet scuffed across the damp slate toward a small candelabra-lit table holding three tall glasses and a pitcher.

A shiver tingled down her spine as her fingers grasped the glass's slicked surface. For a moment the scent of the flowers clinging to the humid air smelled as overpowering as spilled perfume.

What would happen here tonight?

"Despair's coming off you pretty strong, Romy," Louisa said mildly, "and it's not all yours." She sat back in the chair, eyes closed, holding a drink in her ringed fingers. "You need unwinding."

"But you're not even looking at me," Romy remarked as she glanced toward Louisa.

"A person doesn't need to look to see," her hostess responded. "If only the world could look beyond the eyes to really see."

Romy studied the older woman. As magnificent as ever, Louisa was not so much large as bountiful, her substantial girth seeming to house a wealth of experience along with a spirit twice as broad.

Tonight in a flowing loose gown that could easily be silk chiffon, she looked every inch the queen—the queen of mystery, wisdom, and something else Romy couldn't define.

"No, perhaps not."

"You drink and relax now. The bourbon in the julep ought to help with the unwinding. We're waiting for Joquita. After she arrives, we'll talk about what brought you here."

"Jo's coming?" Romy asked as she poured herself a drink with fingers trembling. Low blood sugar, she thought. No food for hours and hours. "She said she wouldn't come so I wasn't expecting to see her."

"Well, I'm expecting her and she knows it. She'll show. She needs to hear this, too. I told her I expected her here within the hour and by my reckoning she's got fifteen minutes left." With that, Aunt Loo pushed herself to an upright position and turned to gaze at Romy.

For a few moments, Romy could feel those inscrutable eyes probing her as if from some satellite overhead. Finally, she met the woman's gaze, acknowledging the instant of connection.

"So," Louisa said softly, her voice edged with wonder. "It's true."

"What's true?" Past the alarm, past the little ping of strangeness, Romy felt something, too, something deeper than her definition of "familiar."

For a few seconds the world seemed to shift, like wind brushing the reflection in a pool, and she thought she stood someplace else, someplace unknown yet half-remembered, a room with a cross against a stark white wall. A pain stabbed her between the eyes and she gasped.

"It's all right, child," Louisa's voice said, her tone soothing like a cool hand on a fevered brow. "Imagine my garden, the fire, the taste of mint in the drink you're holding. Try to use your imagination as the rudder to anchor you back to now."

Romy followed those instructions until she could drag herself back into the comfortable mystery of Louisa's garden. "What's happening to me?" she whispered.

"Life, death, and the pursuit of absolution, that's what," Louisa said softly. "Your soul has work to do. Don't worry. I'll explain all in good time. I've been waiting for this encounter for a long while now. I just didn't recognize you were the one until this moment. All the times we met before, the time wasn't right."

8

Joquita strode onto the patio carrying the food trays, her energy shattering the moment. "Is this all we're having for supper, these fish thingies?" she called out.

Romy turned toward her, dazed.

"Those 'fish thingies' are crab sandwiches with homemade mayonnaise and my own baked bread," Louisa told her, swinging around. "And if you think I'm going to let you gnaw on celery sticks while you're here, think again. Look at you. I have a lamp pole out here with more width to it. Eat."

Jo made a face. "Yes, ma'am." She cast a glance toward Romy. "Aunt Loo, can you sort this one out? She's in deep shit."

Louisa shot her a stern look. "Don't go using that language around here, Joquita Maria Bonita Dupré, especially not in the presence of food."

Joquita, looking as if she was accustomed to this exchange, took a mock bow. "Sorry again. No swearing, references to sex, or any other appetite not associated with food."

Aunt Loo rumbled a laugh. "Good, then. You understand. Now, offer the sandwiches to our guest and sit yourself down."

Joquita obeyed, winking at Romy as she settled into one of the cushioned chairs. "There. Get comfortable and eat up, my friend. I have a feeling we're in for a long night."

"You came," Romy said.

"My presence here is by command. Auntie," she said over her shoulder, "I told her you were an expert on the paranormal but I had no idea what to tell her to expect. Certainly not a séance, I know that much."

"Child, you don't know how little you know. For once, try to listen and learn something that doesn't come packaged in a book. And no scuttling out the back door when the discussion delves deeper."

"But I'm fixin' to go on a date later," Jo remarked. "He's a hottie and I don't want to be late."

Aunt Louisa laughed again. "So, what else is new? My guess is he means no more to you than the last twenty you've strung along. Call him up and send your apologies. Say you have pressing business concerning your education and you're giving him a chance to escape with his heart intact."

Jo shook her head. "You make me seem like some modern day Delilah."

"Ahuh." Louisa nodded.

But Jo didn't argue further and trotted off across the garden, cell phone pressed against her ear.

Only later, after they had eaten most of the sandwiches, munched their way through a mixed green salad, and left a crater in a dish of pecan bread pudding, did Louisa ask Romy to give her version of the events she'd been experiencing.

By that time, the fire had burned low in the grate, the tea lights had winked out one by one along the mantelpiece, and a mellow mood washed over everyone.

Until Romy began summarizing recent events. "So, you see, in the past three weeks I've been experiencing this strange phenomenon. Sometimes it's as if I'm actually transported to the past and sometimes it's more like the past is influencing me here in the present."

"Go on." Louisa nodded.

"After last night, I finally have names—Claire and Antonio. Is this possession? Nothing about this feels like what I think I know about possession but I don't have any other ready explanation. What's happening to me?"

It took a few moments for the woman to respond. Louisa sat with eyes closed and hands folded in her lap. "Not possession but more like progression. This is your soul's attempt to move on its journey. What's messing with you in the here and now is an earlier version of your soul's unfinished business and a pile of anguish keeping her locked in a kind of spin."

"What?" Romy and Joquita said in unison.

"Claire is you, Romy. She's your soul's memory of another lifetime."

"You're saying my soul is somehow stuck in a life it's lived before?"

"I said Claire is your soul's memory, not your soul. Brains have memories, hearts have memories, and souls have memories. Think of it as an imprint, an internal ghost, if you like. Your soul has unfinished business to attend and it's haunting you."

"My soul is stuck?"

"Something powerful is keeping it from going forward—keeping it from letting go—some traumatic event your soul can't forgive herself for, or perhaps for which others can't forgive. It keeps going over the memories like a video on constant replay. She can't find peace. She can't move on, and because she can't move on, neither can you."

Romy and Joquita looked at one another. Romy swallowed hard. "I'm being haunted from the inside. Is my soul in a kind of purgatory?"

"Think of purgatory as only one way of looking at things," Louisa said, "but only one way. Call the light 'heaven,' if you want; call pain and suffering 'hell'; call all the in-between part 'purgatory'—doesn't matter. Different beliefs use different metaphors. Fact is, souls are on a journey and there's a pile of work to do along the way. Most of us keep right on going unless we get stuck. That's what's happening to your soul, Romy. It's stuck, all right."

Romy sat upright in her chair, struggling to comprehend. "I'm stuck," she repeated. "Okay, I can believe that. I certainly feel like I'm spinning my wheels, but what about Adrian? Where does he fit into this?"

"Right smack in the middle, to my way of thinking. His soul's memories are tied in with yours. Your two souls are probably well acquainted, maybe across many lifetimes, which is why you're susceptible to uncontrollable behaviors when you're around him and why his reaction to you may seem so odd. Something happened between you two."

Romy nodded. "He's Antonio de Ulloa, isn't he?"

"Sounds that way to me," the older woman said.

"Part of me believed that from the beginning," Romy acknowledged.

Joquita whistled. "No way the good professor will ever believe that."

Louisa let out a low rumble of a laugh. "Not yet, perhaps, but he will. That man's got a lifetime of preconceived notions to overcome first, same as you."

"But he's always kept me physically at a distance," Romy said, "as if he's not attracted to me."

"Do you really believe he's not attracted?" Louisa asked.

"No, but he behaves as if he's not, which is twice as bad. That means he's lying to both of us."

"And on more than one level," Louisa said with a nod. "He senses some pull toward you beyond his conscious understanding and it doesn't quite fit with who he thinks he is in this lifetime," Louisa continued.

"How male of him," Jo said with a sigh.

"So, not only am I burdened with another lifetime's baggage but so is he?" Romy asked.

Louisa agreed. "And others, too, but the two of you are at the center of it all. Your spirit is more guilt-ridden and thus more toxic. You have a powerful spirit, Romy, one that has bound others to you throughout the centuries. You've got to resolve whatever it is that keeps Claire from letting go and by doing that you'll unlock all kinds of things about yourself and maybe others, too. Plenty of people have a stake in this, child, but only you can figure out how the pieces fit."

"That's a huge responsibility," Romy protested. "How can I do that?"

"I'll help but I want you to tell me something first. Tell me about your parents." Louisa leaned forward, fixing Romy with her inscrutable gaze.

"They both died when I was a child and my memories of them are pretty sketchy. There was a lot of pain, I recall that. My mother died of cancer and my father of a broken heart, as best I can tell. I went to live with my mother's brother after that, Uncle Gerard—a sweet, wonderful man. He died two years ago but I still miss him." She raised her empty glass as if toasting the air, her vision blurring with unshed tears. "You see, a simple tale, after all."

"Now listen, Romy," Louisa said, taking her hand. "You've had a ton of grieving to do and so has Claire. She is part of you, too, though on a much deeper level. We'll begin with her. Know Claire and you'll understand yourself."

Romy stared at the embers in the fireplace. "You've probably also picked up on how, on some subconscious level, I don't think I deserve happiness because, if I did, my parents would never have abandoned me in first place. Despite my stellar academic success, I suffer from massive low esteem. In other words and using modern psych babble, my inner child is a mess. That pretty well sum it up?"

Louisa sighed. "Sounds like you've had counseling, though maybe not the kind you need."

"I have."

"And has it helped?"

"Not one bit. It's just given me a few reasons for what ails me, and a couple of tidy words to apply to my syndromes, but no cures."

"All right, then, now we're going to try healing your soul. All the previous assistance dealt with the mind, which is only organic circuitry, when all's said and done. Your soul is the heart," Louisa told her. "Once Claire's free, the rest will follow."

Romy gazed at her. "You make it sound so easy."

"Believe me, honey, it will be the hardest thing you'll ever do."

9

"So, what do I have to do?" Romy asked. "I must continue on my quest to go back into time, don't I? I have to find that woman who was me and the man she loved."

"Yes, and it may just be the hardest thing you'll ever do in this lifetime or any other but it's got to be done. You ready?"

"Yes and no," she whispered.

"A good honest answer," Louisa said with a satisfied sigh. "Find out what Claire can't forgive."

"To have a soul obsessing away on past traumas like that is enough to drive a person wacko," Jo muttered.

"Perhaps some mental states are interpreted that way. When people begin to behave in ways they can't understand or hear voices and see visions, their trouble may not be one of the brain but of the soul." Louisa tapped her substantial bosom.

"I always knew psychiatrists didn't have all the answers," Jo said, sitting up.

"I'm not sure anyone's got all the answers but modern science is not equipped to deal with the crux of it," her aunt remarked. "They usually deal with one lifetime instead of all the complex layers that lie beneath."

"But how to you argue with that?" Jo asked.

"Maybe you don't. Maybe you just live your own life your own way. To science, what can't be proved doesn't exist. What do they know? They think they can fit every human experience into tidy little boxes that can be explained from A to Z. Sometimes, when they can't find something that fits one box, they invent a new one and slap on a label to make us little folk feel all impressed."

Jo shook her head. "Those little boxes, as you call them, make sense. They're explainable, quantifiable. Personally, if it can't be proved, I get twitchy."

"You need a good dose of faith, child," Aunt Loo countered.

"Faith in what?" Jo asked.

"Faith that the universe is bigger than evidence, faith that your soul knows what your mind can't grasp."

"But things should make sense," Jo answered back.

"They do make sense but not the kind you expect."

"What's that supposed to mean?" Jo asked.

Romy said, "It means that you need to look at things differently, take everything you think you know and turn it upside down. I'm experiencing the past—know it, feel it, have my own evidence to prove it, even though everything that's happening to me is supposedly impossible. I'm learning the rules as I go." She turned to Louisa. "But why is my soul's memory only affecting me now? Why not back home in Nova Scotia? Why not somewhere else?"

"Because the memory triggers are strongest here and so the soul remembers. Many of the souls involved in these same life events are also drawn back to New Orleans, too, like Dr. Adrian. There are more connections than you could ever imagine."

Romy stared at her. "Like Adrian," she repeated.

"Like Adrian, and I'm in this, too," Louisa said.

"You are?"

"I am. And so is Joquita."

"Wait a minute," Jo exclaimed, throwing up her hands. "I'm just the observer, the spectator on the sidelines. Leave me out of this, okay?"

"You're in it already, child," Louisa said, "only I haven't figured out how or how deep. I expect Romy will discover that through Claire's life."

Romy grinned at Jo. "Sorry, girlfriend."

Jo frowned. "I don't believe this. I haven't seen any ghosts or suddenly been transported into another age to have sex with some drop-dead gorgeous Spaniard. Now that would be worth believing in reincarnation. I can't wait to hear what Dr. Countway says when you tell him he's Ulloa."

"When I tell him?" Romy repeated.

"He'll have to hear it at some point," Louisa said with a nod. "I suspect this has been going on for a long time between you two, maybe across many lifetimes."

Romy sighed. "Unrequited love in purpetuum."

"Every life brings new opportunities, Romy. Don't go thinking that you have to live every life in the same old groove. Make this the lifetime your soul breaks free from the pattern and claims love for your own. Tell yourself you deserve it and will make it happen, no matter what."

"But how? What do I do?" Romy asked, almost afraid to hope. "And how do I fight Claire's life inside my own?"

"Why can't she just tell Claire to go away like as in an exorcism?" Jo asked. "Tell her the error of her ways and send her packing?"

"You think we should just cut her a ticket and help pack her bags?" Louisa asked, her gaze directed at Romy. "Claire is not aware she's moving in this century. She's caught up in her own sorry loop, obsessing. She's helpless and locked into a traumatized state. You're seeing events as Claire's seen them."

"So, what then?" Romy asked. "She's becoming stronger every day and causing me to enact her behavior. How do I get control?"

"First, we need to figure out just when and where you slip into Claire's head." Louisa rose to her feet and towered over Romy, arms crossed. "We need to recognize the triggers so you can protect yourself from going back at an inconvenient time. Think about it. When are you having these experiences?"

Romy gazed up, trying to remember. "At first, it happened at the end of my Frozen Angel performances but last night was different."

"Let's just focus on the Frozen Angel routine first. That was when they started, yes? Something about that angel is important. What do you do when you go into your angel state?" Louisa asked.

Romy hesitated. So much of what she did, she did without thinking.

"Well, I try to settle myself into a quiet frame of mind and focus on something."

"Focus on what?" Louisa pressed.

"It varies. Usually I try to fix my gaze on some faraway spot and think of the past."

Louisa frowned. "What kind of things in the past? No, wait, better yet, show me. Get into the angel position right here and prepare yourself as if for a performance."

Romy scanned the patio, wondering if she could manage without her props—the wings, starched gowned, pedestal, everything that helped her "freeze."

Reluctantly, she got to her feet, walked to the center of the flagstone space, and got down on one knee with a hand resting on a thigh and the other stretched out as if holding something—a scepter or staff. "It doesn't feel right wearing jeans."

"Where'd you see that pose now?" Louisa asked.

"It's as if I've always known it."

"You probably have."

"I used to freeze as a child and the kids would count the minutes before I blinked. The first time I struck this pose as an adult was in Adrian Countway's office. I told him about my strange childhood 'gift' and he asked me to demonstrate. I thought I had experienced a brief sense of being somewhere else even then but decided I had to be imagining it."

"What is it you think of when you get yourself into the freeze?"

"I think of cemeteries and the stillness of stone. I think of this stone angel staring down into forever, still as death, no, stiller than death—unchanging. She wants to fly but can't; she wants to break free of stone and just be but can't."

"Now, if that's not a description of the soul's quest, I don't know what is. Something there is opening the door to Claire's memories, one of the triggers," Louisa said.

"Let's find another."

"The headaches," Jo prompted.

Still in her angel position, Romy grimaced. "The migraines. Yesterday, I'd been fighting one all day and then I ended up with a sexist lout in the tour group. By the time I reached the last stop at Pat O'Brien's, I knew the headache would strike hard and it did. I began behaving uncharacteristically—first I saw Adrian and panicked, then I pushed my client down the stairs. Can you imagine me doing that?"

"No way," Jo marveled, "but I sure enough wish I'd been there to see it."

"The event must have been witnessed by at least fifty people, including Adrian. Imagine him just happening to be at O'Brien's at that moment? I—"

"Wait," Louisa commanded.

Romy looked up. "You're going to tell me that it wasn't a coincidence."

"I was just fixin' to do exactly that." Louisa chuckled. "The universe may seem chaotic but it's anything but. There's a pattern but it's far too complex for us to understand in its entirety. Adrian was there because he's part of what's happening to you, he's part of the pattern. Remember, we're all connected."

Romy stared. "Of course."

"Synchronicity," Jo said. "Like that song that Sting sings?"

Louisa swung toward her niece, hands on hips. "Why is it my own niece sees the world through the eyes of popular culture? I thought you were a scholar?"

"I am a scholar but one who lives in this particular culture," Jo protested.

"Touché. But remember that Police band didn't invent the term 'synchronicity.' Sting probably read Carl Jung, for a start, and maybe you should, too."

"I don't have time to read Carl Jung. I'm too busy studying slavery," she countered.

"There's more than one kind of slavery in this world, Joquita. Only you can set yourself free."

"What's that supposed to mean?" Jo protested.

"Shush up, Joquita Bonita. This isn't about you—yet." Turning back to Romy, Louisa sighed. "Lost my equilibrium for a moment. Sorry 'bout that. Go on, child."

Romy glanced from Jo to Louisa. "You two have a little cycle on replay all your own, don't you?"

"That we do," Louisa acknowledged. "That's what happens between families: we fall into this spin of trigger and response that's mighty hard to break out of, but enough of that. Carry on. You were talking about your migraines."

"Right, well, the migraine took over. That's when all the really strange things began. The migraine must be a trigger."

"Hard to say. Could be the past life experiences are provoking the headaches, making you susceptible."

"Or there's something about migraines that cause my brain to hit the necessary state to have these past experiences. They come in clusters. I may have none for months, then suddenly I'm plagued by them for days on end. Lately, I seem to be getting them a lot, which coincides with my recent past life encounters. It's hard to say which is intensifying which."

"All kinds of things may trigger these jumps back. There are countless things that trigger even regular memories."

Romy climbed to her feet. "Like a smell or a thought or seeing something that connects with something in my past life?"

"Exactly," Louisa said. "The same kinds of things that trigger regular memories could be causing yours. Could be anything. Most folks encounter a lesser version of this when they experience déjà vu but yours is just much more vivid."

"In living color and surround sound," Jo muttered.

Romy stared out across the darkened garden. "I feel as though I've been dropped into a period film, only someone else is saying the lines from my lips."

"Well, you're going to have to learn the script as you go," Louisa said.

"My God, if this is true, you really could be reliving the past," Jo marveled. "Think about it."

Romy turned to her friend, her heart thumping in both fear and exhilaration. "All my life I yearned to travel back into the past to taste another age and live what the people experienced back then. Every time I hold an artifact in my hand, I try to feel the resonance of those who used it long ago. When I stand in an old, hallowed spot, I practically ache to be transported back for one instant. And now—" she took a deep breath "—and now that it's happening, I swear, I'm more terrified than anything else."

Louisa walked back over to the chairs, her movement graceful despite her size. "Bad enough a soul has to go through the wringer once let alone live another life over again and again. Claire lived in dangerous times and whatever happened to her has left everlasting scars. It won't be easy reliving that."

Romy followed Louisa back to the fireside.

"I'll help prepare you," Louisa said. "Though you can't control the events that impacted Claire, you need to at least be the one to decide when and where you go back to experience them. Right now, you're just getting jerked back every time a connection is made. That's dangerous. That's got to change."

"Can I control the order in which I experience these events, too? So far, the memories are completely out of sequence. At first, I saw Antonio wounded but some of last night's events seemed to have occurred before that, when he and Claire were still lovers."

Louisa took another sip of her julep. "Memories don't occur in any particular order unless you're consciously controlling them. When you go back for a longer experience—more than an hour at a time, let's say—the memories might be more sequential. No guarantee, though. I don't advise you to try going back for more than an hour at any given time, anyway. Too dangerous."

"You've been back yourself, haven't you, Aunt Loo?" Jo said.

"Sure enough I've been back," Louisa admitted, her eyes fixed on the fireplace. "But it's not something I do lightly or often but I did so to clarify my own soul. Recently, I try not to go back at all. Every time a soul goes back in time, there's a danger it will get entangled with the old memory and get stuck there forever. That's one way a soul gets lost."

Romy felt a sudden chill. Her uncle used to call it "someone walking across your grave" and, in this setting, the old saying held special meaning.

"What would that look like in the body left behind?" Jo asked.

"Either empty or mad, depends on the person."

Jo shook her head. "Empty as in trance?"

"Empty as in comatose. Whether the person is revisiting the past for a short time or is lost for good, the way their body behaves back in current time remains consistent for each person. For example, I go into a deep sleep and can't be roused. My body just stays here kind of comatose. Some folks have a more dramatic reaction. Their body walks around speaking and behaving just as if they were back in their past life. They're acting out their soul's past right here today, but inside they're gone."

"Like me at times," Romy said in a small voice.

"Like you at times." Louisa nodded. "You do need to know the risks, Romy. Fact is, the stronger the soul's memories, the greater the influence it will have on your current life. I'm afraid you're getting close to that point now."

Romy's shivering increased. Getting up from her seat, she stood before the fire's grate, trying to leech the ember's last warmth into her icy fingers.

"You have a strong though a damaged soul," Louisa continued. "When you go back, you could get so wrapped up in Claire's life that you forget your own—if you don't take precautions, that is. You *will* take precautions, though, 'cause I'm going to teach you how. Don't fret now. We'll spend some time schooling you for the trip tomorrow."

Romy glanced at Louisa. "Tomorrow, not tonight?"

"You need rest first. Being overtired makes you vulnerable, makes it harder for you to come back."

"Are there other alternatives? I mean, what would happen if I didn't go back and focused on trying to stay anchored in the here and now instead? Couldn't I learn to live with those ghosts moving around inside my head or, better yet, shut them out entirely?"

Louisa looked pained. "You know it's too late for that. Claire's already worn a groove into your brain."

She did know that, damn it. Romy rubbed her eyes, suddenly feeling exhausted. Burying her face in her hands, she staved off the fresh urge to cry. "It was a desperate hope. If I don't go through with this, not only will my soul bang itself into a wall for eternity but I'll go crazy." When Louisa didn't respond, she lowered her hands. "I have no choice."

"You have a choice, right enough," Louisa responded. "And only you can make it."

"Risk my sanity or lose my mind? Not much of a choice."

"Still, you can choose the how of it."

Romy nodded, so weary she felt she could sleep for a week. "If I'm going to do this, I just want to get it over with. When do I start?"

"First, you go home, gather some things, and return here tonight. I want you both to sleep under this roof so I can keep an eye on you until this business is finished. I don't want you to go imagining the eighteenth century at all, do you hear? Turn it off. Focus on something benign. Avoid the triggers. Get rested. Joquita Bonita, keep her distracted."

Jo nodded. "Distraction is my specialty."

Louisa smiled. "Now, tomorrow morning, bright and early, we'll get started with the preparation. By the afternoon, I'm fixin' to have you ready to go back, Romy. We have to be strategic here. No time to dawdle. I fear Claire's getting too strong a grip on the present and every day wasted will put you in more peril."

10

Romy and Joquita took a cab back home to gather their things, fare paid compliments of Aunt Loo.

"I just can't believe we're preparing you for a past life regression," Jo remarked as the car sped through the streets. "Still, when it comes to Aunt Loo, I've learned not to argue, at least not all the time. She's usually right about most things. Now, all I have to do is get my mind around the possibilities—life after death, deceased souls muddying up the present. My life as a historian may never be the same."

Romy, who had been leaning her head against the back of the seat, gazed out into the city night, too weary to talk. The cab began to slow down as it wound through the narrow streets of the French Quarter.

"This the place?" the driver called over his shoulder as the car eased into the curb. Both women remained silent, studying a car with its engine running parked outside their cottage. Romy leaned forward. "Who's that?"

"Police," Jo whispered, peering at the dark sedan.

"How'd you know?" Romy stared at the unmarked car. Something awful must have had happened to someone she loved. Only there wasn't anyone left.

Jo peered through the window. "The guy on the driver's side who's getting out is Detective Thelonious Brown. I dated him for a while. He rates as my longest-standing boyfriend, in fact. So, why don't I just pay the driver while you see what's up? Maybe one of us has overdue library books."

But Romy was already out of the car walking toward the two men, one in uniform, one in plain clothes, her heart galloping. The only time a policeman made house calls that time of night meant something was wrong, but what?

By the time she reached the front step, the officers were waiting.

"Ms. Landry?" the taller of the two men addressed her. Romy looked him right in the eye, seeking signs of a man preparing to deliver bad news. Then she saw her purse in his hand.

"You found my bag!" she exclaimed. "Thank you! I thought I'd never see it again!"

He cleared his throat. "I'm Detective Brown from the New Orleans police—" he flashed his card "—and this is Corporal Howell. You say this is your bag?"

"Yes, absolutely. I lost it last night and reported it missing this morning." She reached out for the item but the officer made no move to pass it over. Romy let her hand drop. "Do you need me to identify it, is that it? I could go inside and get my passport."

"Since when do the police hand-deliver missing property, Brown?" Jo asked, coming up behind them just as the cab pulled away from the curb. "This is better service than I used to get from you; though, I'll admit, when it came it was worth waiting for."

The tall officer stiffened but kept his full attention fixed on Romy. "Ms. Landry, let's step inside to continue this, shall we? No need to involve the neighborhood."

Romy glanced at Jo and nodded. "Yes, yes, of course, but Jo and I are roommates, in case you thought she came with the neighborhood. Come in."

Minutes later, the officers had each taken one of the old battered club chairs in the narrow living room while Jo and Romy occupied the couch on the opposite side. The women sat, tense and waiting.

By now, Romy realized the return of her property was not the sole reason for the police's interest.

"Would you please confirm the contents of this bag?" Detective Brown requested.

After a deep breath, Romy listed everything she remembered putting inside the small, sleek purse the evening before. It didn't hold much, so remembering was easy. "Is the money all there? I had a fifty-dollar bill and some small change," she asked.

No response. "Did you say a Swiss Army knife?" Detective Brown asked, looking down at his notes.

Romy nodded, wondering where all this was leading. "Yes, but I think of it as a nail file, pair of scissors, and bottle opener all in one—incredibly handy when taking tour groups around. Somebody always seems to need something at one point or the other. I never use the knife part." God, how she babbled but his interest in the little tool made her squirmy. "There was just enough room in my bag to stuff it in."

Brown stopped writing and glanced straight up into her eyes. "Where were you last night between the hours of ten-thirty and two-thirty, Ms. Landry?" The question affected her like being splashed with ice water. She'd watched enough television to recognize the language of alibis. "I—I don't know exactly," she began. "I mean, I led a tour group out that evening, and after I finished up at Pat O'Brien's, I walked home."

"Alone?" Detective Brown inquired.

"Well, yes," she began, thinking back to her mad run down Bourbon. "I mean, I think so, at first, yes." How could she even begin to explain this one? "Is there something wrong?"

"Is there anyone at all who can confirm your whereabouts during that timeframe?"

"Wait," Jo interjected. "Are you accusing her of something, Brown? If so, maybe she needs a lawyer."

"Do you have someone who can confirm your whereabouts, Ms. Landry, yes or no?" Detective Brown insisted, talking over Joquita.

She had to tell the truth as she recalled it, as pitiful a tale as it would seem. "Well, yes. A man tried to hit on me, one of the men from the tour, Stan somebody," she said, realizing she didn't know his last name. "But I didn't feel well," she continued, scrambling to make sense of this account. "I had a migraine and was having blackouts. Halfway home, he attacked me in an alley, which is where I think I dropped the purse."

"Which alley?" the detective asked.

"I don't remember exactly, I was so confused by then. Somewhere on Dauphine, I think. I was going in and out of consciousness by then—my migraine. I managed to get away and made it home."

"Do you have blackouts often?" the detective asked.

"Yes—no, I mean, lately, yes."

"Romy," Jo interjected, her voice tense. "You're too tired to think straight. You need a lawyer."

"But I haven't done anything wrong!" she protested. "I'm confused and I didn't know what to do. I was going to press charges for assault but—" she shrugged "—decided not to because everything is too confusing."

"Romy, the detective knows you should have a lawyer present."

"But I have nothing to hide," Romy hurried on. "You could try contacting this Stan fellow, though. He's part of the FlashTeck group attending the conference. I think they're all staying at the Hyatt. He might be honest enough to admit what he tried to do. Did he say I did something to him, is that it?"

Swallowing hard, she gazed straight ahead. No, that wouldn't be it. Something else had happened, something worse.

"What is this really about, Detective Brown?" Jo demanded.

"Stanley King was found murdered in an alley just off of Ursulines Avenue," the detective said. "The possible murder weapon was found at the scene—a Swiss Army knife plunged with amazing accuracy right into his heart. This bag was found nearby."

11

It had rained overnight. When Romy stepped onto the balcony overlooking Louisa's garden, she could have been gazing down on some steaming jungle a thousand miles away. For once, that knowledge brought comfort rather than irritation.

Breathing deeply the scent of the yellow trumpet-shaped flowers dangling nearby, she leaned against the railing and gazed out below. What else could she look at, think of, to keep her mind away from the past? All thoughts of the murder and Claire's life were too treacherous. Flowers and the weather seemed safe enough.

She pushed herself away from the railing and padded barefoot back into the bedroom where she quickly took off her night tee, threw on a light cotton shift, and slipped her feet into a pair of flip-flops. She pulled her hair off her shoulders and into an untidy knot on the top of her head.

Focusing on the present wasn't as easy. Half her waking life had been tethered to the past, whether leading tour groups, performing her stone angel stint, studying the Acadians in colonial Louisiana, or writing her thesis.

No wonder imagining past scenes had come so easily with all that practice. Now, like a powerful engine buried deep in her brain, her imagination had to be locked down in case it sent her into another dimension.

She left Jo asleep in the adjoining room and tiptoed out the door and down the old servant's staircase at the end of the hall. While trying to keep her thoughts concrete and fact-driven, she reviewed recent events.

Stanley King was dead. Poor Stan. No matter how boorish, she certainly hadn't wished him dead. And now she was under suspicion of his murder, *murder*. As if she could do such a thing. On the other hand, what if she *had* done it? Nothing about her police statement sounded convincing, even to herself.

Though her little knife may have been the weapon, surely she didn't possess the physical strength and fury to jab that thing into a man's heart over and over again?

The nausea threatened to return. She continued down the narrow stairs, grasping the banister. To consider, even for a minute, that her hands may have committed such a horrible act was almost more than she could bear.

Had Claire done this thing and, if so, why? How? No, no—she couldn't think about Claire, either. Any stray thought might summon her soul's memory to wreak more havoc.

Romy gripped the banister to steady herself. Louisa had immediately brought in a lawyer from the firm she used and that man, rotund, grizzled-haired law expert that he was, had said not to worry. Was she really to be comforted with phrases like "temporary insanity" or "self-defense"?

She had been released into Louisa's care. Not yet charged. Regardless, a man was dead and, one way or another, some part of herself could be responsible. Life and sanity teetered on the edge.

And today was the day she'd be immersed in Claire's existence? She'd go back in time? Overwhelming.

Reaching a side door to the garden, she hesitated. The scent of fresh-perked coffee and the jangle of silverware coming from the kitchen warmed her senses but food could wait. She needed time to think, as treacherous an activity as that had become of late.

No, not think, she realized as she pushed open the door. For once, she craved respite from thought.

Outside, wet fronds brushed her shoulders as she ducked under the overhanging palms and strolled deeper into the jungle garden's cool, dappled shade.

A twig snapped somewhere behind her followed by an odd, chilling, tapping sound that seemed familiar in a distant, dream-infused way. She swung around. "Jo? Rae Dawn?"

A bird called from somewhere across the garden. She stood listening with a fierce sense of being watched, a feeling similar to what she had experienced two nights ago.

Then the tapping resumed, sounding like a stick being jabbed into the earth punctuated by occasional vicious whacks of the nearby foliage. The sound grew closer, both alien and familiar all at once. A jolt of fear hit.

Breaking into a run, she slipped down the first pathway, following its winding route, past pools and rivulets snaking through the undergrowth, past a hothouse brimming with orchids and pitcher plants, down stone steps leading to a moss-paved grotto, up the side of a small hill beside a Balinese pagoda, down by a naturalized lagoon-shaped swimming pool, and along a gravel trail, her feet crunching underfoot.

Once, just once, she thought she heard footsteps directly behind her and a whack of something strong enough to shake the palm fronds. Swinging around, she almost chastised Jo for frightening her but the words died on her lips. There was no one there.

Panting and bathed in sweat, she carried on, moving more quickly now, powered by adrenaline. When she finally turned the corner and dove for the sanctuary of the Katrina forgiveness garden, she plowed headlong into a substantial form standing in meditation.

"Whoa! What's getting you, child?"

She looked up into Louisa's startled face as the woman attempted to recover a spilled mug of coffee.

"Somebody's following me! I heard footsteps, felt myself being watched." She pointed behind her toward the garden path.

Louisa narrowed her eyes and gazed in the direction of the garden where Romy pointed. "Nobody there now," she said after a moment, "nobody you can see, in any case."

She raised one hand, her voice a command. "Stay back! No one enters my realm without invitation. I only invite healing spirits and guardian angels." Her arm dropped. "Just as I thought. It's retreated now. She doesn't like me much, either, it seems."

"She?" Romy nearly squealed.

Louisa linked arms with Romy and drew her into the courtyard toward the fireplace. "Whatever's following you doesn't have a corporeal form but it's female. Don't fret now. It can't touch you in this place and time."

"A ghost?"

Louisa stared, pursing her lips. "A bad spirit, whatever you want to call it. The universe contains both good and bad in constant struggle."

"I felt it. It feels evil."

"Something dark is tailing you. She's angry. I sensed it last night but didn't want to pile on more than I thought you could handle. It stayed away from our circle, that's all I cared about."

"But what is it?"

"Look, child, energies both good and bad exist everywhere, as do ghosts. We live among them. Most of us can't see them or, if we do, we brush the experience off as some twitch of the imagination. Oh my, don't they love trauma and crises."

"Why is it chasing me?"

"Because it has unfinished business with you. It's probably part of this whole loop you're caught up in."

"Good God," Romy said, collapsing into a chair, her heart banging away inside her chest. "I don't need more ghosts or bad energies or whatever they are! Claire's enough. Can't you make them go away?"

"No, but you can. In time."

Romy glanced up at the woman, panic galloping in her chest. "Maybe it's Stanley King's ghost chasing me? That night, he did follow me in real time and now he's dead. I may have even killed him myself while in Claire's mind."

"Hang on just a minute. I admit, when I heard about Stanley King's death, I realized this whole business just got a pile more complicated in this timeline, but I don't believe for a minute that Claire killed King in either timeline."

"How do you know?"

"Because if your hand killed somebody, your victim's ghost would be clinging to you so fresh it would seem like a bad smell. Murder victims hang about their killers emanating fury and despair, especially soon after the event."

"But couldn't that thing back there be a murder victim?"

"Possibly, but not from this timeline. A fresh victim would scream out to be identified, not hide and stalk the way this lot is doing. The ghosts of the murdered want the truth to be known. They don't hide unless they are after some kind of other revenge. No, if you killed Stanley King, he'd be up front and center, wailing to be heard."

"Then what's following me?"

"I don't know yet. This spirit isn't so fresh. It's something else, someone else, a female. Someone Claire probably wronged in her lifetime. You'll find out eventually. I sense it's linked to Claire's life, not yours."

Romy shivered. "Does it mean me harm?"

Louisa nodded. "Probably. It's very, very angry but it's not in corporeal form so can't hurt you."

"But for a twig to snap like that, something has a material form!" It took every scrap of Romy's will to keep from screaming.

"Strong energy can manifest physical phenomena, Romy." Louisa, dressed this morning in a long silk muumuu in shades of deep purple, eased down into a chair and tipped the remains of her coffee onto the flagstones. "But nothing can hurt you if your will is strong."

"But I don't know if I *am* strong enough."

"Of course you are and you're going to find out the identity of these entities soon enough, believe me. I can't tell you how, I just know you will. Most things happening to you are tied in with Claire and Antonio's life. Stay calm and let the story unfold. Stay focused on the task ahead. Don't let these competing energies distract you, hear?"

Stalking energies a "distraction"? But Romy clung to the woman's words. Maybe her sense of balance would increase over time. "Okay," she said, brushing a strand of hair from her eyes before clasping her hands in her lap. "Where do we start?"

"With breakfast. Come along with me."

THE SUN CLIMBED HIGHER, INTENSIFYING THE HEAT THAT FELL OVER THE garden in a breathless shimmer. Romy followed behind Louisa, admiring the older woman's surprising grace, trying to keep her mind clear of Claire,

Antonio, and Adrian, until a sharp, unexpected pain stabbed her in the temples.

For a blinking instant, she thought she glimpsed another, much shorter woman standing in a dark room. Both vision and headache disappeared so quickly she couldn't catch the details.

"I just had another very brief regression," she whispered, staggering slightly. "I saw a woman dressed in a dark gown."

Louisa stopped, her back still turned away from Romy.

"Were you thinking of the past?"

"I was thinking of you."

"You say this woman wore black?"

Romy nodded. "Black with a white hood of some kind."

Louisa sighed, turning around. "That woman would be me. Well, not me exactly, but one of my soul's manifestations. Romy," she said, fixing her with her deep brown gaze, "as I've said, you and I have shared some small piece of the past. We have known one another before."

"You knew Claire?"

"Not me, my soul. It's an important distinction because individuals are made up of their own life experiences as well as unconscious memories of their past lives. Watching me just now slipped you back to a time when our souls shared the same timeline. I became a trigger."

"Who were you, Louisa? Who was Claire?"

"I can't tell you that. You need to take this journey yourself."

Romy fought back desperation. "Will you be coming back with me, then?"

"It's not that simple. When you go back, you'll be an observer only, just like I am when I revisit my soul's memories. We can't talk, we can't control where we go or what we see. And we certainly can't communicate. We're only passengers, understand? You'll be alone yet still closer to another individual than you've ever been before. You'll be inside her mind."

Romy stared at her, realizing the implications. "You mean, I can't communicate with anyone, not even Claire?"

"I never could—loneliest damn feeling in the world. Think of Claire's memories as that DVD I told you about last night. It's been recorded. It's fixed, done. Nothing's going to change what it does or how it acts. You're just sitting there watching the show, inside the show but not a part of it."

Romy shook her head. "But I'd hoped I could influence Claire in some way, keep her from doing whatever horrible thing she did to Antonio." Her tone came across half-plea. "I need to try."

"No." Louisa took a step back toward her. "Sit back down over here for a moment." She led her to a sitting nook where two chairs had been positioned for private conversation and wedged her generous body into one of the iron seats.

"First couple of times I went back," Louisa told her, "I thought I'd just try tinkering around, too. I didn't much approve of some of the things my soul let happen back then. I tried and tried but it couldn't be done, shouldn't be done, either, as I later came to realize. Who'd I think I was, trying to finagle history? The past is over, can't go changing it, no matter what. If we could, we'd probably just make a mess of things. The present and future are all we have to work with."

"But we could make the world a better place," Romy asked.

"More likely we'd just make it a different place, no better, no worse. The real change takes place in the present and moves on into the future, starting with us."

"But I need to try."

"It's only a memory you're seeing. No way you'd get to be in the director's chair. All we can do is go back and learn from the past so as to fix what's wrong with the present. The present's all that's ours to change, that and the future, our future. Nothing else."

Deep in thought, Romy stared across at a marble statue half-submerged by a pool of ferns, a small dragon crouching in the undergrowth. "I need to try. I just have to." She turned to Louisa. "Tell me about Claire."

At that, Louisa leaned so far toward Romy that her arm nearly toppled the mug she'd sat on the table between them. "How much do we really understand about another person, even those we think we know? Everything I could tell you would all be interpreted through the eyes of who I used to be back then—a woman of a certain time and place, part of her own social restraints, almost three hundred years ago. You don't need that. You need to discover and interpret Claire for yourself, not see her through my eyes."

"But I need information. This has now become a murder case."

"Yes, and only you can find the clues by retracing Claire's steps.

That's where you'll find the key to Stanley King's murderer and maybe this other entity dogging you, too. But I can't go with you or influence your perspective and I can't be lying to you, either. It's a dangerous path."

Romy wrapped her arms around herself. "What if someone else is reliving their soul's memories the way I am with Claire's, like whoever killed Stanley?"

"Exactly. Whoever you thought you sensed back in that alley last night may be totally unaware of what their body's been up to, as well," Louisa said. "Then again, Stanley's death might be about something completely different. That's what I mean to find out."

Romy shot her a look. "You're going to find out? But didn't you just say that only I can put the pieces together by going back in time?"

"Yes, but while you're catching up with the past, I'll be pulling in favors in the present. You think the local police force is going to know how to factor in paranormal influences? No way. I have to do my thing, sure enough."

"Looks like both of us will be playing detective," Romy said.

"We'll get started after breakfast. Don't go putting eating on the back burner. I give it star billing 'cause it's important. The more rested and fed you are, the better your past life trip's going to go. A fatigued, hungry body could negatively influence your ability to stay clearheaded and return from your past life."

Romy's stomach rumbled. "I hear you. I make it a point never to turn down food, anyway."

Louisa smiled. "Smart woman. Now let's go eat." She heaved herself to her feet and turned toward the house. "We'll talk as we go."

Romy followed Louisa toward the French doors. "What should I be looking for back in Claire's past?"

"You're going to see what Claire sees and feel her thoughts while attempting to remain consciously yourself. First sign of trouble or confusion, you just start thinking about here, my house, and try to bring yourself back. Sometimes that works."

"What if I can't bring myself back?"

"I intend to guide you through a few practice sessions so you'll learn how. It's not easy but it can be done and it's a little bit different for every person. Staying calm and focused, that'll help. The blackouts are most likely caused by panic."

"Panic," Romy repeated. "So, I'm in danger of losing control when I'm frightened, like two nights ago?"

"Right enough."

"What if Claire's terror affects my own?"

"Fight it. I don't know how, but try."

"What else should I remember?"

"Try not to stay in the past too long. You need to be strong. You need to recognize when you've been gone too long and then force yourself to return. Ever tried to wake yourself up from a sleeping state?"

Romy frowned. "A few times. I can remember my conscious self recognizing my body as sleeping and wanting to wake up. I've pulled myself up to consciousness but it's very tough."

"Well, that's the way it will be bringing yourself back from the past—very tough—but if you don't do that while you're still conscious, you'll be totally at the whim of Claire's memories or, even worse, could get stuck back there forever. You need control. Stay calm and remember who you are inside Claire's memories—that's critical."

"Right."

"I'll begin by describing that moment in time we shared, which we'll use as the trigger to take your soul's memories back. You'll stay only briefly that first trip, then bring yourself back. Got that?"

"Yes."

They were almost at the breakfast room doors. Romy could see the table set with a bowl of fresh flowers on a sunny orange tablecloth and smell something cooking inside.

She had gone a few steps ahead of Louisa and turned to face her. "I've remembered something about the place I just glimpsed—a bare room painted white with a cross on the wall."

"Wait, Romy, don't trigger—"

But the warning came too late. At that moment, pain struck her forehead again, knocking Romy backward while simultaneously pitching her ahead into a strange past.

Seconds later, she found herself staring into an unfamiliar room dominated by a woman silhouetted against a wall, her black gown a stark contrast to the white plaster.

A nun, she realized with a shock. The woman walked toward her, speaking in a language both familiar yet difficult to understand. Romy tried to avoid her path but her feet refused to move.

"Are you prepared, my child? I fear your wild spirit will lead you astray, despite our tutelage. Do not let it be so. Do as you're told, for once." Archaic French, Romy realized as the woman took her by the shoulders and shook her so hard the world quaked. "Do not let us down. Our lives depend on you. Do exactly as I instructed. Do not speak until I give you the signal, yes?"

Another woman spoke from somewhere behind Romy. "She is very clever, is she not, Mother? So she will do what needs to be done. She has learned much."

The sister lifted and dropped her hands in a gesture of resignation. "It is too late, in any case, Sophie. The men will soon be here. Our fate is in God's hands now, yes? Let us pray that He has found a worthy soldier in this girl. We can do no more." Still gazing at Claire, she added, "Stay here and be quiet, child, as you've been bid. Touch nothing. Sophie, let us make ready."

"Romy, can you hear me?" Louisa's voice came from a long way off, like a radio dial trying to fix a channel. Romy struggled to focus on her voice but Claire's feelings swamped her own.

And then, understanding flooded into Romy along with Claire's consciousness, an understanding awash with desperate intent. At that moment, she understood what Claire planned to do and knew she had to grip hard on to the past with all her might.

12

Claire held a single candle aloft to illuminate the books lining the cramped space—nothing but convent records with leather bindings pitted by damp. And Romy realized that she'd been pitched into yet another chunk of Claire's memories and for a moment struggled to return. But then what lay before her eyes was too intriguing to fight...

The stark white room had gone, replaced by a cramped room covered wall to ceiling in books, a closet-like space barely illuminated by a tiny window.

And Claire seemed to be looking for someone—no, waiting for someone.

Romy tried to sort through Claire's thoughts and emotions like an eavesdropper in time. She could read the passing thoughts. Yes, Claire waited. She had been ordered by Mother Superior to stay here until the time came to be presented to the plantation men and priests. The girl's pique churned her stomach. She was to be presented like a prize cow.

Mother Marie had counseled Claire against pursuing convent life, though Claire had wanted to become a nun very badly. Apparently she had been told that she was unsuitable to be a bride of Christ. But why? Romy wondered.

She felt Claire's anger at being barred from what she believed to be the doors of Paradise and tried to fathom why Mother Superior refused to accept her. Oh, Romy realized as she picked up on Claire's thoughts: too headstrong, too willful, too angry. To demand answers from God, from Blessed Mother Mary, was not the path of a nun.

Resting her forehead on the cool glazing, Claire stared out into the courtyard. The night hung thick and heavy in this swamp of a land. The animals slept and all seemed at peace except the watchman's pacing beyond the gates.

She, on the other hand, would never know peace again. Now that Mother had confirmed that she could not be a bride of Christ but a whore of the Devil.

Quickening footsteps ended her reverie. Below came the whispered mumblings of men. Pushing the casement ajar, Claire listened. They had arrived. They would proceed in stealth, lest some spy of the Spanish king realize that the sisters of the Ursulines had more business than God's work on this night. Her heart quickened. Claire swung around as the door opened behind her.

Madame Letourneau slipped her gowned self through the hidden doorway, her red silks rustling and the air scented by the distillation of jasmine and spice she dabbed about her person. "They come, *chérie!*" she whispered, finger to her lips.

"Yes, Madame," Claire said, curtsying.

"You are ready, yes?" Madame's hand swept over Claire. "A fine accent, a beautiful woman in a flattering, if sober, dress—you do indeed look lovely. One glance and they will know that you can seduce any man. Remember, you must keep the farm from your tongue and the peasant from your manners. Mother Marie may have taught you about God but from me you have learned everything of worth, no?"

Including brothel tricks, Claire thought. Half of her days of late had been spent either peering through the peepholes of Madame's establishment or learning how to cook and manage a household from the convent's cooks and slaves. Training to be housekeeper had proven exhausting but learning the ways of men and women overwhelming.

She had studied the art of seduction. For that part of her upcoming role, she had only watched wide-eyed while burning with shame and excitement at the lewd intimacies between men and women. She had never understood what went on in her parents' bed, though, as a farm girl, she certainly had seen the couplings of the animals.

Now she knew the difference. Now she felt more whore than virgin, now she believed herself to be both.

"Yes, Madame." *Never let anyone know what you are really thinking.* That much Claire had taught herself.

Men's voices grew louder from the other side of the thick cedar door.

"Hush!" Madame whispered.

Pushing past Claire, Madame removed a large wooden cross and pressed her eye against the wall. Another peephole! The walls were riddled with them.

For a moment Claire stood watching Madame, eager for a glimpse of what was going on in the other room, but the older woman had no intention of sharing the view. Bristling with impatience, Claire tugged on Madame's lace sleeve.

"What is it?" the woman said, turning around.

"Madame Letourneau, would it not be best for me to gaze through that hole also to better prepare myself for what lies ahead?" she whispered.

"Oh, for heaven's sake! Go on, then!" Taking the candle holder from Claire's hand, Madame gave her a little shove toward the wall.

Eagerly, Claire stared into the spacious room beyond. Candles perched on massive candlesticks and many more burned in sconces on the white walls. The room glowed with more candles than Claire had seen anywhere in all her years. Mother Marie must wish to light the dark deed she plotted this night.

Standing in the middle of the room and directly in line of sight, the woman herself appeared every inch the Mother Superior with hands tucked into her sleeves and expression benign and watchful.

Nodding to the delegation of men and dark-robed priests, she bid them to sit in the chairs provided while the slave girl, Lulu, served wine from pewter goblets. All the real silver, Claire knew, had been sold.

Romy yearned to study every detail of clothing and to scan the room with a historian's eye but Claire strained her attention toward the five men. The girl knew two of them and the other three were priests from the church of St. Louis. Claire scrutinized the first man, the obvious spokesman.

Monsieur Campeneau was a wealthy plantation owner Claire had seen at Madame Letourneau's, a regular customer who asked only for the services of Madame herself and spoke of days when he, like Madame Sophie, had lived the grand life back in France.

But the other man interested her more. Claire knew Jean d'Entremont to be an Acadian. Despite the clothes—torn breeches, filthy shirt, and scraggly hair not even tied into a proper tail—her heart warmed at the sight of him.

Here was one who had once shared her homeland and had known her father, had even been one of those ripped from his farm in Acadia as her family had been. He, too, had been forced to leave that life of honest hard work to crawl in the bayou like a bottom-feeding catfish. Now he made his living among smugglers and thieves, the soldiers having stolen his life the way they had stolen hers. They shared those scars.

"Ah, excellent wine," Monsieur Campeneau commended Mother Marie as he sipped, "A 1751 Bordeaux, is it not? I had always heard that the Ursulines kept a superior cellar."

Jean d'Entremont, Claire observed, was guzzling his wine as if from a flagon instead of a glass. Gone in two gulps!

"We have no such cellar now, monsieur," Mother Superior told him as she took her seat across from her guests. Mother Marie rarely touched wine herself, Claire knew. "I have been selling what cases we have left to purchase supplies for the sisters and our charges. We can ill afford but few luxuries these days—a bit of salt, here and there. I fear a few weeks longer and our stores will be exhausted. Our king has forgotten us, leaving us to languish far from France."

"Times are most difficult since the Spanish arrived, are they not?" Monsieur was saying. "They choke our smuggling routes and impose rules designed to cause starvation. And this governor—curse the blasted mongrel."

"The mongrel!" Jean d'Entremont erupted. "This man, he is a curse, no? He takes our life!"

The mere mention of the Spanish governor seemed to have caused the little Acadian to explode into furious coughing that did not cease until he had spat out a wad of phlegm onto the floor.

Mother Marie looked aghast. "Monsieur d'Entremont, I implore you to remember where you are!"

"Oh, pardon me, Mother Superior. I lost my head, I lost my head! Pray, forgive. Here." Falling to his knees, he untied the kerchief from his neck and wiped the spit from the floor.

Claire stared at his rump with its patched breeches. Poor Jean. To come to this. *Do not grovel.*

"Forgive me, Mother. It is that Spanish dog, no? I hear his name I go crazy mad! *Sacre bleu.*"

"Monsieur, such blasphemy!" Mother Marie's face had changed to the color of boiled crayfish. Her skin being as pale as bleached sand, every emotion showed. Lifting from her seat, she towered over the little man as if she intended to shoo away a rabid dog.

"Mother Marie, our Holy Mother," Monsieur Campeneau implored, rising to intervene. "Please forgive my friend here. He forgets himself," and to the Acadian he added, "Jean, pull yourself together, man."

"Mother Marie, monsieurs," said one of the priests sitting beyond Claire's view—Father Dagobert, she guessed by the timbre of the voice. "We must speedily proceed to the matter at hand. Time passes, no? Fathers LeTour and Blanche have labored to ensure the Jesuits and Spanish priests sleep deeply this night but we cannot guarantee that they have each consumed sufficient laudanum. One of our Spanish brethren often forgoes the evening drink and is known to pace the grounds at night. Let us quickly proceed. Should he awake and see that we are missing..."

"Yes, of course, Father," Mother Marie said with a nod. She resumed her seat but kept one eye fixed on the little Acadian as if he might wet on the furniture at any moment. "We are ready to introduce you to the girl who will do our work."

A mumbling of Hail Marys came from the priests while Monsieur Campeneau nodded in satisfaction.

"She has been schooled by our convent but trained by Madame Letourneau in matters of the flesh—all very circumspect, I assure you. The child is prepared to do what is necessary." Mother Marie frowned as if even uttering those words pained her.

"Trained by Madame Letourneau?" Father Dagobert gasped. "A peddler of the flesh?"

"But of course, Father." Monsieur Campeneau turned to the priest. "Who better to teach a woman the ways of espionage than the king's former mistress? The court studies intrigue, does it not? We must use every weapon in our arsenal, employ every trick to trap the Spanish governor."

"It is true." Mother Superior nodded. "It was a sacrifice the girl is willing to make in the name of God."

"Nothing can stand in the way," Campeneau continued. "We cannot waver where our mission is concerned, no? We must use the governor's weaknesses to bring him down. A beautiful woman is just so equipped and a beautiful woman who is clever and wily is best suited for the task. Pray continue, Mother Marie. My curiosity brims."

Mother Marie regarded him with her fierce blue gaze. "Yes, monsieur, but first I wish to see our agreement in writing, as we discussed."

"But of course." The man pulled a letter from his coat pocket and passed it to Mother Marie. "I have listed those items upon which we have agreed should this girl prove suitable and bring us something of note. I state here, before all of you worthy brethren of God and France, that I, Richard Dean Denis de Campeneau, do pledge an annual sum of five hundred gold pieces to the Order of Saint Ursula for as long as I shall live. It will state also in my will that my sons are to continue the bequest on my behalf. If the girl proves to my liking and, should she bring back something useful, I will seal."

Mother Superior had already scanned the writ before the man had finished. Satisfied, she tucked the parchment deep into her sleeve and rose to her feet. "Good. I shall call the girl in for your inspection."

Claire felt a jab in the ribs. "Come, *chérie*, time to dance, no?"

Taking her by the hand, Madame Letourneau tugged her from the room and down the hall toward the door of the receiving room.

"Remember all that I have told you," the woman whispered. "Even priests are men. Remember what moves them beneath their breeches and cassocks is all the same for every one of them, soldier or priest, all the same."

"ROMY!" A WOMAN'S VOICE CRIED OUT. "TRY TO RETURN. TRY HARD!"

Mother Superior calling. What had she done this time? She had not yet performed the mission and already she was being shaken so hard her teeth rattled.

"Romy, get your mental butt back here, will you?"

Not Mother Marie, Romy realized, shaking off the remnants of Claire. She pulled her will together and steered herself forward into the present. Befogged, Romy found herself gazing up into Jo's face. Her tongue felt packed in cotton, her brain on ice.

Louisa leaned over her and Romy read the concern furrowing her forehead. They were in the breakfast room.

"What was I doing?" Romy asked.

"You were walking around talking to people we couldn't see, that's what," Jo told her. "I had to hold you to keep you from ramming into a wall. You were speaking French, so I couldn't understand a hell of a lot more than the occasional '*Oui, madame.*' It was the scariest damn thing I've ever seen."

"Watch your language, Joquita Bonita," Louisa admonished.

"Mother Marie," Romy said as she gazed up at Aunt Loo. "Louisa Dupré, you were Mother Superior of the Order of Saint Ursula in 1767."

"What?" Jo said, her mouth agape.

"It's true," Romy said.

"You, a white nun?" Jo turned to her aunt. "I presume the Ursulines in New Orleans were color coordinated to the ruling class of the day?"

Louisa fixed her niece with a stern look. "Souls do not follow racial lines, girl. Of all the things I've tried to teach you over the years, have you missed the most important point? Yes, my soul was once housed in the corporeal form of a woman of God, though probably one of the most conflicted in the history of the Order of Saint Ursula, and yes, she was Caucasian. Do not assume every past incarnation had you as black, either. Souls don't chase color, humans do."

With Jo briefly silenced, Louisa returned her attention to Romy. "And you, child, it worries me the way you went into Claire like that."

"I couldn't stop myself," Romy told her while rubbing the bridge of her nose. "First came the pain and then suddenly I was somewhere else. I understood what was happening but I couldn't pull myself into the present, though I admit, I grew so involved I didn't try very hard."

"You must try harder. Maybe we won't know exactly what will trigger your regressions or when. With the past so close to your consciousness, there's too many ways to spark it off. You need to find a way to return at will."

Romy struggled to sit up. "I know, I know. I'll find a way somehow. It's just that it happened so quickly and then I just kept getting drawn deeper in. I believed at first that I could return whenever I wanted but it's not so easy."

"The problem exactly," Louisa said with a nod.

"But I recognized you this time, I recognized your soul." Romy pressed one hand to her mouth. "You were preparing me for something...something awful."

Louisa closed her eyes. "My poor Mother Marie tried so hard to follow God's will but failed to realize that following the will of church and state are not the same thing as following God. It's been my soul's journey to follow spirit beyond religion and doctrine."

Romy swallowed hard. "But not before you sent Claire to the dogs."

"What are you two talking about?" Joquita intercepted. "Let me in on this, will you?"

"Don't judge her, Romy. This journey is about forgiveness and you still have a long way to go. What do you think it will be like when you're knee-deep in Claire's trauma?"

Romy crossed her arms. "You trained her to lure the Spanish governor in some way."

"Not me, Mother Marie."

"Your Antonio ghost?" Joquita asked.

"Hush, please." Louisa held up her hand. "What triggered you to return this time?"

Romy tried to remember. "The moment Claire's attention wavered, I think. She was being called to meet the conspirators and at that moment I heard your voice calling me."

"Transitions, then, maybe. You've got to figure out those doors if you're going to gain control. You watch yourself, Romy. This is no game you're playing. These lights can go off and on without you knowing. You could fall headfirst in this particular story and never come out sane. The longer you stay, the harder it is to leave."

Romy sighed. "I know."

"Okay, so what have you learned this time?" Jo interrupted.

"Claire is..." Romy pondered. "Confused and very angry. And hurt," she added. "She burns with a resentment that I don't quite understand. There's a plot concerning Governor Antonio de Ulloa cooking that I was just about to discover more of. And Claire's Acadian! Unbelievable. I've learned enough in that hour to write twenty books."

"Hour?" Jo exclaimed. "You were gone maybe ten minutes."

Romy stared in amazement. "I was?"

"You're starving and weak as a result," Louisa said. "Maybe that's why you left so suddenly. You need to get food in you so you don't get the body stressed along with your mind. We don't want you going back on an empty stomach and insufficient sleep." Aunt Loo plunked a plate of croissants before Romy. "Eat."

"Look, I guess there's no good time to bring this up," Jo said as they settled down for breakfast. "Thelonious Brown, the detective with the amazing body and miserable disposition, left a message on our answering service. He wants you down at the station for more questions ASAP."

Romy chewed the croissant, hardly tasting its buttery richness. She swallowed hard. "I don't know what more I can tell him, seeing as he doesn't believe a thing I say."

Louisa passed over a plate of scrambled eggs. "As soon as I get a chance, I'll be having a word with that young man. In the meantime, I'll ask my attorney friend to be there just in case. I'll give him a call and have him meet you down at the station. I don't like you being alone with Mr. Brown. He knows a heck of a lot less than he thinks."

"My thoughts exactly," Jo said between nibbles. "I tried to tell him that countless times. However, he's extraordinarily skilled in other departments."

Her aunt shot her a look.

Romy, relieved not to be discussing her own problems for once, turned to her friend. "What is it between you and Thelonious Brown, anyway?"

Joquita managed to flip her cascade of tiny cornrows in a dismissive gesture. "My troubles with Telly are simple compared to your convoluted past life relationships. Let me put it to you in the most basic of terms: I was really into him and he into me, literally and figuratively, only I was seeing another guy on the side—nothing serious, you understand, just someone to scratch that itch while Mr. Policeman was off chasing bad guys. Telly found out and broke it off. End of story."

Louisa rolled her eyes as she buttered another croissant. "And so the past replays itself over again and again."

"Auntie, what are you implying now, that Telly and I are having these past life events, too?" Jo asked.

"You'll find out soon enough," her aunt replied.

"Ah," Romy said. "So, to sum up an already shortened tale: you still really like him only he's not having anything to do with you."

"Well, that's kind of it in a proverbial nutshell," Jo agreed. "He hasn't spoken to me since."

"And do you have any difficulty understanding why he took offense to you fooling around?" Louisa asked her niece in a deceptively mild tone.

"Auntie, as I've told you before, I didn't fool around so much as got distracted. Besides, it's not like I signed an exclusive deal with this man—or, at least, I didn't think I had. We were getting pretty intense, it's true, but we hadn't made any declarations or anything. I might have been willing to try monogamy for the likes of him if he asked nicely but from his perspective it was too late."

"Thelonious does tend to make his mind up pretty quick, to my way of thinking," Louisa agreed, "but I tell you, child, you strained his patience."

Jo shrugged. "With Telly, if you do wrong, you're out. Romy, I'm coming to a point here and it's this: I know this guy. He's a good man—better than good, in fact—but he sees the world in black and white, in more ways than one. If he thinks you're lying to him or holding out, he'll cut you off so fast you won't know what hit you. You don't want to go getting Detective Brown on your case. He'll go for the jugular."

"Detective Brown's already on my case and aiming for my jugular," Romy pointed out. "I can feel his teeth in my neck as we speak."

"He was actually pretty tender in the one-on-one department but not in a professional sense."

"Joquita!" Louisa admonished.

"Okay, okay." Jo threw up her hands. "So, we've got to get you downtown so you can show him you're on the up-and-up. It's already been over three hours since he phoned. He's going to think you're hiding something."

"I am hiding something," Romy said as chewed a mouthful of egg. "I'm hiding the fact that I periodically slip into someone else's life and live out her memories, often without a clue of what I'm doing."

"You have to tell him about this past life stuff plus the ghosts, whether he believes you or not, that's what I think. What do you say, Auntie?" Jo asked.

"Right enough. Gerald will be there to keep the questioning steady, in any case." Romy could tell that Louisa's attentions were clearly fixed on something else. "We need to get as many people as possible to understand what's going on around here if we're going to solve things."

"Besides," Jo continued. "So what if he thinks you're a nut? Can that be any worse than having him think you're a murderer?"

"He thinks I'm a murderer, anyway, and why not? I'm the prime suspect with both probable cause and opportunity. The murder weapon belongs to me and plenty of witnesses saw me shoving Stan downstairs, which links to motive."

"You read too many mysteries," Jo commented. "You should stick to heated romances for your reading pleasure like I do. Better endings."

Romy pressed a hand to her temple, staving off a stab of panic.

"Look, Romy," Louisa said, placing a steadying hand on her arm. "Why don't you just finish your breakfast and go with Jo for a little stroll in the garden to clear your head? That'll give Gerald time to get himself to the station."

"In the garden with that stalking ghost?"

"What stalking ghost?" Jo asked.

Romy filled her in about her experiences earlier that day, causing her friend to mutter under her breath. "Fact is, I'm almost afraid to go out there now."

"Make that two of us," Jo chimed in.

"I warded the garden pretty strong. You'll be safe there now. Besides, Romy, you need to work out what you're going to say to Mr. Brown and get yourself evened out," Louisa said with determination. "You don't want to be going down to the station with your brain all in a stew. Now why don't you take that stroll while I make a phone call or two?"

When Jo and Romy finally made it outside after getting dressed, the rain had evaporated into a haze of hot white sun with steam rising from the jungle floor.

"What did this ghost do, anyway?" Jo asked, glancing over her shoulder as they made their way down a cooling fern-lined path.

"Made tapping noises and gave me the sense of being stalked."

"How comforting."

They ducked under the palms toward the grotto, favoring routes that took them near a cooling pool or fountain. This time no tapping sounds followed Romy so she put her mind to the upcoming ordeal with the detective.

"Jo, my fingerprints are all over that knife," she said as she sat down on a stone seat beside Louisa's half-moon lagoon. Behind her, golden orange koi flitted in the water, and the iridescent shimmer of a dragonfly sparked in the sunshine.

"So, it's yours, isn't it? Did you use it for anything?"

"A bottle opener, mostly."

"They can't pin a murder based on something like that. People use their belongings, so what?"

"Maybe the 'what' part comes in if they don't find anybody else's prints."

"Stop panicking."

"I'm not panicking so much as facing the worst possible scenario and then panicking. Your aunt doesn't believe Claire killed Stan and I desperately want to believe that. I checked my black dress before I handed it over to Detective Brown but I couldn't find anything that resembled blood, not that stains show up well on black crinkle fabric."

Jo sat down beside Romy and dipped one hand into the water. "Look, I saw you first thing that morning, right? You didn't have blood on your hands or anywhere that I could see, only that wicked bruise on your cheek."

"That's true."

"Did you sleep with your makeup on?"

"No, it looks as though I went through my skin routine that night, brushed my teeth, everything. I keep asking myself, if Claire really committed murder, would she have the presence of mind to wash afterward?"

"Maybe in her own time she'd scrub up in the river or a washbasin or something but use modern day plumbing and skin products? I don't think so. From what Aunt Loo's been telling us, that's not how it works. Claire would go through exactly the same motions she would have gone through in the past with no updates, which includes no toner or moisturizer for T-zones. If you thought you'd been cleaned up down in the Mississippi, it might make more sense but that's not what happened. You used the sink, maybe on autopilot, but it had to be you doing it."

Romy nearly sagged with relief. Of course, logically, this all made sense. "You're right," she whispered.

"Furthermore, I agree with Auntie that your hands didn't murder anyone," Jo continued. "It's got to be pretty damn hard to kill a guy with a pocketknife unless you know exactly what you're doing. That's got to take strength as well as fury. No way. Hell, I've watched *CSI*. I think you've got another killer out there, but let's face it, that's damn worrying, too."

"Hi, y'all. You out here looking to give me some help?"

Romy and Jo glanced up, startled. Rae Dawn stood with a shovel in hand.

Jo waved. "Hi, Rae Dawn. How's Dawn Over Dixie going?"

"Just grand, Joey, as far as landscaping companies go, only your aunt keeps me going half the time just doin' her stuff. I got no time to handle all the clients she keeps sending me. Shouldn't complain, though—pays good."

"Rae Dawn, you wouldn't have been outside here early this morning, would you?" Romy asked. "You know, maybe tapping on something?"

Rae Dawn made a face. "Hell, no. As much as I honor Queen Louisa, I don't get to work before ten. Why, you hear something out here?"

"Well, yes, actually. I just hoped it might have been you."

"Nope. Probably some bird. Hey, you girls want to see the new garden I'm working on? You know what a mediation garden is, don't you? It sure ain't the same as a meditation garden. I found that out the hard way."

"We'd love to," Romy said, dragging herself to her feet, "but not right now. I've got an appointment to keep and I'm running late. Maybe next time?"

"Sure thing."

Moments later, as the women made their way back to the house, Romy thought she heard the faint tap-tapping sounds on the path behind them. "Wait!" she said, grabbing Jo's arm. "Do you hear that?"

"Hear what?'

"That sound, like someone hitting the ground with a stick just a few steps behind us."

"Hell, no," Jo said, suppressing a shiver. "It's Rae Dawn digging, that's all."

Romy swallowed. "I hear the digging, all right, but something else besides. Come on, let's get out of here."

13

"Now let me just clarify this some, Ms. Landry," Detective Brown said in that Southern drawl that coated tongues in treacle and rum. Only, in his case, Romy detected an acidic undertone. "You say you think a woman from another age may be visiting you from the past and messing with your head?"

Romy struggled for calm. Thelonious Brown's cool, professional demeanor combined with a skepticism he couldn't quite keep in check, bothered the hell out of her but could she blame him? She didn't expect him to believe her but it was tough nevertheless. "Look, Detective Brown, I know how this sounds. Why do you think I didn't tell you the whole story the first time around?"

Because you hadn't invented it yet? his expression seemed to say. "I have no idea, miss," came his response.

Both hands palm-down on the table, she leaned her body slightly forward. "Because I knew you'd react exactly as you are doing, with total disbelief. I am not crazy, Detective, despite what you may think, and I'm not making up some bizarre story just so I can cover up stabbing one of my clients with a pocketknife."

Sitting midway between the detective and Romy, Mr. Thomas Graham Murphy, Louisa's lawyer, studied the exchange with a watchful eye. He was not supposed to intercede or interrupt unless Romy's rights were violated but he had already made it clear to her that, since she was not an American citizen, the issue of rights remained a bit murky, to his way of thinking.

"Miss." Thelonious steepled his long-fingered hands and for an instant Romy thought of them pleasuring Joquita. She said he'd been good on the job, very thorough. Oh, hell. What a time to think about sex! "Nobody's accusing you of anything just yet. I'm only asking questions and trying to understand. It's not my job to make decisions on whether what you say is wrong or right. Should you be formally charged, that will be for the courts to decide."

"Should" and "yet" sounded ominous all on their own but at least he was still speaking in terms of possibility rather than probability.

"But in the meantime," Brown continued, "it is my job to ask questions, maybe even the same questions over and over again, until I understand what it is that you say happened."

Romy swallowed. "I understand."

"Good. So, let's just go back to the night in question. According to your statement, you were at O'Brien's with a tour group when you and the deceased had an argumentative exchange. The matter concerned whether or not you would dance with him. Is that right, so far?"

"Yes, though actually he made it clear he had more than dancing on his mind."

"But you said no, and Mr. King became insistent so you pushed him downstairs until one of the employees, a Lucas Wilkins, escorted him off the premises."

"Right."

"After that, you went upstairs to the ladies' room where you began seeing strange phenomena and experiencing blackouts. You believed you saw Governor Ulloa—" and he paused to check a detail on his notes "—circa 1766. After that, your memories are very disjointed but you recall coming to an alley somewhere with Mr. King attempting to sexually assault you. Then you blacked out again and woke up in your own bed alone."

Romy swallowed hard. "Correct." It sounded utterly ludicrous.

"Anything else happen back at O'Brien's you forgot to mention, Ms. Landry?" Brown inquired.

She gazed across the table into the man's face—handsome, intelligent...

guarded. There was something she hadn't mentioned, she knew, something excruciatingly embarrassing, but it hardly seemed relevant to Stan King's death. Still, if he knew something and she said nothing... "Well, my former professor, Adrian Countway, followed me up there. He'd been waiting to drive me home."

"Dr. Adrian Countway."

"Yes." What did Adrian have to do with this? She had the sense that he'd been waiting to mention him. Romy kept her voice steady. "I didn't mention him before because I didn't think it important. The two men had no contact with one another."

"And I reminded you, Ms. Landry, that I am the one to decide what's important and what isn't. Your responsibility is to tell me everything you observed. Or thought you observed," he added.

"An oversight on my part."

"Dr. Countway was your thesis adviser until recently, wasn't he?" Brown asked.

Thelonious knew more about her life than she had told him. He had scrutinized her, probably normal police procedure, but still. "Yes," she said.

"How would you describe your relationship to Dr. Countway?" he prompted.

Oh, Lord. She hesitated. "Cordial but distant. I'm taking a hiatus from my doctoral studies and he's not pleased with my decision."

"No romantic entanglements or sexual relations between you two?"

Hell. Romy could no more stop her cheeks from flaming than she could from breathing and knew exactly how it made her look. She took another deep breath and spoke with care. "I left the program partly because I was attracted to the professor and felt that put us both in an untenable position."

"Witnesses say you were in a very untenable position with Dr. Countway outside O'Brien's ladies' room that night, Ms. Landry."

"An inappropriate statement," Mr. Murphy asserted in his big, basso voice, sounding like a volcano rumbling to life. "This is not about the young woman's morals."

"Tom," Detective Brown said, turning to the lawyer, "we are not in court here so nix the objections. Besides, I'm simply assessing a relationship that may have a critical influence on this case. Ms. Landry is not being straightforward with me here, are you, Ms. Landry?" He turned back to Romy.

"All right, all right," she said. "I didn't mention that incident because it was hideously embarrassing and I figured you wouldn't believe me if I explained the details. Besides which, I didn't think it relevant." She took a deep breath. "It wasn't me doing that to Adrian but her—Claire, the woman from the past."

"The one you say is possessing your body?"

"Yes but no. It's not possession, really. It's more like my soul's memories influencing my current physical self. After that embarrassing incident with Dr. Countway, I left O'Brien's, alone, and haven't seen him since. I don't understand what he could possibly have to do with this."

Detective Brown turned his brown eyes to Romy and she sensed a tensile strength there that made Jo's warning even stronger. "Because, Ms. Landry, you were seen in Dr. Countway's company after you left O'Brien's. On Ursulines Avenue, to be exact."

14

"I have to talk to Adrian," Romy said in a harsh whisper as she strode into the police station waiting room and out the door.

Jo scrambled after her. "What's happening?"

Romy leaned toward her while still on the move. "Brown has witnesses who've placed Adrian with me on Ursulines Avenue the night of the murder."

"You're serious?" Jo asked.

"That's what he said. Could Adrian be doing things completely unawares, as I have been? Hell—" her steps faltered "—what if he's the murderer? Your aunt could tell, couldn't she? She'd see Stan King's ghost hovering about."

"Whoa! Just slow down a minute," Jo cautioned, trying to break Romy's headlong pace. "What did Brown say exactly?"

"Not much, believe me. He doesn't have to tell me everything he knows, does he? I, on the other hand, have to disclose everything, no matter what. I have to talk to Adrian. I have to know what he remembers." And thinks and feels.

"Wait." Jo grabbed Romy's arm. "Maybe this only means something as innocent as Doc Countway passing you on the street with neither of you remembering."

"If a person had recently been on her knees fumbling with your fly, wouldn't you remember?"

"Good point but stay calm. If you panic, you could bring on one of your past life event thingies and I sure don't want to be chasing you around the streets with you babbling in tongues."

"Right, of course—calm, my elusive moving target." Romy stopped dead in the middle of the sidewalk, lifted her face toward the sun, and took several deep, even breaths. "Okay, I'm now slightly less frantic but I can't promise calm. How do I do get calm when my life's such a catastrophe? Rhetorical question. Let's find Adrian. What time is it?" She checked her watch. "Three p.m. Where would he be?"

"Do you know his home number?"

"I don't have it with me. He must be in the White Pages. Wait—if the police interrogated him, surely he'd try to call me? He has my home number."

"What a slice it is to listen to you run through all that deductive reasoning," Jo said as she pulled out her cell phone and punched in their home phone number. "I'll check our answering service."

While Romy waited, the heat thickened around her heavy and oppressive while sunlight on the cars' chrome seemed to pierce her eyeballs. Fear coursed along her spine. Another headache loomed on the edge of her brain as the past began to press in around her. "No," she whispered. "Not now!"

Jo, ear pressed to her phone, didn't notice. "He's phoned twice and left his cell number. He says for you to call ASAP." She passed the phone to Romy.

Romy took the phone without thinking, still trying to anchor herself in the present. Her emotions buzzed with desperation, her head whirled with questions. When she realized he wasn't home, the turmoil mounted.

"Adrian," she said to his answering recording. "I just found out how you and I were seen together after leaving O'Brien's last night. I've been staying with Louisa Dupré. Please call me on Joquita's cell as soon as you get this." She gave the number, clicked off, and passed the phone back to Jo.

"All right, so let's get you back to Aunt Loo's so you can rest."

Rest? How could she rest now? "Why don't we research Claire at the Old Ursuline Convent Museum instead? It's a perfect opportunity. There must be a convent archivist or maybe even a librarian who could trace Claire back through the records. If I could find out if she might have known Ulloa, maybe more pertinent facts might emerge. The convent building withstood the fires so there could be a wealth of material there."

"Okay, but take a deep breath—in-out, in-out. *Think*. You are not supposed to be researching or doing anything that screams PAST, get it?" Jo stood on the sidewalk, hands on hips, her warrior princess stance. "You're so riled up I wouldn't be surprised if you popped into Claire right on the spot."

Romy dug her knuckles into her temples, trying to press back the tension. "I know, I know, but I'm just so agitated that resting's going to feel like standing still. I have to do something."

Jo swore under her breath. "What can I do to distract you? Want me to describe how good Telly was in bed?"

Romy looked at her. "You talk sex and I'll just think about Adrian or maybe Antonio, too, and how would that help?"

"Wouldn't."

"Exactly." Something was tugging at the back of her mind, knocking away at her brain with twitchy desperation. "Let's go back to the house. Slap me if I start acting strange because the emotions I'm feeling right now aren't my own. I feel a migraine coming on."

"Shit!" Jo started scanning the streets for a taxi. Then, seeing Romy struggle, she thumped her friend on the back and muttered: "Leave her alone, you long-dead bitch."

Afraid Jo might try dislodging Claire with the Heimlich maneuver, Romy backed away just as a cab slid to the curb.

"Talk to me, talk about anything outside the forbidden zone. Distract me, will you?" Romy begged as they climbed into the car.

"Right, here goes." Jo began babbling as requested. She told Romy about her affair with Detective Brown and she discussed her problems finding a good man, describing everything and anything to keep Romy distracted. Romy tried to fix on every word while the streets flew by.

"See what I mean?" Jo was saying as she gazed out the window toward Decatur Street. "I can't stick to one man and I don't know why. I don't believe that old adage about not finding the right one. I found the right one and I ruined everything. As soon as he got serious, whoosh! I blew it."

"You have some past life shit of your own going on," Romy said, feeling as if she was speaking from far away.

"I'm thinking so. Maybe most of us do, only not to such an extent as you."

"I'm probably an extreme case yet." But when Romy turned to her friend to make a point, the world shifted and an overpowering scent of jasmine and spice filled the air.

Madame Letourneau was sitting beside her, whispering instructions in her lilting French.

She wasn't ready for this! Romy tried to force herself back to the present, to fix in her mind the sound of the streets, the smell of the air freshener ball dangling on the driver's rearview mirror—pine, maybe? Jo's face turned toward hers, the traffic noises...

"Rom, what's happening? Finish your sentence before I shake it out of you!"

15

All the conspirators stared at Claire—Mother Marie, Campeneau, d'Entremont, and the three priests—and Romy could not pull herself from this moment. Not now, not on the brink of discovering the nature of the plot against Ulloa. Instead, she settled in for the ride of her life as an eavesdropper to history.

"This is she?" Campeneau asked, stepping forward to inspect Claire. His breath reeked of onions and something sour but she had been told to keep her eyes cast down and so she would.

After a moment of scrutiny, he asked: "This girl, though comely enough, why would we choose her? She is but an Acadian peasant," Campeneau said.

"You doubt our choice?" Mother Superior's voice.

"Mother, but we must be assured that she is able, no? I do not think her beauty so grand, is all. If we are to entice Ulloa we require a woman of great skill, much like Madame Letourneau here. I have met the Spanish mongrel and he is a cold fish unmoved by much of what we French offer. He holds us in contempt. He will not be easily enticed by a mere morsel."

"Just so," said one of the priests. Not Father Dagobert this time, but the rotund Père Michel, who occasionally sent for Madame Letourneau's girls to be smuggled into the back door of the chapel. Claire could feel his eyes on her now. "Though not one familiar of the ways of the flesh, I must insist we adhere to one who knows something of these things. Perhaps she should lay with Monsieur so that he may return with the account?"

The bastard. Romy yearned for a good look at these men. All she could see was their feet, the muddy shoes and hems, splattered breeches. And the smells! She had little prior exposure to this reek of sweat and unwashed bodies—the odor of humanity in a time when bathing had not become commonplace. And there was another scent, too, incense, perhaps. Yes, that was it; Mother Superior was burning incense to mask the odors that seeped into this sanctuary.

Claire's heart beat quickly—in anger, Romy realized, but she couldn't focus on that just now. The Acadian was speaking.

"But that is petite Claire Landry!" Jean d'Entremont exploded. "*Mon Dieu!* But I did not recognize her at first! What her father would do to see her turned whore!"

"She is no whore," Mother Marie stated, her tone strong and resolute as an ax beheading a chicken. *Thump! Do not argue with me!* "She is a soldier of France, is she not? Do not men kill in the name of our Lord to protect our shores from conquerors? Women do what we must to defend our land, too, and use what weapons we have to serve. Here is a soldier to be sent forth into battle to do the work of France and God."

"Besides." Madame Letourneau's melodious voice poured into the room like molten gold over gravel. "She is a virgin still, unsullied by any man. Of that, I assure you. She has been taught the ways under my watchful eye but I permitted no man to lay a hand on her."

Claire stomach twisted. *Virgin in name but whore in knowledge. This is what you have made me.*

"As you will see, she does not have peasant manners, monsieur, and what skills she offers are precisely those needed for our task," Mother Marie said.

"Respectfully, I must be the judge of that, Mother," Campeneau insisted. "You are not so familiar with what entices a man, is that not so? She is very pretty, I agree, but I believe there are other women at Madame Letourneau's more delectable. Perhaps I should test her skills?"

"She is to remain a virgin until she makes the ultimate sacrifice!" Mother Marie insisted. "Do not think otherwise. Though not immersed as you in the ways of sin, Monsieur Campeneau, I do understand politics, which I fear is much the same."

"But—"

"The governor is not interested in prostitutes. He is a Christian man and needs to believe the girl pure and so she remains. I assure you, Claire Landry has been educated precisely according to our needs. She is extremely clever and reads with ease all manner of books."

"Not just the Bible?"

"No, monsieur. For this child, we allowed access to the library. She was quick to learn and excellent with languages. Since she was not to be a nun, we did not restrict her readings."

"Precisely so," Madame Letourneau added, sweeping forward in a rustle of red—red for Tuesday. "And this governor is a man of letters, is he not? He will not be enticed by some colt who does nothing but whinny when a man is about." She tapped her coiffed blond head. "All great courtesans know that an educated man yearns for brain as well as body. She will make better progress if she can speak to him of books and fine ideas so as to pry his thoughts free along with his breeches."

"Madame!" Père Dagobert exclaimed.

Poor Father Dagobert would be shocked at that, Claire thought. He, at least, followed his vows.

"Oh, forgive me, Father, but I have studied our governor," Madame explained. "Though he does not bring his custom to my house, many of his soldiers do and speak of him when lulled with wine and our soothing attentions."

Father Dagobert's displeasure soon subsided and Romy, following Claire's every thought, remained enthralled by the events unfolding. For an instant, she considered what her own body might be doing back in the present but soon became too engrossed to give it another thought.

"I understand the Ursulines teach women more than just about God," Campeneau nodded, gazing around. Claire lifted her gaze but remained fixed on the plantation owner, taking in his brown linen jacket and stained jabot, the calculating glitter in his small brown eyes. "I have never understood why you waste your efforts on women. Why, my wife has been ruined by such thoughts. She babbles on about things she has no need of knowing and I have had to use my belt on her upon occasion to still her tongue—your fault, Holy Mother, for teaching her things other than humble servitude."

Mother Marie pressed her eyes closed. Campeneau took the opportunity to step closer to Claire, which almost caused her to gag. Such a pig! His body blocking the view to both Mother Superior and the priests, yet in full view of Madame, he pressed his filthy paw against Claire's bodice and squeezed one breast.

How she longed to slap his face but she had seen far worse under Madame's roof and had prepared herself accordingly. She must gain this disgusting creature's approval or never be admitted to the governor's house. Endure, endure, she cautioned herself, her fingers flexing at her side, while Romy sat tucked deep inside her head, seething equally.

"Not large," he mouthed at Madame as he removed his hand.

Madame leaned forward and whispered: "Not every man likes to suck the cask when a glass of fine claret will do. Stop this, you scoundrel. Come to me later and I'll give you what you want for nothing, yes?"

Campeneau grinned, revealing teeth blacked from tobacco and too many sweets. Turning away, he addressed Mother Superior. "Holy Mother, assure me that this girl has the skill we require."

Mother Marie rose and strode toward Claire, her expression a mask of endurance. If she knew what had just occurred, she did not acknowledge it. "To answer this, you must hear her story from her own lips. What you ask of her is to orchestrate the downfall of a powerful man. You ask her to commit treason, is that not so? What kind of woman do you believe can manage such a mission, monsieur?"

Monsieur hesitated, as if searching his mind for a response, but, of course, he did not have the brain to outthink Mother Superior.

"Let me describe her to you, if you please, monsieur. We need a woman who is intelligent and educated enough to navigate the forces that rule Ulloa's Spanish household. She must be a woman who burns with fire, the fire necessary to perform treason—*treason*, monsieur!"

Campeneau cleared his throat. "And the girl has this fire, Mother?"

Mother Superior turned and gave the signal. Claire felt as though she had been rehearsing for this moment half her life. Shrugging off the demure mantle she had assumed, she stepped forward.

"Monsieurs, Holy Fathers, I stand before you, Claire Comeau, an

Acadian, yes, and proud to be so. Ten years ago, I lived a happy life with my parents, brother, and grandmamma on a little farm in Grand-Pré, in the land of Acadia many hundreds of miles away."

Only now did Romy pick up the faint hint of the Acadian dialect in Claire's voice. "We were simple folk. We farmed the land and built dykes to keep the sea at bay and toiled from noon to night for our crops. My parents' one goal was to have a little house, snug and warm against the cold winters of northern climes. For years, that was our longing: to move from our shack to a proper house!"

"Yes, yes, get on with it," the plantation owner said.

"No, monsieur, you must hear me out. You think you understand, but you do not. Our land, like this one, fell from sovereign to sovereign, back and forth, English to French, French to English, until the day came when the British arrived, their coats blazing like the crimson of a bleeding wound. Thump, thump, thump, we hear their boots marching down the road."

"The British, yes." Père Dagobert nodded, as if recalling some old grief.

"The British," Claire acknowledged. "They lived among us for years, watching and guarding. We came to know them. We grew comfortable with their forts and barracks. We sold them food and some even ate at our tables like friends. Yet it was all a lie, a lie, you understand? The day came when Sergeant Sewell, who had befriended my father, said that something was afoot. He said that we would be asked to sign a writ claiming we were subjects of the King of England."

Claire walked about meeting the gaze of each one of her audience's faces, daring someone to interrupt, while Romy studied the details of the men's faces.

"But," she said, "no Acadian would agree. My father, he said, 'Though we are French in soul, we do not sign allegiance to any sovereign but Christ our Lord. Who is the King of England to demand such of us when the King of France has not? For years we lived on this land, we tend this soil. It is to Acadia we vow allegiance now and no sovereign across the sea! Tell your king we will not sign but tell him also that we will not take arms against any flag. If the French king asks us, we will refuse him also. Leave us in peace and in peace we shall stay, no matter who the monarch.'"

Claire heard an exhalation of breath—from Jean d'Entremont, she suspected. Yes, the little Acadian would beat his heart in tune with hers. "We refused, and for that, we were punished," she continued. "There came a day when the soldiers called the men to a meeting in our little church." For a moment, a memory of St. Charles, its stone walls afloat as if in a sea of grass and wildflowers, swamped her heart. She struggled with her voice but went on. "We were told to leave. The land we worked so hard would be confiscated, our belongings taken, and all of us shipped away in boats, to God knew where, across the sea."

"We know this, child," Father Dagobert said gently.

"Yes, Father, you know this in your head but I need you to know this in your heart, yes? I need you to know that, on the day the soldiers set fire to our homes, my mother collapsed on the doorstep. Her unborn child screamed to come into this world and she could not be moved, but it mattered not to the soldiers."

And she said "soldiers" as if the word named a scourge, a disease more deadly than any pestilence. Romy felt the quiver of hate run through her, understood the depth of Claire's repulsion.

"As they dragged her to her feet, my father intervened and they struck him an evil blow and hauled his senseless body to a ship. In the chaos, my little brother, Petite Jacques, for my father was Grand Jacques, was put upon another boat. I was struggling to stay with my mother, who was bleeding and screaming in pain, and knew not which way to turn."

She was crying now and it took every bit of her will to force the words out of her throbbing throat. Romy experienced that trauma—not her own and yet completely hers in some profound way.

"My mother died untended in the dirt as our new house burned. I remember seeing her blood staining the dust, hearing the village women crying out to help her while the soldiers pushed them on. I remember running through the press of people being separated from their lands and families, and finding Sergeant Sewell, my father's friend. I asked him, 'Why?' as only a child could ask. 'Why do you let them hurt my mama and papa? You liked them, yes? You said they are fine people and yet you let them be hurt! Help my mama, monsieur, please!' And to this he answered, 'I cannot, child, for I am soldier and a soldier obeys his orders. Now, get on a boat, for God's sake!'"

The tears ran unchecked as Madame Letourneau patted her on the back, shushing her as one would a child, while the men hung their heads.

It was Father Dagobert's voice that broke the silence moments later. "But, my child, all this tells us is why you despise the British not the Spanish."

Claire dabbed her eyes with the handkerchief Madame pressed into her hand. "No, Father. It tells you why I despise soldiers, no matter who the sovereign. They all behave the same. Soldiers do their duty, no? And their allegiance is never to the people but to the rulers who care not the common folk."

"Tell the rest of the story, Claire," Mother Marie's voice said, not unkindly.

Claire nodded. "I was taken care of by the Beausejoir family, good people who treated me well, and our boat's passengers settled in the bayou. I stayed with them for many years until Madame Beausejoir thought it best I go to the sisters of Saint Ursula to cure my soul. You see, I could not forgive—cannot forgive still—and Madame Beausejoir, she convinced me that living close to God would help."

"So, Claire came to live here, as one of our girls, though we soon realized her unsuitable for convent life and could not form her into a Bride of Christ," Mother Marie said. "The emotions run too strong for the life of piety, chastity, and humility to which we aspire. God has other work for her to do."

Claire managed to hold her tongue.

"Go on, child," Mother Marie urged.

"Over the years, we heard word that some Acadian ships had sunk and many more sailed to other places, both north and south. I understood from one news-bringer that Petite Jacques died of fever not long after sailing but I had heard nothing of my father, my dear papa, for years. Then, just months ago, I heard he was alive still, though very confused from the soldier's blow."

"Your father, he is Jacques Landry? I had not heard whether he lived or died," Jean d'Entremont remarked.

Claire was careful not to meet his eyes in case she began to cry anew. "The news-bringer said his boat had had trouble finding settlement, monsieur, that the Acadians on board would disembark for a few months only to be forced away again. Their ship was often low in provisions and the people sick from the constant hardship."

"This is our fate, is it not?" Mother Marie sighed. "As the French either war or trade back and forth with England or Spain, so we are traded, too, the fortunes of French-speaking peoples changing by the day. We become foreigners in our own land and then again in our adopted country, like now with the Spanish. Continue, Claire. Tell the gentlemen what happened to your father."

"Nearly a year ago, we heard that my father's boat was sailing here to Louisiana. The captain had been told that Louisiana, being French, was one of the few places where Acadians would be welcomed."

"Word must not have come to this man that the King of France had already traded us to Spain like we were no more than sacks of sugar and barrels of whiskey," Campeneau muttered.

"We are worth nothing to France, no?" Madame Letourneau scoffed. "Louis, he never saw the value of only part of a colony unless he could dominate an entire continent. He thinks we cost him money. France sleeps with Spain, yes?"

"Continue your story, Claire," Mother Marie urged.

"Yes, Mother. It is true the settlers had not heard of this latest change of fortunes for new French settlers. They made their way down here, weary but hopeful that, at last, they would find a home."

"And you heard that your father lived still?" Father Michel inquired.

"Yes, a man who had met these Acadians at one of the places where they tried to settle, it was he who brought word that my father was alive. He said he was not well, being sick in heart and mind. But how I sang with joy when I heard he lived still. To think we would be reunited after all these years!"

"Was that the ship that came but eleven months ago?" Jean d'Entremont asked.

"Yes, the same. I was here at the convent by then and stood with other Acadians down by the river. The ship dropped anchor just offshore and the settlers sent a rowboat forward to greet the governor on the wharf. I borrowed a man's spyglass and believe I saw my father on deck, though I could not be sure after so many years. He had changed so much. As I waited and waited for the boat to disembark, I realized something was wrong. This Governor Ulloa, he was standing on the wharf saying something to the men who had rowed in to request permission to land."

"And?" prompted Father Lucien, who had been silent until now.

"And that bastard cur, he sent the boat away, did he not?" Jean d'Entremont said. "No more French allowed here, he says! This land, it belongs to Spain, yes?"

"Yes!" Claire cried out. "He sent them away! My father died on board with many others, do you understand? Died! Gone! Dead! Murdered!"

She swung her fierceness toward the men, "I hate them, do you see? I hate all soldiers. They care not for the men and women and children. We are but fodder, pieces in the game. They play us about like our lives do not matter. They speak of strategy and care nothing for heart. This Ulloa, he, too, is a soldier in a governor's guise, yes?"

"A naval officer, yes," Campeneau said.

And then Claire steamed toward Monsieur Campeneau, skirts swishing. Shifting her accent, she smoothed her expression and spoke the Spanish she had strived so hard to learn. "Señor Campeneau and Holy Fathers, look at me now and you will see a woman prepared to go to battle, as fierce a soldier as has ever walked. I carry the sword, yes? I carry the sword to vanquish our enemy the way enemy soldiers have vanquished us. Governor Antonio de Ulloa, he will suffer at my hands as he and others like him have caused my people to suffer. He will be the one to bear the consequences of pain and sorrow as I crush him in my hands, heart and soul."

"Is that Spanish she speaks?" Campeneau whispered.

"Yes," Claire proclaimed, changing back to French because she knew no one in that room understood much more than a few words. "I have learned Spanish right here at the convent from a nun who grew up in Madrid. So, you see, I can read the governor's most private correspondence without him knowing. I can listen in on conversations when they'll think I cannot understand. Who else do you know who can do this?"

16

"Who else?" she demanded. "I ask you, monsieurs, am I not the perfect one for this task?"

"Romy!" the voice said. Someone shaking her, shaking her. "Snap out of this! Come back, for God's sake."

The voice, male, spoke perfect Spanish and something about its timbre caused her thoughts to stumble. "You are not Claire, do you hear me? You are Romy Landry and we need you back here now."

Backing away, she stood gazing around. Slowly, item by item, the room came into focus: the books lining the walls, the oriental carpet's jewel hues, the carved Chinese tables against the wall, the scent of furniture polish and gardenias—Louisa's library.

She became aware of the presence of three people as a whiff of bay rum brought her sharply to attention. "Adrian?"

"Thank God," he muttered, rubbing a hand through his hair. He looked as if he wanted to touch her but held himself in check. "I thought you'd never come to."

She gazed at him, confused. "I'm not sure how I did. How'd you get here?"

"I received your message and came to Louisa's just as Joquita was bringing you home by cab. You were apparently having some kind of 'event.' We had to restrain you so you wouldn't wander off and, for the next half hour, I, along with Joquita and Louisa, have observed you walking about this room, talking to yourself in archaic French mixed with Spanish."

"Not talking to herself," Louisa, standing nearby, corrected, her tone stern, "but enacting a life she once lived as another person, as I've been telling you."

"Right, of course. My apologies." Adrian squeezed the bridge of his nose. "I'm having some difficulty getting my mind around that point. Apparently you were walking around enacting a past life, all the while speaking in either an archaic Spanish dialect or equally French. Do you remember any of this?"

"Of course," Romy said, trying to gather her wits. Jo passed her a glass of water. They exchanged a quick, pointed glance. "I—sorry, I mean Claire, an Acadian, was trying to convince a group of French conspirators that she made a perfect spy because she could speak Spanish and wanted revenge for her family's deaths. At first, I was so involved I admit I didn't even try to return."

"Didn't I warn you about that?" Louisa muttered.

"You're actually conscious during these episodes?" Adrian asked.

Episodes, he thought these were *episodes*. Romy glanced away to assess Jo and Louisa. Sipping the water, she tried to shake the last dregs of another century.

"I was—am—conscious in a way, yes," she explained after a moment. "I mean, I'm very engaged in the events taking place back there, too engaged, obviously. I'm inside someone else's body and brain, listening to her every thought and feeling, experiencing life over two centuries ago. Who wouldn't be? And yes, sometimes I forget myself, literally, and I'm totally unaware of what's happening here in the present. Yet, most of the time I know who I am, unless I have a blackout, that is. Does that make sense?"

He turned away, striding across the room while digging his fingers into his scalp. "If you only knew how desperately I want to believe you."

"You have just witnessed Romy in her past life state, speaking and acting as a woman who lived long ago," Louisa pointed out. "You have seen this with your own eyes, Adrian. What are you having difficulty believing?"

"Everything," he said, swinging toward them. "So far, nothing I've seen here this afternoon proves to me that I have just witnessed a long-dead

Acadian girl speaking from across two hundred and forty years." He turned his green eyes directly on Romy and it took everything she could muster not to flinch.

"Listen to me, Romy," he continued, his tone pained. "I could translate every word of that Spanish dialect you were speaking and the French, as well, and you are, after all, a brilliant linguist, not to mention a talented woman and stellar student of history."

"Don't slap me with a backhanded compliment by implying it's all an act," she told him, fighting to keep her voice even. My God, how she loved this man, but every word he said left a wound.

"No, of course not an act, exactly, not an intentional act, in any case. I believe you're delusional. Everything you said—all the detail about Père Dagobert and the other conspirators, most of whom are well-known plotters in the insurrection against Ulloa—could have been plucked straight from published writings on the topic, don't you see?"

Suddenly Romy needed to sit down. Collapsing into one of Louisa's club chairs, she gazed up at Adrian. "Of course I see. How could I possibly expect you to believe me? After all, only documentation and evidence matter in this world, right? Nothing of value exists unless we can measure it."

He winced. "I'm just saying I'm not convinced, that's all."

"Because it's so much easier to believe I'm crazy," she said quietly.

"Wait," Louisa interrupted, holding up both hands. "Please, both of you. This is not helping and I absolutely do not want you, Romy, to be getting further upset." She glowered at Adrian. "And as for you, Dr. Countway, I suggest you stop thinking you know everything about the universe 'cause all your degrees are no better than alphabet soup when it comes to deeper matters. Pry open your mind, why don't you? Think like a human with a spirit, not a scholar."

He grimaced. "But I am a scholar."

"You are also a man with a soul."

"Why don't you talk about the night Stanley King died?" Jo suggested as she paced about the room barefoot. "That seems pretty pressing right now."

Romy nodded. "The police have at least one witness who said they saw us together after I left O'Brien's, Adrian. I certainly don't remember seeing you later that evening. Did you see me?"

He turned away again, his long legs taking him across the room, nearly colliding with Jo. "No, I certainly did not. The police's sources are mistaken, as I've told the detective in charge. After you ran out of the restaurant, we did try to follow you—Veronica and I, plus one of the restaurant staff, that is—but we lost you on Bourbon. We walked down the length of the street looking and even went so far as to wait outside your cottage, all to no avail. After I dropped Veronica off at her hotel, I continued my search alone—very concerned, you understand—but I never did meet up with you."

Louisa, standing with her arms crossed, shook her head. "So you think. And you have no soft spots in your memory, no fuzzy bits?"

"Absolutely none," he insisted. "I recall every action I took that night." He paused as if gazing back into his thoughts.

"Regression affects different folks different ways, Adrian," Louisa said, her eyes fixed on his face. "Did you go to sleep any time that night?"

A startled expression flashed across his features. "Briefly. I was completely exhausted and, after I'd dropped off Veronica, I went home to bed. I was concerned, very concerned, and I saw that lout grab you on the stairs so I feared the worst. In any case, I couldn't have snatched more than three hours' sleep before beginning my search again, but with no success."

Romy gazed at him. He cared that much?

"So, you don't have a conscious memory of every hour you spent that night, after all. You can't be telling me you know exactly what your body gets up to while you're sleeping 'cause I know it's not so. My guess is you went sleepwalking," Louisa said.

"I don't sleepwalk," he protested.

"That you know of," Jo pointed out. "Hard to know these things when you're asleep."

"Are you saying that I got up out of bed and left my flat to wander around the French Quarter sound asleep?"

"Your conscious self may have been sleeping but your body was wide awake while animated by your soul's memories," Louisa pointed out.

"And possessed by Antonio de Ulloa, I suppose," he said, his tone incredulous.

"Someone besides Stanley King followed me that night, Adrian," Romy said, trying to shrug away the vast weariness pressing down around her, "someone besides Stan. I heard two male voices and then the sounds of a struggle. Somebody interrupted Stanley as he was attempting to rape me. I heard voices just before I went under."

"Before you went under?" he asked, turning toward her. "But I thought you remained conscious as this Claire person?"

She gazed up at him. "I said for the most part. Look, I don't understand every detail of what's happening here, either, but is it so outside the realm of possibility to think you might not know everything?"

He looked at her, stunned. "Well, of course not. I'm not a complete intractable, close-minded clod." He hesitated. "Am I?"

"The jury's still out," Jo said.

Louisa intercepted quickly as she sailed toward him. In a moment, she stood eye to eye with him, one red polished nail tapping his chest. "Like it or not, Dr. Countway, forces are at work that you don't understand. Doesn't matter that you don't understand them; they'll keep happening, anyway. Seems to me if would help mightily if you were to stretch your world view some and try to get on board. Think outside the box, as they say."

Adrian took a deep breath, his eyes locked on hers. "Louisa, believing I'm the reincarnation of Antonio de Ulloa is so far outside the box it may as well be in another galaxy."

Louisa nodded. "Welcome to the universe."

"Look, guys," Jo interrupted. "I hate to be the voice of reason but it seems to me the point is this: a person's been murdered and maybe the culprit doesn't know he or she is a killer. Perhaps it is you, Doc."

Adrian turned his shocked expression toward her. "Like hell. I'd do anything to defend Romy but I'd damn well remember doing it."

"Actually," Louisa began, "you did not kill Stanley King any more than Romy did, Adrian. His murdered spirit is not clinging to your soul, either. I'd know. No, someone else murdered Stanley King, a third person who probably has no idea what their body is getting up to every hour of the night and day. We've got to find and identify that someone in two lifetimes."

Adrian rubbed his eyes. "I don't know whether to be relieved that you don't think I'm a murderer or further boggled by that remark."

"Try both. Until recently, general confusion worked for me," Jo suggested. She took a deep breath. "Look, I didn't believe all this stuff at first, either. Now I do because what I've seen doesn't make sense any other way. Now I believe in reincarnation."

Adrian gazed at her. "I've been so misguided I actually thought ghosts and reincarnation canceled one another out. Still, I promise to try very hard to suspend belief."

"Good," Louisa said. "That's all I'll ask for now. So, you'll have no objection to staying here as my guest until this is settled? I figure we'll need all the help we can get to sort this thing through and your translation services could be mighty handy when Romy speaks as Claire. Agreed?"

"I'd be delighted to stay and make myself useful." He kept his eyes averted from Romy. "And provide whatever support I can. Despite my skepticism, I'm thoroughly intrigued—dumbfounded, but intrigued. What do you propose happens next?"

"Sleep," Romy responded, getting to her feet, "for me, anyway. I'm exhausted. I'll just go upstairs for a nap. I presume you'll all be putting me under house arrest in case I try to wander off speaking to the dead? Perhaps even lock me in my room? Either way, I feel like I'm about to collapse on the spot. Living two lives takes a lot out of a person."

"Locking you in isn't enough, Romy," Louisa told her. "Somebody's got to keep an eye on you all the time in case you start banging into walls and such. I'll have Joquita stay in the adjoining room upstairs again. We'll check on you regularly and listen out should you start wandering around."

Romy nodded, making her way into the hall, too tired to care. She didn't reach the steps before the headache struck.

17

Romy reeled backward, the return to Claire's head swift. Where did she end up this time and could she pull back into the present?

She soon became aware of Claire standing perfectly still, staring at a man beyond an open doorway, but even as the man came into focus through their shared eyes, she heard Louisa calling to her at the edge of her senses.

"Romy, follow my voice," she heard Louisa say, the volume as faint as a whisper. "Tune out Claire's memories and don't get involved. Return right this minute!"

Romy tried. She imagined Louisa's den, thought of Adrian, of both Jo and her aunt as a means to steer her back, but except for an instant of wavering where the room seemed to blur, she remained firmly fixed in Claire.

Another attempt similarly failed. She could not disentangle herself from Claire's memory. Every step Claire took carried Romy with it; every thought, every feeling, became shared emotion. And now that Claire seemed transfixed by this man standing there, so, it seemed, must Romy.

And Romy recognized him in layers—once as Antonio de Ulloa and, once again, as Adrian Countway. She could not tear herself away.

The man stood in the center of the tiled floor, his face half-turned. Claire recognized him at once. Who else could it be with that blue sash across his chest, that ceremonial badge of office? Her heart throbbed. She risked taking a step toward the doorway despite her instructions to wait.

Governor Antonio de Ulloa was not what Claire expected. Seen from a distance that day on the wharf, he had appeared as a turkey squawking in a silver periwig. Yet, as Claire peered at him now, she glimpsed a far different man.

Much older than she, with his own hair tied at his neck, the intelligence of his lean, sharp face seemed to leap into prominence. He had a quick efficiency of manner that sliced across his surroundings like a sword prodding for stowaways. Yet, strangely, he seemed unaware how she watched from the doorway.

She edged against the doorframe, still not too far from the spot she had been told to stand, gazing as he took a seat behind a large desk positioned in the center of the room.

She stared hard. Though not tall, the governor gave the appearance of being very fit with compact muscles well used to exercise and life outdoors. The arresting combination of planes and angles in his face drew her gaze over and over again.

He wore a line of a mustache and a thin, pointed beard, old-fashioned but a style that served him well. With his white linen shirt open at the neck and the jabot hanging loose down the front, he appeared to be a man at leisure yet ready to tie the last knot in his appearance for the public display, if need be.

She leaned far enough forward to gaze at the glass cases of insect specimens and engravings lining the walls, enthralled by glimpses of other objects in the adjoining room. Everything about both the man and his interests seemed most peculiar.

"You have not yet been summoned to my presence," Governor Ulloa said without looking up, his French barely edged in Spanish. "Pray return to the foyer and wait as you have been instructed."

Startled, Claire quickly retreated, returning to the exact spot on the foyer tiles where the footman had ordered her to stand. So, this Spaniard had been aware of her the entire time and yet had said nothing? Not such a simple man, after all.

After a few minutes, she heard voices coming from the governor's room —heated Spanish voices, kept low so as not to be overheard. She crept back to the doorway again to listen.

Leaning forward, she saw a man she judged to be younger than the governor, accompanied by an old woman dressed head to toe in clothing as dark as crows' wings. As the two approached the governor's desk, the old woman tapped the floor with her cane as if demanding the floorboards to applaud her coming.

"I have seen that glossy bit of a thing waiting there. I do not need her!" sputtered the old crow.

"Hush," the younger man warned, raising a finger to his lips, "for she may hear." It took several moments for Claire to realize that this man was the governor's brother.

"She does not speak our language." The woman shot a searing glance in Claire's direction. Claire tried to sink into the shadows. "They have told us she is French through and through and she looks it, too. I beg of you, señor," she said, tapping her cane on the governor's desk, "do not force her upon me!"

"Señora Viscaya," the governor said, raising his head at last, "do not distress yourself. Of course we must accept the assistance the convent has provided. You have not been well and soon we will return to La Balize where the conditions are far worse. Juan and I, we cannot risk the health of the very woman who figured so prominently in our youth. We will not have you so burdened by work. With the girl in place, you can have a well-deserved rest. Indeed, I should not have allowed you to travel so far to serve me."

"But, señor," the old woman said, her voice tremulous and both hands clasping the cane as if that was all that held her up. "Have I not served both you and your brother well? Have I not always and forever put your needs before my own? No one can take care of you as I have, certainly not some little French thing. The French, they have no sense. They are frivolous and untrustworthy. Their cooking is inedible—so tasteless! They do not know how things are to be done."

The governor's lips quirked into a fleeting smile. "Señora Viscaya, the French do things differently, which is not the same as doing things incorrectly. We must open our minds to the way of this new land, for to do otherwise puts us at a disadvantage."

"Phaw!" sputtered the old housekeeper with a thump of the cane. "The French are the conquered ones! They must do as you say, Señor Antonio. Tell them to do as we Spanish do."

"Enough!" the governor said, getting to his feet. "You forget yourself, señora. I have said how it is to be and you will do as I bid. I will expect you to train the young woman in the ways of our household but to learn equally well the ways of her culture."

"But—"

"Cease! I will not be governor of a people I do not understand. Rest assured the girl comes from a good French family and, being convent raised, is of sound character. She is also well-educated, I believe, and knows how to read. She can be useful and will do the work that you cannot while assisting you to manage the other retainers and slaves. Perhaps she will even help our cook to attempt some local fare. Now, go!"

The little crow lowered her head, cast her quick pecking glance toward the foyer doorway where Claire remained out of sight. Then she hobbled from the room, her cane banging the floorboards all the way down the hall.

"Insufferable," Claire heard the governor mutter. "You have given her too much license, Juan. How I regret allowing you to bring her along. Her body may be failing but her spirit is as difficult as ever."

"Now, now," the younger brother said, shaking his head but looking quite unconcerned. Though slightly taller that the governor, Claire judged him to be perhaps five or six years younger. "Señora Viscaya is a good woman, if a bit headstrong. She means us well and is completely loyal, which is why I beseeched you to let her attend us."

"Loyal to what?"

"Not to 'what,' Antonio, to 'whom.' She is loyal to us, to you and me, the Ulloa family, or what is left of our noble spirit, and one must surround themselves with such loyalty in the country of our enemy, yes? These French, they are not pleased that we have come. Every Spaniard in this godforsaken swamp is a treasure."

"And our French citizens are treasures also, only one yet to be won." Antonio nodded, gazing at his brother as if trying to bore understanding into his sibling's skull. "Remember, we cannot force Spain upon the

French. This is a colony not gained by war but given in treaty. We must win their allegiance through just leadership, not by pounding them on the heads with our might."

"So you say," Juan said, turning away. "And I have no choice but to follow your lead, but pray remember that respect is gained by power, my brother, not by weakness. You are not a statesman so much as an explorer, as you have said yourself many times. I implore you to leave the management of the staff to me."

"And you would command the soldiers, too, if you could, would you not? But it will not be. I've known battles and courts and more foreign lands than you will ever hope to glimpse, little brother. You are young but make the mistake of believing you know more than you do. You are forever making suggestions as to how to govern this colony. Pray do not presume to judge what you don't understand. I will not risk insurrection to satisfy your notion of power."

"They would not dare rebel against us. What do peasants and renegades know of organizing a rebellion?"

"The French are in command here in all but name, Juan, and we have not the force to make it otherwise. Our king has yet to show much interest in this colony, yet it remains my job to ensure Spain profits from the acquisition. Enough. I weary of this and we will never agree." The governor rubbed a hand across his face.

"But yet we must talk these matters through."

"We have always thought differently, you and I, so let our debate rest for now. I have chosen my approach to this difficult governance and will proceed accordingly. Within the week, I plan to return to my fort at La Balize, in any case—a strategic position perfect for watching the mouth of the river. I believe the French would prefer we remain at a distance. Now, let us greet our new housekeeper and prepare to meet the plantation representatives within the hour."

By the time the governor's brother stepped into the foyer to fetch Claire, she stood, head down, studying the design on the tiles.

"Mademoiselle? Come with me, if you please."

Dropping a curtsy, she swept into the room in what she hoped was the perfect blend of the dignified and the demure. As soon as she stepped over the threshold, the governor's eyes pinned her to the spot. Something hot and deep plunged into her heart, shooting the length of her, and for a moment, she could only stop and stare at him.

Nothing in that intense, scrutinizing gaze indicated that he felt the same impact. His face remained curious, amused, perhaps.

"Welcome to my household, mademoiselle. I am, as you no doubt realize, Señor Antonio de Ulloa, and this is my brother, Señor Juan de Ulloa. You will find us to be men of few demands who ask only that you help run a tidy, efficient, and orderly household. In addition, I will call upon you to offer some insight into the ways of the French in cooking and such and to instruct my staff accordingly. I intend for you to assume the role of head housekeeper so that the esteemed Señora Viscaya may retire from her labors. Have you any queries?"

Queries? *How do I make you love me so I can bend you to my will?* "Yes, yes," she said, nodding far too much. "The language, does anyone else but you speak French, Monsieur Governor?"

"'Monsieur Governor'—I do like the sound of that. I fear the French have other names for me not nearly as pleasing." There came that fleeting smile again. "No one speaks French fluently in this household, mademoiselle, though a few of my staff have gleaned a few words. The slaves we received as gifts speak the language, of course. It would be most helpful if you would learn a little Spanish for I fear my staff is slow to learn the ways of their new country."

"Perhaps it would help if they were to fraternize with more of the locals," she told him. "On market days, I've seen how they arrive only long enough to choose provisions and then quickly leave."

Señor Juan turned to his brother as if to see if he would allow such impertinence but the governor only acknowledged her words with a slight nod. "I will take that under advisement, mademoiselle. That said, you are dismissed. Please proceed to the kitchens where Señora Viscaya will inform you of whatever else you need to know."

Dismissed already? She opened her mouth to speak but couldn't think of what to say. How would she ever win his confidence? Did he not appear to find her alluring, let alone attractive? How would she succeed now?

"Mademoiselle? Do you wish to say something?" the governor prompted.

She curtsied again. "No, monsieur. I will leave you to your business."

❧ 18 ☙

Romy came alert inside Claire and tried again to stage her return. She envisioned Louisa's house, her garden. She imagined Adrian and Jo. She tried to rouse herself from a dream but Claire's memory gripped her tight. She felt herself falling backward, sending her back in a dizzying tilt deep into Claire's mind.

"Señorita," Señora Viscaya called out, her black lace shawl drooping about her shoulders like a shredded bat, "come here at once! Not a week on the job and already you dawdle."

Claire, already halfway across the courtyard, turned and nodded a greeting but continued on her way, pretending not to understand the woman's Spanish. No matter what her assignment, she would not let that creature speak to her that way. She suffered enough of her abuse.

"Come back, I say! I have not given you permission to visit the kitchens. You are to remain in the house until I say otherwise!" The cane could be heard thumping on the tiles as if intent on smashing them with her temper.

But Claire only picked up her skirts and scurried across the courtyard, scattering the chickens as she ran toward the large square building from which wafted the scent of baking bread.

Bursting through the doorway, she paused, her eyes adjusting to the light. Suffocating heat filled the room. Ahead, two slave girls busied themselves, one chopping vegetables on the long wooden table that dominated the space while the other stirred something in a cauldron on the fire. Both girls glistened in perspiration, the air heavy with cooking aromas and sweat.

Except for a brief flicker in their eyes, neither slowed their work or gave any indication of her presence. A man, a Spaniard by the looks of things, stood by, assessing their efforts, and it was he who addressed her first.

"Good afternoon, señorita! You must be the new housekeeper, yes? We wondered when you would visit. Has Señora finally opened your cage? Welcome to the kitchens of Governor Ulloa. I am Ricardo El Cardez, chief cook, a man whose dishes the governor favors so much he brings me with him to add flavor to the new world, *sí?*" Ricardo bowed deeply, his face beaming a merry smile.

Claire smiled back, relieved to find a friendly face in this dour household. Behind her, she could hear the tap-tapping of the cane making its slow way across the courtyard.

Stepping forward, she spoke in French. "I am sorry that I cannot speak your tongue well. I know but a few words. I am Mademoiselle Claire Comeau. I have been instructed by the governor to help bring the flavor of New France to his dishes and intend to start today. Together, we could try some new combinations, something that will tempt the governor's palate, yes?"

Not commanding enough, she remanded herself, and what did it matter if the man could but understand a few words? As housekeeper, she must govern these people, once the old crow got out of the way, that is. If it was true that the household would be moving elsewhere, she must organize that, too. "Pray, let me see what it is you cook."

Ricardo turned to the slave girl stirring the pot, a small, very dark-skinned girl not much younger than Claire. "Odette, what does she say?"

Odette turned to Claire and then back to Ricardo, her large brown eyes quick and knowing beneath the kerchief that restrained her unruly hair. "She says she will make you cook proper French food, Ricardo. No more shells in rice. No more burning spices. No more raw shrimp. We take the tails off first."

Haitian by the accent, Claire thought. She narrowed her eyes at the girl. Oh, she'd have to watch this one.

"What? But the master loves my paella. He does not want all that French cream in his food, he says. Tell her that I will not allow her to touch my dishes until the master says so." Ricardo's otherwise cheerful countenance flushed in dismay.

Odette turned to Claire, her eyes twinkling with mischief. "The cook, he says you go to hell."

Claire stifled a smile. *Oh, yes, Odette, you will need watching.*

"Señorita Comeau!" came a shrill voice from the doorway as the housekeeper huffed over the threshold and tap-tapped her way into the kitchen. "How dare you walk away from me when I bid you otherwise! I have not been supplanted by you yet, you useless French piece of work. Do not dare speak to my staff when I am not present."

Odette stepped toward the old housekeeper. "She speak no Spanish, Señora Viscaya. I tell her what you say?"

"Yes."

And Odette obliged with a reasonable translation, adding only a few threats to further spice up the señora's words. "What you say back?" Odette demanded of Claire.

Claire knew her words would be twisted but she replied, nonetheless: "Tell Señora Viscaya that I apologize but do not understand her language. I mean to do my duty as diligently as possible but only as it matches the role the governor has entrusted to me. I am to supervise the cooking and so I shall."

Surprisingly, Odette recounted that verbatim, even managing some of the more difficult words. Ah, thought Claire, as wily as a fox, this one. Could it be that, in Señora Viscaya, she and Odette shared a common foe?

"You must first come to my room and empty my chamberpots and comb out my hair and massage my legs, French slut," the old woman demanded, her eyes narrowing. "This is all you deserve, for you French are no better than slaves, the lot of you. These tasks you do before I permit you to go near these kitchens, *sí?* You will not talk to the governor or the servants unless I am in attendance, do you understand this?"

Odette translated, adding for Señora's benefit, "But she can talk through me, señora. I speak for her to the others."

"You will not speak for her unless I ask, you tar-faced idiot. You are a slave and entirely too big for your shoes."

And down cracked the cane, aiming for Odette's hand resting on the table edge but the girl snatched it away. Brandishing her cane, Señora Viscaya moved in to finish the job. "Hold out your hand. I have had enough of your impertinence!"

But Claire slipped between Odette and the housekeeper and yanked the cane from the woman's hand. "Odette, translate this for me. Tell Señora Viscaya there will be no more hitting of slaves or servants under this roof. If she tries again, I will inform the master. I suspect the governor does not want the reputation of a man who allows foul-tempered servants to beat his slaves."

Odette recounted the information to Señora Viscaya, adding: "And she says she will not clean your stinking chamberpots or rub your filthy old feet!"

"Or do anything but what I have been instructed by the governor," Claire added before she could catch herself. She stared, aghast. Now Odette might suspect the truth, know she understood Spanish. Good Lord, what had she done?

As Odette recounted her last words, Claire hastily added: "The governor has requested that I assist with the cooking and that is where I shall start today without further interference."

After Odette had finished repeating Claire's words, Señora Viscaya appeared too stunned to speak. It was as if no one in this household had ever dared defy her. It was as if she now assessed the full measure of her enemy, this French chit who dared to contest her authority, and realized the size of the battle ahead. Her worn face, hardened by who knew what hardships, appeared to constrict into a mask of venom.

Yet Claire stood her ground. She had taken a risk in threatening the housekeeper—for what did she know of the governor's ways regarding servants and slaves?—but she sensed he struggled to forge the right impression among his citizens. Also, she realized with a shock, cruelty did not seem to suit him.

So, why had he sent her father and the other Acadians away? She vowed to find out but, no matter what she discovered, would never forgive. Could not forgive.

But her gall in challenging the old housekeeper was rewarded. Señora Viscaya hauled the lace wrap tighter around her shoulders despite the punishing heat, snatched the cane from Claire's hands, and left the kitchen, sweeping the pile of sliced vegetables onto the floor along the way.

"Cow," Ricardo muttered after she'd gone. "Look how she makes us work and tortures little Odette. All my days under her, it is always the same."

"Here, I will help," Claire said in French, gathering up the tomatoes and peppers strewn across the straw.

Romy took advantage of the moment when Claire relaxed into the mindless task of gathering the strewn vegetables to regain her place in time.

It was as if she attempted to swim to the surface of a deep, sludgy swamp, pushing bits of foreign memory from her brain while fighting for air. Though the surface of consciousness grew closer, appearing like a skim of light on the edge of her senses, she could not break through.

For one blinking instant, however, she thought Claire sensed her presence. Claire had been picking up slices of pepper and carrot when she paused, as if listening to something inside her head—a scrap of memory, an invocation of something not quite hers, perhaps. She soon dismissed the sensation as her imagination and carried on with her task, but a thrill shivered through Romy at that brief connection. Maybe, just maybe, she could communicate with Claire, after all.

But she had no time to think. Not only did she remain trapped inside Claire's memories but those memories had begun to chunk into separate episodes as if Claire recalled only the highlights of her days at the governor's house.

Romy clung to vestiges of her own self while scene after scene of Claire's life flashed by.

THE FRICTION BETWEEN THE BROTHERS INCREASED OVER DESSERT UNTIL Claire shooed the servants from the dining area. She would attend the

Ulloas' needs herself, confident they believed her unable to understand Spanish and would speak freely.

"I understand," she overheard Señor Juan say, "that Señora Viscaya has today taken to her bed, very distraught over the arrival of this convent girl here."

"How unfortunate," the governor remarked mildly as he sipped his wine. "It is no doubt time she took a rest from terrorizing the servants."

"She is old and frightened, Antonio. She fears losing her place in our regard."

"She lost her place in my regard when, many years ago, I watched her convince Papa to whip every one of our slaves over some trumped-up slight. I would not treat a dog the way she treats those of different skins. For years I have abided with her temper but I will not tolerate this behavior here. She refuses to change."

"Does she not run a good house? After Father's death, for all those years when you were at sea, I remind you that I managed the estate, Antonio, and her service to me was exemplary. What if she loses her temper at a slave or two or admonishes a servant with the back of her cane? Do they not work efficiently under her rule? Are we ever bothered by poor behavior or undisciplined service?"

"Fewer servants would also ensure good behavior as there would be less to manage. The fact is, both she and this entire retinue should have remained in La Balize. I have no need for such here. I have been assigned a job to govern, not to keep grand houses and socialize."

"You are such a soldier, Tonio. Do you not see how the size of a governor's household impresses the locals? They see what fine servants you keep and that will show your importance. A governor should not live like a pauper. You have been too long at sea and forget the ways of civilized existence. Why not leave this aspect to me?"

"Enough!" The governor got to his feet and tossed his linen napkin to the table. "I agreed to leave the management of this retinue to you and my wife, thus dragging you both over to these shores against my better judgment, but I will not tolerate Señora Viscaya's tyranny further."

"You can't just cast her out."

"You know I would never do such a thing, but perhaps I will send her to La Balize to be with my wife. Those two get on rather well, I note. To honor the years spent in the family's employ, I have reluctantly given Viscaya's son a position of command at your insistence but she will be removed as head housekeeper as of today. That ends the discussion."

"Francisca deserves a say in matters of household management, surely? She should be here with you instead of at La Balize."

"What my wife deserves is my concern alone."

The governor shot a quick glance toward Claire, who busied herself just inside the adjoining room tidying the serving tables. "Keep your voice down. We do not need the servants whispering among themselves."

"As if they do not already."

"I am certain they do, especially at La Balize where my wife has spent an inordinate amount of time in your company, my brother. A less trusting man might speculate that I am not the father of my child."

"Antonio, you can't think for a moment I would ever seduce your wife."

"It is not what I think that matters. Here, I am among enemies where any impropriety might flame the masses. Watch your step, Juan, that is all I ask. Do not push providence. I am tempted to send both you and Francisca back to Spain."

"What?" stormed Juan. "You would remove the only allies you have in this godforsaken land?"

"On most days, you hardly appear to be my allies." And with that, the governor left the table, his sweet rice dish left untouched.

Claire kept her head down and went about her work while her thoughts churned. He had a wife, a child. His brother and he did not agree. So much turmoil.

19

Claire stood in the storeroom checking provisions when the maid approached.

"Señorita," the girl whispered, casting a quick glance over her shoulder. "I have message, ah—how do I say the French?—from Señora Viscaya."

"How is the señora?" Claire asked. "I have heard she remains unwell. She has eaten the meals I sent up? Can I do anything to make her more comfortable?"

Something flickered in the girl's dark eyes but she only shook her head as if not understanding. This girl, Claire knew, was one of the few who spoke a little French yet somehow managed to misunderstand everything Claire said.

"She want you to—" and the girl struggled to find the word "—to go to kitchen building. Yes, yes." She nodded. "She want you go check kitchen door."

"Check kitchen door?" Claire stared at the maid, puzzled. Since when was checking the outbuildings before going to bed her task? "But surely that would be the soldier's job or maybe the yard man?"

The maid only gazed back in incomprehension. "Check kitchen," she repeated. "Go to kitchen now."

Maybe Señora Viscaya had heard that Ricardo had not secured the door or adequately prepared the food for tomorrow's breakfast? The man had proved delightful but unreliable in the two days she had been here.

"Oh, very well." Claire untied her over-apron and left it folded on top of the day's laundry.

She had barely the time or space to sort through the things she had heard over last night's dinner or even decide whether tension between the Ulloa brothers would be of any interest to the conspirators. Most of what she had learned hardly concerned matters of state.

What kind of information would concern matters of state? she wondered as she readied to go to the courtyard. Something about ships, guns, and policies? She needed information to bring to her meeting with Mother Superior and the conspirators Sunday next but her plans to search the governor's quarters had been complicated by the fact the man seemed to never sleep. He stayed up all hours writing at his desk or reading books.

Besides, this business of housekeeping proved to be far more demanding than Claire anticipated. She hardly had time to spy. Not only was she to supervise the meals but also oversee the Spanish maids, who seemed determined to misunderstand even the simplest of directions.

And now there was talk that the governor would return to this La Balize, a swampy area in the mouth of the Mississippi Delta, where presumably he kept his main household, including this wife.

Whatever had to be done needed to be done soon. But how would she ever find the time, energy, or opportunity to both woo Antonio de Ulloa and spy on him, as well?

Unhooking one of the lanterns from the wall, Claire turned to the maid. "If this will make her happy, I shall do so."

The courtyard lay deserted this time of night, though Claire could hear slaves singing from behind the outbuildings—low, strange songs that caused the heart to ache.

She caught the mumbled voices of the Spanish soldiers and retainers out of sight around the premises. All would be taking advantage of the last few hours of evening to share stories and sing songs beside their own cook fires while the crickets and bullfrogs chirped along. The scent of burning wood from the firesides filled the air.

How she hated being outside after dark in this land—too many strange noises, too many odd cries—and though she knew soldiers patrolled the enclosure, the nearness of their swords and bayonets did nothing to dispel her uneasiness.

Halfway across the courtyard, she heard a hiss coming between the stable and the storage shed.

"Mademoiselle, Odette here!"

Claire turned to see the girl huddled in the darkness. "What are you about? You should be in your quarters by now." The slaves occupied their own huts behind the animal sheds and were not allowed to prowl about the courtyard after-hours.

"I come warn you. You must hear. The old woman, Viscaya, in her you make bad enemy."

Claire shook her head. "I am not afraid of an old woman whose only teeth consists of waving her cane about."

"Not her, the son," Odette explained, the girl's thin hands clutching Claire's arm.

"What do you mean?"

"When Señora Viscaya come last year, she brought son, a soldier, very mean, mademoiselle, mean and crazy. You watch out now. He hurt you."

Claire grasped the girl's hands in hers. "Did he hurt you, is that it?"

The girl hesitated, her eyes widening, not so much with fear as perhaps with some remembered pain. "No matter, that."

"What did he do? Tell me."

Odette shook her head. "No matter, I say. He pay, someday I make him pay."

"What do you mean? I hope you're not considering trying to do anything to a soldier, Odette. If you were to even attempt such a thing, they'll kill you, you know that."

The girl nodded. "Other ways, mademoiselle. I know other ways."

"What ways?"

"Voodoo," the girl whispered.

Though Claire had never heard of this term, the sound of it caused a deep foreboding. "Forget this voodoo," she said. "You should let the governor know what this man did to you. He doesn't abide by abusing slaves."

"No, no—say nothing. If I's sold, I go away and never see Papa."

"Your papa? Where is he? Here, in this household?"

But Odette only shook her head. "No. Please, listen, mademoiselle, promise you not tell."

Claire sighed but shook her head. "I promise, but this is a mistake. And Governor Ulloa, why would he sell you? It's not your fault that some soldier in his army forced himself upon you. That is what happened, yes? This man is the one who should be punished, not you."

As if justice played a part where women and men were concerned, let alone justice between servant and master. Claire knew it, Odette knew it.

"I warn you."

"Thank you for your concern, Odette, but thank you, also, for not giving me away with Ricardo."

Odette nodded, smiling a little. "You speak the Spanish."

"A little."

"You do not want the others to know?"

"Exactly. Pretending not to understand the language is very useful but I would appreciate if you would give a fair recount of my words next time, Odette, you understand, yes?"

The girl smiled. "Yes."

"It is difficult enough for me in this household, you know that, don't you?"

The girl nodded. "The Spanish not all bad, mademoiselle. Many good, many kind. Ricardo, he always good to me. Never slaps, never hits, though I—how I say?—tease him."

"You tease him. Yes, I understand."

"Ricardo good man. Spanish girl, Juanita, good, too. If you want friend, find her. The others..." She shrugged.

"I will and thank you again. Now off to bed with you before a soldier catches you about," she said, realizing she sounded just like Mother Marie. "I am just checking to make certain the fires are all doused in the cook rooms." The responsibilities!

As the girl slipped back between the buildings, Claire crossed the rest of the courtyard, passing two of the governor's soldiers standing on guard close to the archway. She greeted them with a nod, paying no attention to their Spanish mutterings.

From somewhere far off, it seemed, someone played a stringed instrument. For a heart-stabbing instant, Claire thought it was Papa's fiddle, but no, Papa's fiddling had been as light and merry as a chorus of bees dancing in sunshine. This was a sad, complex fingering of strings that tugged at her heart and nearly moved her to tears. For a moment, she allowed herself to be entranced before quickening her pace.

Claire paused before the kitchen, surprised to find the door ajar. Doors should not be left open to animals or passing pilferers. Holding her lantern high, she pushed the door open and stepped in.

"Little Frenchie," a man said in Spanish just seconds before a hand pressed across her mouth. "I wait for you."

20

Claire would have kicked out at her attacker had her arms not been held behind her back. The man tightened his grip, wrenching her head back until she could feel the sharp point of a knife pricking her throat.

"Ah, you struggle, no?" said the man in broken French. "I like the struggle, but if you scream, I slit your throat and the slave girl will be blamed. Do you understand my bad French?"

Claire tried to nod but couldn't, only hoping her squeak of agreement would be understood.

"Good." He released her only long enough to slam her into the center table. She turned just as the man took her fallen lantern, sending his face jumping into view—a young man with hard glinting eyes, a man wearing the familiar blue of a Spanish soldier.

"Who are you and what do you want with me, monsieur?" she asked in French. From the corner of her eye, she judged the distance to the door—too far for escape and he had shot the bolt, in any case.

"What do I want? I tell you what I want." He stepped forward, his mouth a cruel twist. "I am Bernardo Viscaya. Now you understand, eh?"

He bore down on her in an instant, one hand twisting her arm behind her back while the other turned her body around again to shove her against the table front-first. An instant of blurring pain followed while the man leaned over her, the weight of his body pressing her against the wood while one hand fumbled with her skirts.

"I give warning," his voice rasped into her ear. "My mother is mistress of this house, not you, French slut." She gasped outrage as one hand moved up her skirt, clawing toward her secret places. "You send my mother to bed. You make her ill and ruin her standing in the house. This I will not tolerate! Who you think you are to act the chatelaine?"

"Who do you think you are?" Claire cried through tears of pain and shame. "I am under the governor's protection! Once I tell him what you have done, you will be thrown into the stocks. Do you understand 'stocks,' soldier?"

He gave her arm another vicious twist and lifted her skirt above her waist, roughly pushing away the fabric and ripping her underclothes. "You will say nothing or Odette will suffer more. Oh, yes. I know you how you defend the slave but she steals food. If I tell, she hangs."

Claire, her face mere inches from the tabletop, stared at the grooved surface unseeing. She could not believe her virginity would be torn from her by this brute. "I swear, you will not get away with this. I will best you, one way or the other."

In answer, he wrenched her around to face him, clutching each of her wrists in his hands and holding them down against the table. "Oh, the little French slut speaks so brave for one with no friends here—no protector, no husband, no nothing. You are nothing, understand? French scum. Learn your place."

With her body bent back and his leaning full against her, she stared up into his eyes and gauged her options. If she screamed, what then? Would her word hold weight with the governor?

But when she began to feel the soldier's hardness prodding her thighs, all thought escaped her. No, never! She'd rather die. Her virginity was to be saved for the governor, her purity critical for the planned seduction.

She spat in Bernardo's face, using his surprise to knee his groin and shove him backward. In the seconds that followed—long seconds where the door appeared leagues away and every object seemed to obstruct her passage—she realized she had made a terrible mistake.

"Bitch! Whore!" He reached her when she was but an arm's length from the door, grabbing her by the shoulders and brutally slamming her against the wall. Pots clattered to the floor.

She should have tried to sweet-talk him, soothe him with false promises, anything but incite this violence.

When he threw her to the ground and fell on top of her, his face consumed with rage and lust and God knew what else, all she could think of was that she had failed Sister Marie, her country, herself. She was to be raped by a soldier, the one insult she had thus far been spared, but as he fumbled with his breeches, a banging shook the kitchen door.

"Who goes there?" a man called in Spanish. "Open immediately on the authority of Governor Ulloa and King Charles of Spain!"

More thumping followed, a girl's high screeching cry rising above the men's shouts. "Thief! Thief in kitchen!" Odette's voice.

Bernardo froze, listening. Claire tried to struggle out from under him but he held her down. Leaning toward her with one hand gripping her throat, he whispered, "Speak of this you die, French bitch."

Pressing her eyes shut, she nodded. She'd agree to almost anything to get free of him.

Moments later, Bernardo Viscaya flung open the door, a smile plastered on his face, his uniform once again in order. He greeted his men in his native tongue while Claire stood trembling at his side. "Angelo! What is this? You try to break down the door?"

Angelo, a plump young man with a serious face and a mass of black hair curling about his ears, peered past Bernardo at Claire. "What is this, Comandante? We have heard that a thief may be robbing the stores."

"Yes, we feared the same thing." Bernardo nodded. "I escorted the señorita here to check the kitchen after we found the door ajar. The pots are in disarray but we have found nothing missing."

"The door was bolted from the inside, sir," Angelo said, his eyes flickering distrust.

"I had to be sure the thief would not escape, Angelo. Enough talk. Do not stand there useless. Search the grounds. The thief probably escapes while you waste time. Move!"

"*Sí*, Comandante." The man, clearly unwilling to challenge his superior, backed away. Turning to his men, he ordered them to spread about the enclosure.

It was then, amid the shifting soldiers, that Claire glimpsed Odette pressed against the wall of the nearby oven house, as if trying to make herself invisible.

Bernardo saw her at the same time. "There she is!" Bernardo cried out. "That slave, Odette, she is the thief we seek! Angelo, catch the little bitch."

Pushing past the men, Claire ran toward Odette, took her hand, and tugged the girl toward the house.

And Romy seized that moment to try again to leap into the present.

21

"Odette, you will bring the wrath of these soldiers upon your head. Hurry!"

"For God's sake stop calling me Odette!"

Though Romy could hear Joquita's voice, her body continued to channel Claire, her mouth saying Claire's words. "We will go to the governor right now, yes?" she said. "He will protect you from Viscaya. Keep moving. Quickly!"

She tried to drag the girl along with her but she broke away from her grip and scrambled into the darkness. "Come back! Odette, please!"

"Stop it! Speak English, for God's sake!" And then Odette slapped her.

Startled, Romy stared, her brain suddenly jerked into the present. Joquita, not Odette. Stunned, she just stood as the video in her mind wound down.

She found herself in Louisa's den clutching her friend's hand. "Jo. You're Odette," she whispered, releasing her grip.

"Don't say that," Joquita said, stepping away. "I have no part in this. I'm just trying to help."

Romy wrapped her arms around herself, attempting to rein in her trembling body, a body primed to run. "You tried to help me in Claire's life, too. You are Odette, the slave girl. I'm as sure about this as I am about anything. I recognized you deep down inside the moment I saw you through Claire's eyes and I can almost see Odette's face over yours right now, like a shimmering overlay."

"No, please stop." Jo shook her head.

Romy continued regardless. "You were a slave in Antonio de Ulloa's household and I think we struck an alliance." Romy paused to take a deep breath, reminding herself that she had returned to the present, that nobody chased her here. "Bernardo has just called the alarm to accuse you of thieving and I'm afraid of what he's going to do to you."

"*Did*, not 'do,'" Joquita corrected. "Get your tenses straight. I do not live in the past, understand?"

Louisa put her arms over her niece's shoulders. "Joquita Bonita, accept the truth. She's found you in the past, just as I said she would, sure enough. Now, Romy, calm yourself. You are safe here at least. Try to stay with us." Louisa loomed before Romy like a bulwark attempting to hold back the tides of time.

"Romy—" Adrian's deep voice spoke inches from her ear "—breathe deeply. Steady yourself. We have been so worried and so damned relieved that you're yourself again."

He briefly touched her shoulder before stepping back. So like Antonio. She turned to meet his eyes, holding his clear gray-green gaze for a moment, searching for a sign that he believed. Nothing. She turned away.

"I've found Stanley King," she said to Louisa, her voice hoarse. "In Claire's life he was Bernardo Viscaya."

"Bernardo Viscaya?" Adrian said behind her.

"A soldier in Ulloa's guard and the son of the governor's Spanish housekeeper," Romy said without looking at him. "I recognized him immediately just as I did Odette."

"All right, this is good, very good," Louisa said as she steered Romy toward the cushions and urged her to sit. "Progress at last. But didn't this incident get Bernardo killed?"

"No, but I guess that's still to come. He tried to rape me—I mean, Claire—and he'll try to harm me—her—again, I'm sure of it." Romy took a deep breath. "It must be in another attempt that someone kills him. I must find out who that someone is and soon." She shuddered. "More deaths are on the horizon. I feel a premonition every moment I spend with

Claire. We're terrified." She fixed her gaze on Louisa. "I have to try to communicate with her."

"Trying will only squander valuable energy," Louisa said. "Energy you may need to return to the here and now."

"But I must." Romy laced her fingers tight. "Somewhere deep in Claire's head, she hears me as if I were a little voice or even an extension of her conscience. I almost reached her a moment ago, I know that much. I have to keep trying." She attempted to explain. "She needs to know me as I know her."

Louisa pondered this. "That's way too dangerous."

But Romy wasn't listening. "I have to go back soon—now, in fact. I have to stay in the momentum of Claire's memories and see this thing through."

Her gaze flickered toward Adrian. "She has met Ulloa for the first time and she's drawn to him but remains determined to spy. She thinks she'll find solace in revenge. She won't. Can I help her realize that before it's too late? I'm going to let myself slip back now."

"Don't," Louisa protested, bending over her. "Don't go back until you've rested. You've been gone too long and your times in the present are getting shorter and shorter. Don't you see how dangerous going back is? I—" As Louisa spoke, her face began to waver before Romy's eyes.

"Didn't you say you couldn't go back when you wanted?" Joquita said from somewhere far away. "Didn't you say you had no control? Rom, get yourself back here."

Romy tried to respond but her tongue had gone numb. "I...I think I can go...back when I want now but...have usually no control over...when I return. It worked this time but doesn't always. I'll try..." She trailed away, unable to finish her sentence. Other sights and sounds were rising all around her, drowning out Louisa's library like background noise.

22

Claire heard the cracking of the whip long before they reached the slave's campfire. Ahead, a press of people gathered in the smoky firelight, people whose faces twisted in helpless fury, anguish.

In a flash of brutal memory, Claire saw similar helplessness in the expressions of her own village folk long ago—the same bleak suffering, the same mute pain.

The sound of the whip seared the air. Once. Twice.

"No!" Claire cried. Pushing through the crowd, she broke into the circle's clearing.

Odette stood bound to a pole, her dress ripped from her torso to expose the fresh angry red welts on her back and across one breast. Blood, pain, moans, and Bernardo with his arm upraised to deliver yet another blow.

Claire scooped up a handful of dirt and flung it at the comandante, screaming as she did so: "Monster! Pig! Such a big man to whip a girl! Are you so small that only a whip makes you grand?" all in French.

"Señorita," cried the governor's brother, stepping forward from where he had been watching the show. "You forget yourself. Such impertinence will not be tolerated."

Bernardo, coughing and wiping his face, cast a look of such burning anger at Claire she felt scorched by his hate.

"You accuse her only to mask your own misdoings! You have attempted to rape me and no doubt abuse her, too," Claire accused. "You are no better than swine."

"What is going on here?" a bold voice demanded. Claire turned to see the governor striding across the clearing. "Who authorized a flogging?" Governor Ulloa called out as he took the space in a few long strides, shattering the scene with the power of his presence. "What is the meaning of this atrocity?"

"That French cow dares to interrupt justice," Juan de Ulloa said, pointing to Claire. "She must be punished. I will ensure the task is performed immediately, my brother."

"You will not." Antonio de Ulloa's voice, unlike the others, came with the terse steel of authority. He stood eyeing his brother and the comandante with such fury and contempt no one could possibly mistake his expression for anything else.

Around them, the slaves shuffled their feet. One old woman broke from the group to help Odette.

"It is Bernardo Viscaya who should be punished," Claire cried. "He attempted to rape me and whips Odette for calling assistance."

"The French wench lies, Governor," Bernardo said before the governor could question him further. "The slave attempted to steal from the kitchens and must be punished."

"On whose authority?" Ulloa demanded.

"Mine," Juan said, holding steady.

The governor turned to his brother. "I will speak with you later, but for now, I will take action against you, Bernardo Viscaya. Henceforth, you are stripped of your command. I have heard enough stories of your behavior to believe the mademoiselle's claim. Now I see the truth with my own eyes. Angelo, throw him in the stocks and be quick about it! As of this point, you will assume command over my soldiers."

Claire barely heard Juan's protest and Bernardo's pleas. She fell to her knees in the dust, helping the old woman untie Odette and lower her to the ground. The girl's eyes were closed but Claire could tell she was still conscious. Her jaw was clenched. The girl refused to cry out and was so rigid with pain she could barely move her lips. The gashes on her back bled, her skin hanging off in strips.

"Water! Bring her water, please," Claire cried, but already the slave community had jumped into action. A pot of warm water was deposited on the ground and a cluster of women gently nudged Claire out of the way. "We tend our own, mademoiselle," said a toothless old woman in French. "You leave now."

❦

"You are intent on making enemies in this household," the governor remarked as he sat at his desk much later.

The candlelight flickering in the breeze from the open window illuminated the exhaustion grooved under his eyes. Even his fierce energy seemed to sag as if worn down by another battle that engaged his mind and body but eroded his soul.

Claire tried not to pity him but everything about this man pulled at her in ways she did not expect.

"I do not aspire to do so, sir," she said while attempting to smooth her apron and tuck a strand of stray hair under her cap, "but I cannot bear injustice. To see it, makes me, how do you say?" She moved her hands as if trying to pluck the right word from the air.

"Interfere? Complicate matters? Incense everyone around you?" he asked with the smallest of smiles.

"Leap, monsieur. It makes me want to leap."

"Leap?" He nodded. "A fitting enough word. Indeed, in the very short time you have been amongst us, you have indeed done your share of leaping into every possible conflict."

"But how can I stand about and allow that swine to abuse that poor girl for no other reason but to mask his own crimes?"

Ulloa sighed, stretching back in his chair. "Many women, nay, most women, would do exactly that, mademoiselle, in the interests of preserving their own pretty necks. You, however, do seem compelled to leap, as you say, frequently and with little regard to your own safety. Tonight you have jumped well and truly into a nest of snakes and, by doing so, have put your self at great risk. I fear your continued presence in this household will not be in your best interests."

Claire's hands clutched the fabric of her skirt. "What is your meaning, monsieur?"

"I mean that, for your sake, it is best you return to the convent, after which I will bid Mother Superior send me a less passionate servant, maybe one a little older. You have made many enemies in the few hours you have been among us and I cannot guarantee your safety."

"But you are governor," she protested. "Surely I am under your protection?"

Ulloa got slowly to his feet. For a moment, his eyes seemed so deeply sunk Claire had to strain to see their spark. "Think, mademoiselle. As an intelligent woman, do you truly believe I can follow you about to ensure your well-being? Even a king cannot protect his subjects in a court where poison can be dropped into a glass of wine in the blink of an eye. Señora Viscaya and her cur of a son have their supporters."

"Including your brother?"

Ulloa frowned. "You verge on impertinence, mademoiselle," he warned.

But Claire did not drop her gaze. She leaned over the desk toward him. "Forgive me, Monsieur Governor, but I have witnessed much in so short a time, yes? I have seen a man who yearns to attend higher matters forced to engage in constant parry with those who should be making his life easier, not more difficult. I have seen a man who knows not who to trust under his own roof, is this not so?"

Claire caught the flash of pride, saw him resolve the inner turmoil beneath a wry smile and a shrug. "I know exactly who I cannot trust, mademoiselle—virtually everyone, in truth."

Though every fresh word might destroy the delicate scaffolding between them, Claire continued. "Your attentions are fractured by a hundred annoyances, yes? As your housekeeper, I see it as my duty to reduce distractions and restore order under your roof. Surely such involves ensuring each slave and servant is reasonably happy with their lot—not bullied and terrorized by those in power? With your support, I will ensure that all are treated with fairness as I model within your house the rule I sense you desire for your colony. I, at least, will be someone you can trust."

He almost laughed. "And why should I trust you?"

"Because I have been trained by the Ursulines, monsieur, and my vow is as one with all that is good in womankind—to fully serve my master with a grace and intelligence that assists, not hinders, his superior capacity. In doing so, I serve God."

Though she feared hypocrisy would throttle the breath from her throat, she managed to say the words with enough conviction to almost fool herself. "I have been raised with no other goal in mind," she lied, "and have lived for the day when I would come to one such as you and serve with every inch of my being."

"Then the convent educates slaves, not servants."

"They educate wives, Monsieur Governor."

"But you come as a housekeeper."

"Do the skills differ so greatly? For me, it matters not the title, for you, sir, are my master, and I your servant, as loyal as any wife. That is my duty. I beg of you, do not send me away."

The silence that followed could be measured by the nightingale's call, by the croak and chirp of a thousand night creatures chorusing in the dark beyond. Claire reminded herself to keep breathing.

"My word," Ulloa said, shaking his head, "but the convent takes its mission to the extreme. Despite the custom, I abhor slavery of any kind but duty I understand well enough."

She dropped her eyes. "Every man needs a wife, yes? And yours is not with you."

"No, she is not." He turned away, looking over his head to where his bookcases marched along the wall. His eyes rested on a small glass case containing a stuffed rodent-sized creature.

"You have been married long?"

"I married by proxy and my bride arrived from Peru escorted by my brother but last year."

"And why is this most fortunate lady not here with you now, sir?"

"She is with child and remains at La Balize where she will be safe. I fear she does not approve of the colony. She finds the local dislike of the Spanish unsettling."

With child. Claire swallowed hard, imagining his wife spread-eagled beneath him as he entered her, impregnating her. "Still, I am certain she must feel your absence sorely."

To that, Ulloa only sighed. "You pry, mademoiselle, but for reasons I can't explain even to myself, I choose to disclose. In truth, I do not offer the kind of companionship to which my wife is accustomed."

"How so?"

"She prefers the light dalliances of society—of dresses and chatter among ladies over tea. Though I have lived for many years in South America and done a fair bit of chattering as necessary as a host, in truth I have been at sea twice as long and spent much of my life exploring the southern hemisphere in search of the unique and extraordinary."

"So you are not well used to chatter," Claire said with a nod.

"Indeed, my days have been spent in the company of men, all caught in the fever of exploration. What kind of conversation can I provide for a lady of style?"

"But what woman would not be enthralled to hear of all those marvelous places, to see through you a whole new world?" And, in truth, who would not?

He turned to face her, and the instant his eyes met hers, she registered again that tremor.

"You flatter me."

"No, monsieur," she said, her words infused with a powerful emotion she could not explain. Is this what good lying was about—believing your own falsehoods? "I mean every word. You have stories to tell, I can see that in your eyes, on your walls, too. Who would not want to hear of these things? Please, tell me of your explorations."

"And is all this interest an effort to ensure your continued presence in this house?"

She smiled. "I do not want to leave, it is true, but it is true also that I crave to know more of other places, other lands. I knew only of my home before arriving here and fear this place will be all I shall ever know from this point forward. At the convent, the nuns opened their library to the girls who could read well and my questing mind found many books to feed my appetite. I...hunger to learn."

"And to experience and to leap without thinking. You are most persuasive," he said. "Indeed, though I would never have believed it in one so young, you appear clear-sighted and so suffused with fervor you burn right down to your toes. I admire that fire, though I cannot begin to comprehend it within your present circumstances. Have the Ursulines truly shaped you so or is there more in your background of which I am unaware? You were born in France, true?"

The lies came so easily now. "In Bretagne, yes. My parents once owned a château—the Château d'Frontenac, do you know of it?" She prayed he did not for she had plucked the name from the air.

Ulloa shook his head. "My travels to France have taken me only to Paris and the port of Lisle. I am certain it was very distressing to leave a château, however. It must have been very beautiful."

"Oh, yes, very," she said with feeling, though her mind filled with nothing grander than an unassuming stone church in Grand-Pré. "Beautiful beyond compare," she said. "But all is lost. My papa was once very wealthy but fell out of favor with the king." She bowed her head. "He believed I might forge a better life in the new world and thus bought me passage to join the Ursulines and God."

"No doubt he believes the combination best for one as comely as you."

"*Believed*, sir, for both parents are now dead."

"My condolences." He bowed his head.

"And your parents, sir?"

"Dead also, both died while I was at sea. I deeply regret never having said the final goodbye."

"As do I," she said, her voice hitching.

Silence settled in around them.

"And so here you are," he said after a moment, "an orphan tossed onto foreign shores."

"War and fate make many orphans, yes?" Claire asked.

"Yes, but time itself makes many more. My own parents would be dead now no matter what the circumstances."

"Age only dims the pain, never ends it, no?"

And then Claire straightened and walked over to his bookcases. "Monsieur Governor, I would like very much to know more of these things you have in cases along the wall. In truth, I have seen nothing like them."

Ulloa watched her in silence for a moment. "Another time, perhaps. For now, I must put my mind to writing."

"Writing?" she asked, swinging back to gaze at him.

"Writing, yes—two hours every evening. I maintain an account of my travels. I have, in fact, printed one in Spain already and plan to do so again upon my return. An explorer owes it to the world to record what he has seen and to do so with precision so those observations will extend and expand man's knowledge of the universe."

"Oh." For an instant she gazed at him, half in wonder. Then gathering her wits, she added, "Do you write of your plans for the colony and its governance?"

"Sometimes but not overmuch. Why do you ask?"

"Curiosity," she said. "You seem an interesting man and I would love to learn more. Please do not send me back to the convent."

He laughed, shaking his head. "I should, you know, but how can I send you away after all you have said? However, you must tread carefully from this point forth, mademoiselle. I will attempt to protect you as best I can but do try to avoid doing anything foolish."

She dropped a curtsy, her heart fluttering with relief along with some nameless happiness. "Oh, thank you, thank you, sir. You will be pleased with my work."

"Regardless, I fear your continued presence will only increase the strife, despite your claims. Now, please leave me. I have much writing to do before dawn breaks."

She noticed his paper and quill ready on the desk. "Yes, sir." Halfway to the door she paused. "Monsieur?"

"What is it?" He was already sitting down, dipping his quill into the inkpot.

"Each Sunday I must return to the convent for mass. I have given my word to Mother Superior that I would do so."

"And so you should. Be assured that I, a mere mortal, dare do nothing to interrupt the will of God and Mother Superior. Go with my blessing."

"I would also like to visit with my sisters and, of course, have Père Dagobert hear my confession. I will not be returning until late afternoon, like as not."

"Of course, of course. I often take excursions after Sunday services myself and sometimes the citizens invite me to dine here and there. Thus, I have the pleasure of spending many uncomfortable evenings skewered by their distrust."

"They do not want Spanish rule."

"No, they do not, but our kings have exchanged this colony in treaty and so we must make the best of it. Good night, mademoiselle."

Claire's hand hesitated on the latch. "Good night, Monsieur Governor. And, monsieur?" He looked up, his brows arching in a "what is it this time?" expression. "When will you tell me stories of your travels?" she asked.

He smiled. "Persistent, are you? Come tomorrow evening, mademoiselle, at quarter past ten, at which point I will unlock for you the wonders of the world."

With a flare of triumph, she smiled and left the room, knowing then that she would unlock far more than that.

23

Seducing Antonio de Ulloa would not be easy.

Claire arrived at his door each evening thereafter, often bearing a glass of port and the dessert he had ignored at dinner and always after the clock struck ten times.

As promised, he would set aside his writing to amuse her with stories from his expeditions, of which, it turned out, he had many. She would grow rapt at the things he had done, the places he had seen.

On her first evening in his study, a visit where he insisted the door be left ajar, he read his writings as a priest might recite a dry sermon. Thus, he managed to avoid eye contact and completely eclipse the wonder of his tales under a sonorous monologue.

Claire could not bear the way he avoided looking at her, the way his attention sought refuge in his journal, and how his gaze would glance off her face as soon as she entered a room.

He'd fix his attention firmly on the ceiling or the floor or any place that did not require him to acknowledge her presence. He spoke, of course, but that was the extent it.

Madame Letourneau, her tutor in the ways of flesh, said once that a woman always knew when a man was interested. The smallest of mannerisms would give him away—how long he held her gaze, his tone of voice, the way in which he smiled or anticipated her every need.

In rare circumstances, Madame claimed, a man would avoid looking at a woman altogether. In such cases, he might not only be very attracted to her but quite likely smitten.

Or restrained by propriety, Claire thought. Either way, she knew she would need to break down the governor's walls with an arsenal of her own.

By the second visit, she launched her campaign. She asked questions, beginning with innocent requests for clarification that soon grew into bold interruptions that dared challenge his statements. By the fifth visit, she had grown bolder still.

"I tell you," he said in the middle of an account of his travels to the Caribbean, "I watched the natives for well over six hours and they absolutely did not know of my presence." His face had flushed a furious crimson, the color of arousal, the color of passion.

"But why, for heaven's sake?" she asked as she paced circles in his study, closing the door along the way. "Why not tell them you were there and eager to learn of their ways and thus observe them openly?"

"Because that would only cause them to feel more inhibited and I would learn nothing."

"Of course you would learn something," she countered. "You would learn of rituals the natives performed when guests were present instead of spying on their most private and intimate ceremonies."

Oh, how brazen and hypocritical she felt at that remark but what a thrill it was to challenge him!

"I am a student of discovery," he sputtered. "I will not learn if the subject is aware of my presence. This is one of the principles upon which scientific investigation of our species is based. Besides which, this happened to be a marriage ceremony to which outsiders were forbidden."

"There! So, in the name of discovery it is acceptable for a man to spy, to behave in an ungentlemanly manner, and thus reduce human beings to 'subjects' just because they live in a manner different from your own?"

He opened his mouth to say something, stared her straight in the eye, and then tilted his head to one side. His face creased into a wide grin. "I believe you deliberately provoke me, mademoiselle. The question is why?"

She stood there wetting her lips, imagining him reaching for his sword, an image instantly transformed into envisioning him naked, mounting her, ready for a skirmish of another kind. The thought enflamed her with feelings so much more ardent than any she had experienced with her eye pressed to Madame's peephole. "Because I enjoy seeing you spar, monsieur, and suspect you well enjoy it, too."

A brief pause followed after which he broke into a hearty laughter, the kind of laughter that shoots a man's face full of a bright light. "I believe you have assessed me too well, mademoiselle, for, in truth, I seldom back down from an opponent as worthy as yourself."

She smiled. "Then I shall not hesitate to prod you again."

After that, on Claire's subsequent visits, Antonio de Ulloa ignored the journals and told his stories from memory. He also began to stare. At first, his eyes would rest briefly on her face, her breasts, and then flicker away. After the tenth of their storytelling sessions, his gaze rested more often and for longer periods until she heated under his attention. By the fourth, she knew the time had come to make her move.

"I do not understand what this 'Arc of the Meridian' is you mentioned last night," she told him as she rested the tray on his table and set the glass of port beside him on the desk. His eyes had not left her from the moment she entered the room. "It has puzzled me to such a degree that all last night I could barely sleep. I still have no idea what it is."

"And why should you?" he asked, smiling. "It is a term for mariners and scientists, not beautiful women."

She frowned. "So, you do not think a woman—beautiful or otherwise—should have a mind to think with? Can we not be mariners or scientists?"

"I am not saying that exactly. In fact, what a marvel it would be for a woman to employ her mind in just such a way, for her to be educated for such vocations and not imprisoned within those voluminous skirts. Yet our society does not encourage such a path and most women I have known would have little interest in science and exploration."

"Then perhaps you have not known the right woman until now?" Her eyes challenged him.

"Perhaps I have not, at that." And he laughed such a full-throated rumble that it caused her to burn in all her secret places. "Are we to spar again this night, mademoiselle?"

She swallowed hard. Her task was to seduce this man and yet she found herself being seduced. Still he made no move. "Perhaps, but I have yet to choose the weapon. Tell me about this arc of yours while I think. Consider yourself in the company of a woman with both a mind and an interest."

He nodded and picked up his quill, a smile still warming his face. "As if I have not learned that much in these last few evenings. The Arc of the Meridian is an imaginary line that runs true north-south. Drawn anywhere on earth," he said as he sketched out a curve on a sheaf of paper, "and, providing the line is surveyed with accuracy, the curvature of the earth can be measured."

"The curvature of the earth?"

"Yes, we can thus measure the fact that the earth is round and, more than that, how big it is."

"Surely one cannot measure the earth without pacing it out north to south, which itself is nearly impossible?"

"Not so. With mathematics and science, all manner of things can be measured without ever having to engage in the more physical aspects."

"I did not think that possible."

"So much is possible that man did not at first believe. Explorers and scientists open the universe to our understanding."

She leaned over the desk and stared into his eyes. "Teach me."

He looked up from his sketch. "Teach you what?"

"To be an explorer."

"Mademoiselle—"

"Claire."

"Claire." He hesitated, seeming to savor the taste of her name on his tongue. "I hardly know how to begin such a task, seeing as an explorer must engage in years of study and build myriad skills from a very young age, including navigation, a knowledge of the spheres, and so much more besides."

She smiled. "Then we'd best begin, yes? Perhaps we might start with something simple. A—how do you say it—demonstration? Yes, that's it. Show me, monsieur. Show me how a brave mariner embarks upon a voyage of discovery as though the whole uncharted ocean rolls out beneath her feet."

He laughed. "Some of the ocean, indeed a large part of it, has been charted, so I—"

"Pretend, monsieur. This is a game, no? Is that not how children learn?"

"Well, yes, I suppose it is. But how do you propose to play this game, mademoiselle?"

"Claire."

"Claire."

Her hands had grown very cold and, if he regarded her closely enough, he would see her trembling. As usual of late, he regarded her closely. "Would you stand against the wall for me, Monsieur Governor?"

Frowning, he rose slowly to his feet. "Are you thinking to measure the distance between us using the same procedure used to—"

"Forgive my impertinence, monsieur."

"A bit late for that."

"But please try not to speak for a moment. Pray just go to the wall and stand facing me." She pointed to the only piece of wall in the room not covered in tall bookcases—a brace of bare stucco above which a crucifix hung.

Even the cross would not stop her audacity.

The governor moved to the wall as a man embarking on a mission of which he knew nothing. He could be doomed to sail off the lip of the earth or about to uncover a treasure of magnificent proportions and his manner could be the same no matter which. "I have a nephew who, when younger, tied me to a chair in a game of—"

"Monsieur Governor."

"Yes," he sighed. "Silence, as one assumes when facing a firing squad." He took his position and turned to face her, his hands clasped behind his back.

She stepped toward him. "Hands like this," she said, holding her arms outward from her body. "Pretend your wrists and ankles are outspread and bound. You will need to lean full against the wall."

His expression appeared puzzled, even troubled, but she sensed excitement in his slight flush. "Will you give me some inkling of your intent, Claire? Will I be skewered in the name of your explorations?"

She swallowed, stepping forward to press her finger to the center of his chest. "You are not to ask questions. This is my voyage of discovery."

His eyes widened, the full impact of her words seeming to strike him in multiple ways. His mouth opened as if to protest but she had already insinuated a finger between the buttons of his shirt to toy with his chest hairs. That alone was enough for him to groan. "Claire. Do not do this. I am... married. I am..."

She stepped back. "A man, yes? An explorer. What explorer does not set upon his voyage knowing he sails into possible danger? What scientist is unwilling to try new things and to open his mind to extraordinary experiences?"

"One who obeys his God and honors his vows."

"How do you know what God says? By reading words written centuries before by men who did not know the world is round or how the earth can be measured without having to pace it out from end to end?"

Oh, she had become a heretic, too.

Closing his eyes, he let his head fall back against the wall and positioned his limbs as bidden. Now he looked like a man tied to a stake. The sight provoked a powerful desire. "I am doomed."

"Not doomed, perhaps only undiscovered. You must not touch me no matter what I do. Promise."

"I promise." He spread a charming grin. "Just say that you will not stab me with my sword, though, in truth, that might be preferable."

"Hush." She stepped to within inches of him until she could see his breath rising and falling in his chest. "Only speak if I ask a question. I am the navigator, remember, you are the ocean."

She heard his sharp intake of breath as she ran a hand along the full length of his arm and sent inquisitive fingers to stroke the firm muscles under his shirt.

He did not move, though his body seized rope-tight beneath her hands.

She smiled, toying with the lace at one cuff. Growing braver, she stroked the hard muscle of his upper arms in small circular motions, watching how her hands brought a look of blissful agony to his face.

"Do you not enjoy my touch, monsieur?"

He nearly wrenched out the words. "Why would I not enjoy those little hands making their slow progress across my body while I stand helpless?"

"Do you...fear me?"

"A wise captain always fears the ocean."

"But you are not the captain here."

"Still," he continued, "I feel my waves sparkling beneath your touch, feel a tender longing to reveal all my secrets for your asking." His voice had turned all husk and smoke. "Your touch sends me quaking and I fear...loss of control."

"Ah." She nodded. "That I understand."

An intoxicating power rose in her also, a strange, unfathomable desire. At last and for once, she had the freedom to do her will. He stood still as she trailed a finger from his wrist back over his arm, across his chest and over to the other side.

Her breath quickened. She stepped back and unpinned her hair, letting it tumble about her shoulders, and then loosened her shift to expose her breasts. Then she returned to give him a swift kiss on the lips, tasting port and smoke and something intangibly delicious. He leaned forward in a desperate bid to fix her mouth on his but she withdrew with a laugh. "No, no, Monsieur Governor. I will set the pace in this."

"Claire!" Her name came off his tongue like a tortured plea but she simply moved about her business unconcerned. "Let me run my fingers through your hair, take you in my arms!"

"No!"

Her gaze dropped to his throat. The lace jabot at his neck had to go. His eyes widened as she unfastened the gold pin and undid the tie.

"Do you plan to undress me?"

"Do I hear a touch of hope in your voice? Well, I will not answer you." She stopped her task long enough to press a finger against his lips. "The power is mine, Monsieur Governor. You must just wait to see what I will do."

She finished untying the jabot and tossed it to a chair, after which she deftly undid his waistcoat and picked open the pearl buttons of his shirt one by one. He gasped in some kind of blissful agony when she swept aside the silk brocade with the palms of her hands and leaned her bare breasts into his chest.

"For pity's sake," he groaned.

She answered him with a single kiss to his chest followed by a gentle lick where her fingers had played. "Forget pity," she murmured. "You have had power all your life as captain, officer, soldier, and man whereas I have had none. Tonight, I take charge," she murmured. "Besides, look at me: I hardly know what I become as I bare myself to your gaze and heart. Before

I came here I was a convent girl, now look how I behave? So, accept my exploration like a soldier and stop whimpering."

She marched an army of tiny kisses across his chest, loving the feel of that hard muscle under her lips, the warm musk of his scent, the way the curly hairs brushed her lips. "You smell rich and intoxicating like wine fermented in eternity."

Hearing more grunt than reply, her tongue slipped a trail back upward until she reached the little hollow at the base of his neck. Framing his face in her hands, she lowered his head until her eyes met his. "What are you thinking, Governor Antonio de Ulloa?"

She waited patiently while he struggled to form the words. "I can barely contain a…coherent thought. Claire…I am…lost."

She smiled. "Good, for I am also, though I must say, the wilderness in which I find myself is quite amazing." Her gaze fell on his throat and she sighed.

When she pressed her mouth to that hollow, she could feel the race of his pulse beneath her lips. Amazed, she pressed her ear against his breast to listen to that strong, racing heart, entranced by the warmth of him against her cheek. Sighing, she rubbed her hair against his chest, realizing how his breath had grown ragged.

"Claire, Claire, Claire. I am a married man."

"Married in name only for she is not with you and I am. Now do stop moaning and tell me what I shall do next," she murmured.

"Put a knife to my heart and put me out of my misery."

"That does not bear saying, monsieur, but perhaps I should undress to aid your thinking?"

"Drive me to distraction is more the truth."

Though the thought of disrobing before a man should have sent her in a tremor of embarrassment, impropriety did not enter Claire's head.

She loosened the ties of her bodice as she had seen the women at Madame's do and slipped from her dress. The under-slip soon followed. Then, as his eyes widened in wonder, Claire again framed his face with her hands and brought their lips together. The fierceness of her desire met his as his urgent tongue plunged into her mouth. He moved his arms to hold her and she succumbed, body and soul.

Finally, she pulled away, leaving him flushed and panting against the wall. He swore softly under his breath, using words that seemed so foreign to his usual restrained propriety.

She swallowed hard, hands pressed against her heart to steady her breathing. The emotion running through her threatened to tear apart everything she thought she knew about herself. This abandon, this powerful force that made her body cleave to his, shook her in every way. This was not about some mission to fulfill for others; she acted on her desires and no one else's. She wanted him.

She stepped forward and boldly cupped her hand over the straining bulge and whispered, "It is time we explore together as one."

"Then, for God's sake let us lock the door!"

Which she did. And what they unleashed that night as they rolled naked across the parquet floor was more passionate and more joyful than anything Claire had ever known.

This was not and could never be a sin.

24

Romy awoke in the dark, her body slick with sweat. Heat left her feeling damp and heavy as if she floated in a steamy fog.

Lying still, she listened to the crickets in the dark, heard a fly buzz, a fan whizzing from somewhere. An electric fan...not in the past, then. Good. But her blood sang with Claire's passion.

Deep inside her mind, she could feel Claire remembering—synchronous yet apart, awake and yet still oddly connected. If she tried hard enough, she could even see Claire's imagination playing out at the back of her mind like a movie projected on a blank wall. Antonio naked...

Claire dreaming, or maybe remembering? Oh, God. Romy tried to shake her brain clear and sat up. Nothing felt immediately familiar. A skimpy slip clung to her body and she could feel a firm mattress with lots of sweet-smelling linen sheets beneath her.

Across the room through an open door, she could just make out the shape of someone sprawled on top of another bed. Joquita? Louisa's, then. Had she returned to the present while still connected to Claire? The thought of the two of them becoming one alarmed her. She had to remain herself. That was critical.

Claire, can you hear me? But Claire was busy, very busy, dreaming of working over Antonio in some very imaginative ways. Romy licked her lips, thoroughly aroused yet alarmed. How could she be reading Claire's dreams now? Even Aunt Loo hadn't warned her of this. She needed to speak with Aunt Loo now.

Romy climbed out of bed, trying to suppress the tangle of confusion long enough to think. The voice inside her head intensified.

I crave him, I want him...over and over again.

It took a few moments for Romy to realize that Claire had awoken. Or something. On the other side of this strange boundary that separated the past from the present, her alter ego, or whatever Claire was, lay awake and listening to the voice in her head—Romy's voice.

Claire?

Leave me be. I do not need you to tell me what to do or who to love. I lay with him and, in truth, it was so much better than what I had imagined. Not like Madame's, never like that. I did not feel dirty or ashamed but full of life the way I have never felt before. No, I am not wed but my heart is his, no matter what I do next. A soldier can both love and destroy.

Romy froze as still as her stone angel. Claire believed Romy was her conscience?

I have chosen my path and will follow it to the end. Leave me alone.

How was Romy to handle this one?

Carefully, she moved across the room, trying not to dislodge Claire in the process. The outer door to the hall did not open when she tugged on the knob. Locked.

Turning, she padded back across the room to the adjoining bedroom where Joquita slept spread on top of the bed in the heat, sound asleep. Inside her head, she sensed Claire quiet and watchful, believing herself in the grip of another strange dream.

Romy tiptoed in front of Joquita's sleeping form to that bedroom door and grasped the knob, cheering silently when it opened in her hand. Just like Joquita to forget to lock it.

Soon, she had slipped into the hall where a series of night-lights shaped like fairies glowed in the electrical sockets along the wall. Romy smiled as she crept silently along the corridor linking the upstairs bedrooms. What would Claire think of those? She soon had her answer.

Little...candles...in the wall? Why are there no flames? What kind of thing captures the power of candles within little casings of glass—magic? Oh, but I would so love there to be magic, but what kind of dream is this?

It took all that Romy could muster not to answer. At the end of the hall, Louisa's room dominated the entire wing of the house. Romy had stayed overnight at the mansion many times and had always been given the guest room overlooking the back garden with Joquita taking the adjoining bedroom.

She paused, gazing behind her at the line of closed doors, fifteen altogether—ten bedrooms, three bathrooms, and assorted cupboards. Where would Louisa put Adrian for the night?

Who is Adrian?

Romy stopped, startled. Claire could literally hear her thoughts. *In this dream you think you're having, Adrian is Antonio.*

Claire thought on that one while Romy trawled for bearings. On the same side of the house, also facing the garden and leading to Aunt Loo's room, was another guest suite.

Didn't she recall Louisa referring to it as "the gentleman's suite"? Yes, yes—it had an Indonesian ambience, she remembered, with a hand-carved Bali bed, exotic textiles, and an en suite flagstone bathroom complete with huge glass shower stall—very manly.

Glass shower stall? Claire asked in her thoughts.

Romy felt Claire marveling all the way down the hall, but the moment she paused before the door of the gentleman's suite, the buzzing in her head stopped and, for whatever reason, Claire evaporated.

Romy stood alone, surprisingly bereft. What now? What did she plan to do, anyway? Introduce Claire to Aunt Loo? "Hi, Louisa, this is Claire..." It was all so ridiculous and impossible, impossibly ridiculous.

And then the door to the gentleman's suite opened. She took a step back as Adrian's tall form filled the doorway. He stood dimly illuminated by the hall's night-lights wearing nothing but a T-shirt and boxers, looking tousled and sleepy, yet strangely intense.

Romy held her breath. "Adrian?"

He crossed the space between them in one stride, enfolding her in his arms with all the passion she'd imagined a million times—the strength of his arms, the eager lips, the desire, the want, the need.

From the moment she met him, she'd been craving this man, this moment. "Adrian," she whispered. "Adrian." She'd sink into him, let him envelop her, be his forever and ever...

"Claire," he said, his lips buried deep in her neck, his kisses trailing to her ear.

Claire? Romy stiffened. She wrestled from his embrace and stood back. "I'm not Claire," she whispered. The man muttered in archaic Spanish, begging her not to tease him so. He was just a man of mortal flesh, he said.

"I am not Claire!" she repeated. "Wake up, Adrian."

"Claire—"

"Adrian! You are Adrian and I am Romy. This is 2021!" Then, realizing he might not understand English under the circumstances, she repeated her words in Spanish. "Come to, wake up!"

"Claire, why do you torture me so? Return to my bed, permit me to envelop you in my arms. Come, I beg of you."

Romy turned and walked away, heart banging in her chest. Perhaps if she wasn't near him, he'd disconnect from the past. She had almost reached the bedroom door when she smacked into a soft object standing in the hall.

"Romy, wake up." Joquita's voice. Her friend grasped her shoulders and shook her.

"I am awake," Romy said, shrugging her off. "I'm not Claire."

"Okay, okay," Joquita said, pulling back. "You can't blame me for not being sure, and why in hell is the good doctor standing in his underwear?"

Romy turned and made introductions. "Jo, this is Antonio in Adrian."

At that moment, a light came on down the hall and Aunt Loo came sailing toward them like a rose silk steamboat. "What's going on?"

"The past arises!" Joquita exclaimed. "The doc thinks he's a Spanish governor."

And then all eyes turned to Adrian still standing transfixed in bewilderment.

"Sorry, Doc," Joquita said. "I didn't want to interrupt you two just now."

Adrian gazed around him as if trying to figure out where he was, who he was, while running his fingers through his hair. "What are you talking about?"

"I'm talking about that dive I saw you just make on Romy—I mean,

Claire—while speaking Spanish in that wickedly sultry accent. Hot. You were in full passionate Spaniard mode, Doc."

"Joquita Bonita," Louisa admonished, arriving on the scene. "Stop teasing the poor man. Adrian, are you all right? Sleepwalking can be pretty disorientating."

"So can sleep kissing," Joquita added.

"Sleepwalking? I don't—" But he stopped himself, looking down at his bare legs before back up at Aunt Loo. "I don't remember getting up."

"Well, you did, all right," Joquita told him. "I arrived on the scene just in time to see you and the Romy-Claire duo getting into it."

"Kissing?" Adrian's gaze found Romy's and held. The moments stretched between them counted in heartbeats. She saw the confusion in his face mingled with something else. Desire? Maybe, but not for her. His blood rang with the shared memory of Claire and Antonio's passion.

"I'm exhausted." Romy turned, passing Jo and Aunt Loo, heading for her room; only when she reached the knob, she forgot that her door was locked. The moment her hand tugged at the knob, pain blasted her brain. *No*, she cried. She didn't want to go back so soon.

25

Claire perched on the edge of her narrow bed waiting for the household to settle for the night. Antonio had left for a dinner engagement with his brother just before seven o'clock. Thus the staff had slightly more time on their hands—no serving of meals, no cleaning up or folding of linen.

Señora Viscaya, however, had thumped the floor with her cane and kept the maids hopping for at least the first hour. The old woman's angst over Bernardo's incarceration knew no bounds but, finally, she fell silent and presumably slept.

Claire listened for the clock to strike ten times before leaving her room and hastening down the hall, the house now dark and silent. The clock's gongs masked her footfall should any squeaky floorboard betray her intent. She took particular care when passing Señora's room at the top of the landing but then practically bolted downstairs in her stocking feet, holding a single taper to light the way.

Downstairs, she crossed the long corridor that ran behind the stairwell toward the rear of the house, turning often to check for followers. The house remained still.

Once she paused for many moments, her senses peeled for the sound of footfalls. Nothing. She continued on, but before reaching Antonio's study she stood again listening before proceeding. But the house sat dark and hushed, enveloped in humid air that seemed thick enough to suffocate both man and beast.

Perspiration beaded her upper lip and her pulse throbbed at her temples. At times, it felt as though the very air clotted at the back of her throat.

Forcing in a deep breath, she fished the chatelaine of keys from her pocket and inserted one into the lock with trembling fingers. The resulting click seemed to echo all the way down the hall. She turned the knob and entered, shutting the door quickly behind her.

There.

Holding the candlestick aloft, she gazed around the room. Antonio's study appeared strangely empty without his presence, as if a singer had been parted from the song. And she missed him, felt for him in her heart, and yet could not falter.

Gripping the candlestick more tightly, she stepped across the floor, heart throbbing loudly in her ears. She must calm herself or risk missing something of import.

What would Monsieur Campeneau seek? What would enflame the colonists and how would she know if she'd recognize such a thing?

She could not fail.

She scanned the bookshelves across the room, wondering if anything of note might be found amid the multitude of books the governor carted about. No, she decided. Correspondence would be much more interesting and timely.

Her eyes fell to his desk where the papers had been tidied into neat piles beside the inkpots and quills. The leather-bound diary in which he so often wrote sat full center.

Tiptoeing to the desk, she hesitated, one hand hovering over the book. His most private thoughts and affairs. She thought of how he looked, head bowed, intent about his writing—so studious, so deep in thought, and not at all like a warrior planning brutal acts.

Instead, he'd be unlocking the puzzles of the universe. Her mind strayed to memories of the passion that ignited them in this very room, of how he felt deep inside her, riding his passion into her heart. She shivered, imagining the warmth of his lips. Enough!

And here she stood ready to plunder his secrets. Her lover, her love. She shook her head. That, of all things, she must not think about. Soldiers do their duty.

Soldiers are warriors by vocation and lovers only in the interludes between bloodletting.

Soldiers do not waver.

Soldiers live to serve.

Fortifying herself, she forced her mind on task. Seeing the letters, she sat the candlestick down and quickly riffled through the bundle knowing, even as she did so, that her efforts would be useless.

Everything had been written in Spanish, of which she could not read more than a few words. On that point, as on countless others, she had lied to the conspirators and no one had ever questioned her. She could understand the spoken word but not the written form. Even Mother Marie had not demanded proof there.

She perspired so heavily her undergarments felt drenched. Now what? For a brief, foolish moment, she had dared think she'd find some correspondence in French or even understand a few words of Spanish because she could at least read in French. How did the two languages differ so much?

Enough, it seemed, for sheaf after sheaf of paper flashed past in a series of meaningless squiggles.

She tossed the letters down in frustration, then caught herself and straightened the bundles to the way in which she had found them. Only then did she reluctantly turn to Antonio's diary. This would be no different. He wrote in his mother tongue. Yet, she must find something.

Lifting the volume with something akin to reverence, she carefully leafed through the pages, wetting her lips as she gazed down at his strong, energetic script that reminded her so much of the man himself.

Even the manner in which he crossed his *t*'s brought him achingly to mind—the cross marks flying from their stems like pennants caught in a brisk sea wind. A mariner's hand, she thought, recalling his touch. A captain, an admiral, a commander of all that heaved beneath him, whether it be ship or woman.

Call it lust, call it desire, but she knew something else had ensorcelled them both, something she would now forfeit forevermore.

Oh, Mother of God, what am I doing? Her fingers trembled.

She made herself study the structure of the entries and slammed the door on every other feeling or thought. Each entry had been dated but some sections covered several pages. Though Claire could not read the words, she could distinguish dates, numerals, and some places, names, enough to know this was no a daily diary but his memoir.

Nothing, however, would be of use to Campeneau and his conspirators. She needed evidence, something to indicate Ulloa a devious scoundrel who would force the French colonists into the yoke of submission. Ignoring her self-disgust, she flipped the pages with increased resolution until she found something promising—drawings.

Drawings? She stared wide-eyed at the sketches Antonio had made throughout the journal. Most were beautifully rendered but indecipherable—lines, circles, strange numbers with little dots and dashes between—but a few seemed ominous. One in particular caught her attention.

Two men stood on what looked to be a hilltop with a strange circle of light beaming down from overhead. She gazed, not comprehending.

What did it all mean? She tried to think. Nothing came to mind but explosions—great bursts of light designed to wound and maim. What else would a naval warrior sketch? Though Antonio did not seem interested in devising new weapons and had never mentioned warfare in any of their conversations. In the absence of anything better, this would have to do.

Of course, it would be risky to tear the drawing from its bindings but, since it appeared dozens of pages from the front, perhaps he would not miss it until much later, a chance she must take.

With shaking fingers, she carefully cut the page from its fellows using a letter opener and folded the piece into her pocket. As she finished, the clock struck eleven times. She completed her task as the gongs echoed inside her head.

One, two, three... Done, it was done.

Only when she turned, candlestick back in hand, did she see the figure standing in the now open door. She gasped, nearly dropping the candle. But she had locked it!

"Yes, I have caught you, haven't I?" the old woman snarled in Spanish, dangling her own chatelaine of keys. "You filthy spying tart! The governor will hear of this and that will be the end of you! You will hang, traitor! What have you there? Pass it over."

The old woman, dressed in a white lace nightgown, her nightcap pulled low over her head despite the humid evening, advanced on Claire with her cane upraised.

The old crow told the truth: only death awaited traitors and spies, no matter what the bond between Antonio and herself. Once he knew how she used him, all would come to an end.

Claire took a step back, desperate for sudden insight on what to do.

But she couldn't just remain there; she needed to move, maybe even run for the sanctuary of the convent before the governor's return.

Bolting past the old woman and narrowly missing the cane's downward sweep, Claire dashed down the hall toward the stairs while, at her back, the old woman's enraged cry clawed the air. Her cane thumped on the floorboards and occasionally whacked the wall as she went.

Surely every maid, every soldier and slave, would hear the ruckus and rush to investigate? But no, Claire thought as she took the stairs two at a time, they'd probably burrow deeper in their beds knowing of the old woman's tyranny and choosing not to hear. And the soldiers outside never paid the old lady any mind.

At the top of the stairs, Claire swung around to see Señora Viscaya humping up behind her, making slow progress with one hand hauling herself up by the banister while the other levered the cane.

"You will not escape your fate, French scum," the woman said between gasps. "You pretend not...to understand but you get... my meaning, don't you? You will die... tramp...and I shall pound my cane upon your grave. Give it back! Whatever you have taken... give it back!"

Claire stood watching her, seized by a horrible realization. Mother Superior might not give her sanctuary if it meant Antonio could point fingers at the convent's involvement. Who else would he assume she spied for if not the sisters?

And Claire did not want to hang. And, above all else, she did not want to witness the shock and pain of that moment when Antonio realized her betrayal—not yet, not so soon.

And did she not have important missions to accomplish—to avenge her family's deaths, to help free her fellow French colonists and contribute to the coffers of the Ursulines and their charges? And what of this old crow, what value did she have besides making others miserable?

Far at the back of her mind, Claire heard her conscience screaming: *Don't do this, Claire! Don't do it!*

She paused, listening, baffled by the little voice that seemed so real; it was as if another person shared her brain. She shook her head as if to dislodge the intruder, her gaze returning to Señora Viscaya. The old woman had just reached the top step and now clung to the banister, gasping for breath.

She still possessed enough vitriol to spit and sputter insults. "Juanita! Carlotta! Get up, I say!" she croaked between coughs. "I have...I have caught a French...whore, a spy. Come—"

Claire, no! Don't!

But Claire didn't listen. She lunged forward and pushed the old woman down the stairs with all her strength.

26

Romy may as well have been trapped inside a cocoon. It was a membrane thin enough to let in air, light, sound, and a storm of emotions besides, yet too strong to rip through.

As a prisoner inside her soul's journey, she could not interact; she could not move. Claire's body propelled her through tortured days with Romy trapped inside, mute and helpless yet screaming with frustration.

And Claire would not listen. She refused to hear. She shoved away every thought Romy pushed at her as if her conscience was attempting to yank away the reins again. Whatever tenuous connection the two had briefly shared snapped the moment Claire pushed the old woman down the stairs.

Murder. Should Romy live for a thousand more lives, she would never forget the desperate terror in Señora Viscaya's eyes. That instant when one human looks out at another and silently begs for her life scars the soul. Romy felt the damage to both her and Claire, but while Claire turned away, Romy mourned.

Nothing justified murder and nothing justified what Claire planned next, the images of which played like poorly edited movies at the back of their shared mind. Seeing those intentions repulsed Romy but it's not as if she could escape, despite constant struggling, nor could she stop what had already happened in the past.

A tourist in another's hell, Romy's sense of self wavered. And to think she had once longed to plunge full-body into eighteenth-century life and walk down the streets of time.

How could she know how much pain that would cause or the need to claw her way back? Every moment spent in Claire's life risked her own existence.

And now an emotional storm unleashed around and inside her. She felt herself being sucked farther down, anchoring her more firmly to Claire as if chained by her ankle.

Far overhead, she could just glimpse light at the surface of her own time, dimly catch the voices of her friends calling her back, yet Claire held her fast, miring her down into her own trauma.

THE LITTLE VOICE IN CLAIRE'S HEAD HAD GROWN MORE STRIDENT AFTER the old woman's death, though the actual murder had been easy enough. At first the señora had clung stubbornly to the banister with her gnarled hands, forcing Claire to pry the fingers from the wood one by one while shoving at the frail body with her own.

She would never forget her face in those final moments—fury followed atop a searing hate—or the manner in which her conscience called out for her to stop. Nothing deterred her, however, and she did not rest until the old woman lay sprawled like a bag of bones at the bottom of the steps.

Briefly stunned, Claire gazed down at the body. *Claire! What have you done? What have you done?*

What had she done? She pressed her hands to her ears in an effort to silence the voice. "Just what any other soldier would do, is all: kill when necessary," she said aloud.

Then, jolted into action, she rushed down to check the body for breath and, finding none, stepped over the twitching corpse, and scrambled back to the governor's study to lock the door.

Moments later, she called the alarm by banging on all the servants' doors and rousing the guards. "Did you not hear the old woman cry for help?" she accused the shocked and sober faces gathered around the lower hall. "I could not understand the Spanish but you could, yes? Finally, I came but too late."

One of the little maids falteringly translated but Claire could tell by the servants' faces that her message had been understood without the details.

When the governor returned later that evening, he listened with solemnity as Claire explained how the old woman had fallen. He made no comment but she could see the pain in his eyes and knew he mourned the woman. She pushed back the trickle of remorse. Soldiers didn't mourn their enemies. Soldiers did what had to be done.

No further questions followed and only in the quiet hours when Claire was alone in her room did that voice try again to gain her attention. While Claire tossed and turned, it seemed to echo within the very chambers of her skull until she thought she would go mad. Finally, it ceased, allowing her to fall into a fitful sleep.

Now, on the dawn of the next day, the household busied itself in preparing for the laying out and interment. Because of the heat, the body would be hastily dispatched to God at the St. Louis church later that day, after which the governor had made arrangements for the Viscaya's earthly remains to be placed in the vacant tomb until he could commission a proper resting place.

In the meantime, the household had been plunged into mourning and those who did not feel grief feigned it well enough.

Bernardo Viscaya's anguish, on the other hand, rocked the stocks into which he'd been tossed. Every slave or soldier in the vicinity heard his threats. He blamed Claire. She trembled when she heard how he cursed her, though he could not possibly know the truth.

The governor, struck by compassion for a son's loss, agreed to allow Bernardo to attend her service as long as he remained under guard. Claire had also confirmed Antonio's permission for her to leave the house to visit with the sisters and forgo the funeral.

Given that many in the household, especially the younger Ulloa, believed Claire the cause of the old woman's misfortune, the governor agreed to give her leave. He did not seem to care that, as housekeeper, she should be in charge of the funeral feast, nor did he meet her eyes, though she craved his attention.

Unbelievably, he grieved or felt twists of some unnamed guilt and Claire suspected it had more to do with their shared passion than his old housekeeper's tragic demise. In the end he agreed to send her off accompanied by one of his men.

She set off as early as was decent, dressed in her most somber gray frock. Before leaving the premises, she planned one quick visit to Odette, confident that the household would be too absorbed to pay her activities any mind.

Until now, she had been kept from visiting the girl and told that her appearance would only further stir the flames. Even the slaves themselves wanted her to stay away. She resisted the urge to plow her way through despite the warnings, but at least she knew that the girl healed well.

Today, with the servants so absorbed with the service preparations, there'd be no one to stop her. Thin plumes of gray smoke curling up from the slaves' fires brought the scent of cooking food mingling with the acrid burning wood as she crossed the yard. She would assure herself of Odette's recuperation and perhaps bring the girl back some small treat from the convent kitchens.

She would not allow herself to think of the murder. She would keep her mind fixed on the day ahead.

Claire wove between the buildings and the outer walls, keeping well away from the stocks at the opposite end of the compound. A tiny cottage and two ramshackle huts made up the slave quarters. Ten people lived under these three roofs—four men and six women, none related except for a husband and wife who tended the animals. No children.

Two fires burned in the little clearing in front of the shacks, each tended by a woman stirring something on a pot suspended over the flames. Aprons, skirts, and a pair of patched men's breeches hung limply on a line strung between two poles while a scraggy dog sniffed at the bush fringing the clearing.

Two pairs of eyes turned in her direction as she stepped into the open, eyes flickering fear and distrust. She could tell others watched her from inside the shacks, too. A shiver of trepidation hit.

She could sense their fear yet could not understand it. She had done nothing to these people. Though a servant herself, she had tried to help them. Perhaps to them she represented one of the oppressors—French,

Spanish, all the same. Her good dress suddenly seemed far too fine in the morning sun.

Straightening her shoulders, she approached an old woman stirring a thick, cornmeal porridge over the fire. "I would like to speak with Odette," she said in French. "Show me where Odette is. Please."

The old woman glanced up, shaking her head. "Odette, she be well soon. She no miss her chores. I do chores today, lady."

"No, no, you don't understand. I am concerned about her. I want to see if she's all right."

"She good."

Claire sighed "Show me where she is now."

Then she caught the movement in the doorway of the cottage to her right and turned. Odette, wrapped in a rag of a blanket, stood there on the planks that served as a porch, beckoning to her.

"Odette!" Claire ran toward her. "I have been worried about you. You are healing, yes?" She searched the girl's swollen face, alarmed to see a hard new glint flickering in her eyes. "I am so sorry for what happened. At least the man responsible is being duly punished, yes? But he suffers more now, for his mother has died. Let me check your wounds."

She tried to turn the girl around but Odette resisted. Shaking her head, she took Claire's wrist and tugged her through the narrow door into the dark cottage where the only window had been shuttered tight against both light and breeze. The odor of unwashed bodies thickened the air. Claire glimpsed a single table in the center of the space and tattered bedding rolled up against the walls in the otherwise empty space.

When Claire's eyes adjusted to the gloom she found Odette staring at the space above Claire's shoulder with so much intensity Claire swung around to see if someone had followed them inside. How foolish; they were alone. "What is it?" she asked. "Why do you stare?"

"The spirit," Odette said with a strange little nod, her eyes wide with fear.

"What spirit? What are you talking about?"

"The spirit stalks you—her spirit, the one you killed."

Claire felt the blood drain from her face. "I don't understand."

"Yes, you do. Señora Viscaya, the one you killed. I know."

Claire's mouth went dry. "But you couldn't have...seen..."

Odette shook her head. "I see dead woman's ghost beside you now so I know," the girl said, gazing wide-eyed into the seemingly empty air. "Bad woman make bad spirit."

Claire took a step backward, all the while turning to search the gloom for signs. Through a sickening dread, she saw nothing. "No."

"Yes," Odette said. "She follow you till you die and beyond the grave, too."

Claire's body trembled in the heat. "Leave me alone, you old witch," she whispered to the air. "You were a horrible person intent on harming me the moment I entered the governor's house and were consumed with hate for all but a few. You received only as you deserved."

"That won't make her go. That just stir more hate," Odette said. "But I try."

Claire wrapped her arms around herself. "What do you mean, you'll try?"

"Voodoo," Odette whispered. "I talk to spirits, ask for their help, send bad ones away."

"I don't know what you're talking about. What is this voodoo of which you speak? Do you mean an exorcism?" The priests had performed exorcisms. That she understood.

"No," Odette said to her, stepping closer. "Voodoo older belief, strong magic."

"Magic?" Would her shivering ever stop? She hugged herself tighter. "I have to go now. I only came to see how your wounds heal and to ask what I could do to help you."

"You help me already. You help punish one and kill other." She nodded toward the corner. "You one that need help now."

"I don't need any help. I am fine." Claire glanced toward the closed door. Could she escape a ghost if she were to outrun them or refuse to pay them any mind? "Your wounds heal well?" she asked, trying to resume normalcy with the girl, who she sensed had more power than she ever gave credit.

"They heal," Odette whispered, her voice raw and harsh as if from crying, yet no weakness softened her tone. "But inside I hurt always. I make them pay."

Claire reached the door. "I must go to the convent now. Could I bring you something back?"

"You go to church?"

Claire hesitated. "You wish me to pray for you?"

The girl laughed but not with mirth. "No, Claire. You take a message to my father?"

Startled by the use of her first name yet knowing she had no right to demand a more formal address after all she'd done, she nodded. "Your father? Yes, of course."

"His name Celestin Picot and he be a free man. He buy my freedom, too, someday he will, and I will be like you."

A free man, Claire marveled. "And he is where?"

"With the stone maker, Monsieur LeBlanc. He give him money to do work. You know him?"

"Yes, yes, his establishment is next to blacksmith's. He does masonry for the governor and it's not far from the convent. What is your message?"

"Say he meet me at Congo Plains. Tonight."

Claire stared. "Congo Plains tonight? But, Odette—"

"Tonight. After dark. I wait."

Slaves were not permitted to roam the streets unless it was about their owner's business and, even then, any caught in town after sundown might be killed. At night the streets of New Orleans were not safe for any woman of any color or status unless they made their home there.

Claire shoved her hands deep into her pockets. "Odette, this is very dangerous. You mustn't—"

"You would tell on me?" the girl asked, that strange smile lifting her lips.

Claire clenched her fists. "Of course not."

Odette smiled. "We are friends, you and me, yes? We are tied together." The girl made a little tying motion with her hands. "So, you will go?"

"Yes," Claire sighed. "But very much against my better judgment because I do not think it safe."

Odette only nodded as she gently pushed Claire toward the door. "Nothing safe for you or me now, sister. Tell my father he must come and I will wait. Tell him he must make his choice."

Claire half ran to the door, her mind beginning to twist as she heard Odette whispering after her. "Remember what I say."

Then a sharp pain blasted her temples and suddenly Claire fell to the floor, clutching her head. "Go away! Leave me be!"

"Let her go," Odette cried in the strangest tongue. "Let her go, you rotten piece of soul scum!"

27

"Soul scum? Soul scum." Romy hugged Joquita hard, her friend returning the embrace with equal fervor. "I've never been so happy to be called scum in any century. I've missed you that much."

"Rom? Finally! Look, we've been worried sick around here. You've been gone so long I wanted to grab Claire and shake you free even if it meant cracking her skull."

"Cracking my skull wouldn't help, I guarantee it, though I wanted to do it myself a couple of times. I thought I'd never return." Romy pulled away, studying her friend. Impossible not to see the strain in Jo's otherwise lively, mischievous face. She gently touched her cheek. "If time and circumstances hadn't driven a wedge between us, you and I would have been besties even back then, Jo. Poor Odette. God, it was such a brutal time."

"Hey, don't start with the Odette thing yet, okay? I just want us to be semi-normal for a while." Jo wiped her eyes on her arm. "Oh, great, you've got me slobbering now." She plucked a tissue from a box on the table and blew her nose noisily.

"But I've just got to say you were one kick-ass woman even then. They whipped you, brutalized you, treated you like dirt—"

"Stop! Do you think I don't know what hell it was to be a slave?"

"You lived it, my friend. You know it deep down in your soul."

"And my people fight like hell to forgive. Please, let's just stay in the now."

"Right. I just want to savor my own world for a while." Romy scanned the room, taking in her bedroom at Aunt Loo's with the bed piled with tangled sheets and the blinds pouring slatted light into the space. Daylight already. "How long have I been gone?"

Jo spread her hands. "At least eighteen hours, give or take a minute or two. Sometimes you prowled the house and sometimes you slept, or at least your body did. By the way you tore up the sheets, I suspect you were busy living Claire's life back there or maybe having another rendezvous with El Spaniard." Jo rubbed her face and sighed. "It's been crazy here. Aunt Loo and I spell one another off so you're never alone but we've been out of our skins with worry. Oh, hell—bad choice of words."

"It's okay. I have been literally out of my mind." Romy ran her hand along the top of the bureau, a lovely Louis XIV gilded commode. Her fingers landed on her cell phone. "God, I missed this century. I can't count the number of times I longed for technology. Jo, the smells, the sights and sounds two centuries ago," she said, wrinkling her nose. "Ugh."

"Are your senses alert the whole time?"

"Completely. Sometimes I thought I couldn't bear another day spent in Claire's body since she washed in nothing but a dish of water once a day. They all doused themselves in perfume to mask the stench and most men smelled of horse or worse. Funny what gets you, isn't it?"

"Yeah, I admit, I never think of how a century smells."

"As historians, we don't think about those details. We're too fixed on the grand events, but since I couldn't do much else trapped in Claire, I took it all in. Oh, I just want a shower with lots of soap and shampoo; I want to plug in an electric kettle or an electric anything and have a close and lasting relationship with an air conditioner!"

Jo grinned, dabbing her eyes "That's my girl—the eternal romantic hankering after an electronic liaison. Maybe if you didn't insist on sleeping with the window open, you could appreciate the AC even more. I've got it on full blast all over the house so you can hear its little whirring heart all you want."

Romy burst into laughter, mirth veering dangerously close to hysteria. She slapped a hand over her mouth. No way could she lose control now.

She caught sight of herself in the mirror over the commode, a bedraggled waif in a limp night-slip with shadow-ringed eyes and lank hair. She dropped her hand long enough to push a stringy tendril from her face. "I'm a mess. Has Adrian seen me like this?"

"I wondered when you'd mention him. If he did, I doubt he noticed. He's been hanging around like a puppy dog. Make that a fretting greyhound, since he's too sleek for anything floppy-eared. He's lost his composure a few times but the good professor rumpled is damn more appealing than the self-contained version. Today, he's taken himself off to his office to do some research but mostly because Aunt Loo banished him for the day."

Romy stared at her friend. "He's been here through all this?"

"Not in the room with you—couldn't have you two jumping one another's bones in somebody else head, could we?—but yeah, more or less. He'll be back tonight."

"Tonight?" The thought of night brought a wave of fear.

"Aunt Loo has a big powwow slated for seven o'clock. She's called together all the players, including Detective Long-Fingered Telly, to discuss the murder case and you. Originally, she hoped that having all these contemporary souls who've played double-duty in the past might dislodge you from Claire. Now that you're home, methinks it will get even more interesting."

"It sounds like a setting for the perfect soul storm." The thought of having all her past life's connections together in one place and time sent shivers down her spine. "Where is Aunt Loo?"

"Out for a while but she should be home soon."

"I think," Romy said carefully, "that my chances of making it back improve when I'm physically among souls I knew in Claire's life—you, Aunt Loo, Adrian." Adrian. She wrapped her arms around herself. "It's like you all give me something to fix on when I fight my way back, a touchstone, maybe. Yet, the moment Claire's memories swerve into events where none of you are involved, I'm trapped."

"From my observation, it seems you're equally at risk when you're with us."

"Yes, it's a conundrum. It's as if our presence opens the portal between the time dimensions in both directions. Oh, God." She hugged herself more tightly. "I don't want to return but I don't know how I can stop this momentum."

"First things first. Shower," Jo suggested, gently nudging Romy toward the bathroom. "Let all that hot water wash that time crap off you and then we'll have lunch. Think girlie things like that new dress you bought just before this crapola started. I brought it here for you. It's there in the armoire."

"'Time crap,' 'crapola,'" Romy murmured as she turned on the shower and tested the flow for temperature. "Are you really preparing yourself for an academic career, Dr. Dupré? Your vocabulary is sure to be an asset. How's it going, by the way?"

"Fine but let's not talk about it, not while your own studies are on ice and your life inside out. I'll just phone Aunt Loo and let her know you've returned to our collective bosoms. There, see? I said bosoms not boobs. My academic career is assured. I'll wait outside."

As the hot water rinsed away the cloud of strawberry-scented shampoo, Romy pledged to never, ever take modern conveniences for granted again. Cleanliness equaled bliss. She stepped out of the shower, wrapped herself in a big, fluffy towel, and sighed in pleasure.

Home in her own skin, walking among her own contemporaries, just became her new definition of heaven.

Now, if only she could stay away from Claire's hell, but how likely was that? They were intertwined and, in Romy's case, chained. She may as well be a prisoner on a day pass.

But, for now, peace had settled around the space inside Romy's mind like a room suddenly vacated after a violent argument. No tortured energy pressed against her temples. In its stead came a sweet reprieve. And then she remembered Adrian thinking as Antonio and the way he reached for her...

No, no, a million times no! Think of something else.

She wiped steam away from the bathroom mirror and studied her face. Claire had been smaller, tiny almost, with the build of a well-developed girl, whereas Romy stood at least a foot taller with a lean, womanly body.

Centuries of better nutrition plus healthier living conditions had genetically changed the population. After seeing life in the 1700s, it amazed her that any of them had even survived. Actually, she thought with a grimace, millions hadn't.

And now here she stood, a woman of the twenty-first century with one foot in the past. She ran her fingers through her shoulder-length hair, separating the curls to let them air-dry. She lived in future past. One thing Romy grudgingly admired was Claire's fierce determination to finish what she started. She was brave and resourceful with a ferocious will to right a wrong.

Romy dropped her arms, struck with the sudden realization that Claire would never grind to a halt mere months away from achieving a goal because of a man, any man. Nor would she give up on that man just because he'd built the Great Wall of China around his long-ago broken heart. And she absolutely would not let her wounded spirit wallow defeated in some kind of purgatory without a fight. If life tossed a speed bump in Claire's path, she'd either swerve to avoid it or barrel right over it, full speed ahead.

Leaning over, Romy swept the mirror clear of steam with her forearm. "Pull yourself together," she commanded her reflection.

Then she threw on a terry robe and stepped into the bedroom while tightening the belt, hair curling in wet drifts around her face.

"We thought we'd lost you this time, child." Louisa rose from the armchair beside the window, her deep purple muumuu emphasizing the woman's regal grace.

"Aunt Loo." Romy embraced the older woman, relieved to be solidly together with her in a shared present. "I couldn't break free, then suddenly and inexplicably I was released. I'm not sure why or how anymore. It's all so jumbled and random, but I know I'll end up yanked away again no matter what I do."

"And so you will as long as there's unfinished business there. You won't find ultimate release until this thing is finally done," Louisa said, stepping back to better study Romy's face.

Romy swallowed. "I don't like the sounds if that. And what is the definition of 'done' in this context? Is it staying entrapped in Claire's life until she dies? Is it me somehow helping her see the wrong she's committed? She murdered an old lady—that's Señora Viscaya's ghost haunting me—and Claire's crimes keep mounting to the point where I can barely stand living inside her skull. She will not listen."

Louisa shook her head sadly. "Try not to judge her, child."

"I can't help but judge her, and what's going to happen next, anyway? Tell me, please."

Louisa dropped her hands, sighing heavily. "I don't know and that's a fact. Our two souls only intersect, not run parallel. You will be the only one who is with Claire to the end, but tonight, Joquita and Adrian will share what research they've gathered over the last few hours. I understand it's little enough considering but maybe this will help."

"Tonight?"

"Yes, tonight. Bringing everyone together is a dangerous but necessary move. These past few days, I've meditated, asking my spirit guides and angels for advice. Again and again they point the way: bring all the interconnecting souls together in one place; seal the space with light, but allow the souls a chance to untangle themselves with shared understanding and love. Nothing less will do. I cannot fix this, Romy, I can only set the stage and enable its resolution. You must make things right."

Romy clenched her fists and stared at the woman in front of her in disbelief. "Me? Aunt Loo, calling together a powerful vortex of energy could suck me right down forever. That's true purgatory: reenacting the same hell on earth over and over again."

"You'll relive Claire's hell no matter what unless you dig deep enough to release her and all the spirits caught in her pull. Yes," she agreed. "It is indeed a soul storm of magnificent proportions. But mind my words, there is no other way."

"Then I will be dragged back into Claire again." Romy gripped the bureau as if that could anchor her to the century.

"Be strong. The risks you face are enormous but you can't escape them. At least tonight you'll have the chance to make things right."

"But how?"

"Only you can find the answer to that. This is your journey. Now you must gather your strength. Get dressed and come eat. You'll need to be well-fortified for what unfolds tonight."

"But I just had breakfast," Romy protested, remembering the wedge of fresh-baked bread she devoured along with a spread of honey.

Her stomach rumbled. She looked down at her belly and up to Louisa with a wry smile. "Oh, right: that was two hundred and fifty-five years ago."

28

Carbs figured prominently in Aunt Loo's world with everything fatty and rich holding court at every meal. Biscuits, savory rice dishes, and homemade sweets wafted their scent throughout the house as Louisa's caterers prepared for the night's event. Soul equaled food and Romy figured she must approach the feast in the spirit in which it was intended. Besides, how could any able-bodied woman turn down brown sugar pie or crab cakes, let alone sweet potato biscuits and gumbo?

Circulating through the capacious kitchen, trying to stay out from underfoot, Romy piled her plate with seasoned gulf shrimp and some kind of rich, cheesy tart. With a glass of iced tea in one hand and her plate in the other, she navigated through the bustling kitchen and outside into the garden.

Jo stood in the fern path with her purse slung over her arm, waiting. She wore that filmy blue dress purchased when she and Romy had gone shopping together only the week before. That would be last week a million years ago.

"You look gorgeous." Romy nodded, taking in the details of her friend's careful grooming. "Where are you going all dressed up?"

"I'm off to run errands for Aunt Loo but who knows how long filling this mumbo-jumbo list is going to take?" She waved a list around before slipping it into her purse. "I figured I'd better get gussied up for the big event first just in case I won't have time when I get back."

Romy settled down on a chair beside a wrought-iron café table and set down her plate along with her glass. "Just in case you arrive back late and a certain Detective Brown is already in attendance, you mean."

"Yeah, you read me like a book."

"One with large type for the visually impaired. Methinks you have the hots for the good detective. What's on that list, anyway?" Romy bit into a sweet potato biscuit.

Jo shrugged. "God knows. Probably eye of newt and toe of frog. I tried not to study it too closely in case it freaked me out. Just know I'm dropping by several shops you wouldn't ordinarily drag me into with a ten-foot pole. But when Aunt Loo speaks, I obey. In fact, I'd better get obeying now before it gets too late. You good? I see you're having a cholesterol love-in."

Romy chewed, relishing the rich, buttery flavors and licking her fingers for effect. "I'm good. For the last two hours, I almost feel normal, or would if everybody wasn't watching me like I'm public enemy number one."

Even as she spoke, Rae Dawn cast surreptitious glances at her through the trumpet tree branches while Louisa hovered by the screen doors, fixing her in her sights and talking on a cordless phone.

"Yeah, they got you covered. Keep Claire the hell out of your head while I'm gone, okay? I'll see you later." And, with that, Jo traipsed off down the path, her bare legs brushing against banks of daylilies.

After Jo left, Romy chewed in silence, focusing on a dragonfly flickering a lazy dance above the Buddha fountain tucked into the ferns.

Louisa's voice continued talking into the phone, at once melodic and persuasive, while bees buzzed, voices murmured, Rae Dawn's shears clipped, and silverware clinked in the kitchen. Everything descended into a cacophony of ordinary, a lullaby to a battered soul. The tension melted away from Romy as she savored being herself.

She yawned. Carb overdose. How long had it been since she really slept? Coffee, she needed good, strong coffee.

Rising, she gathered her dishes and stepped toward the kitchen intent on finding the nearest brew when her feet suddenly refused to move in the direction she wanted. Instead, they veered sharply to the right and sent her bolting down a path deep into the garden, her plate and glass crashing to the ground.

⁂

CLAIRE PROCEEDED RAPIDLY DOWN THE STREET WITH HER SKIRTS LIFTED slightly in a futile attempt to keep the hem clean.

Pods of dung glistened in the heat, foul and pungent, full of rot and attracting flies. Like her heart, she thought. Her conscience kept knocking away at the back of her skull, whispering admonishments and begging for attention, but she shut her mind firmly against the intruder. Her mission ruled her, not her weakness.

Occasionally, she'd glance over her shoulder as if Señora Viscaya's ghost might be dogging her heels. Though nothing was visible, she still felt the old woman's presence wrapped around her like a chill breath—a passenger on her ride to hell. She'd been damned for all eternity. No matter, her deeds had been done for the best of reasons.

Yet, she thought as she walked along, how could sin come so easily? Things she'd never dream of doing were now swiftly plotted and planned. The restraints of church and morals that had once tied her tight now threatened to hang her. She remembered her parents with a desperate ache. How disappointed they would be.

Did God send every soldier to hell? She blocked all that from her mind, resolving to stay true to her goals.

What trees had not been felled to help build the town stood with branches drooping as if burdened by the very air. Though the sun had not yet reached its peak, the heaviness of the summer pressed down upon the streets, clogging every alleyway and courtyard with listlessness.

Sundays did not mark a day of worship for most residents of New Orleans. Occasionally, a carriage rumbled past kicking up dust and a horseman or two ambled by, but most inhabitants still slumbered, their upper-story shutters flung open to catch a passing breeze.

Few would stir until late afternoon. Should the rumor prove true that a magnificent new cathedral would someday replace the Church of St. Louis, such an edifice would surely rise like a beacon against a legion of sinners. A futile attempt to call the wicked to absolution.

And she must now count herself among the wicked.

A man's voice called out to her in faltering French. "Mademoiselle, wait up, if you please! It is Corporal Arturo coming to attend you."

She swung around, annoyed. She had forgotten that the governor had assigned an escort.

"I do not wish you to accompany me," she told the young soldier upon his approach, noting the gleam of moisture above his upper lip. He looked like a boy dressed up in a man's uniform, the heavy serge fabric trussing him like a chicken. "It is not necessary and the sisters do not like strangers hanging about." Let alone Spaniards, she almost added.

He bowed. "My apologies, mademoiselle, but the governor, he insists I come."

She had last seen Antonio that morning offering condolences to Bernardo Viscaya, a man he penalized for cruelty and inappropriate behavior even while offering his sincere sympathies. But as payment for the governor's compassion, Bernardo only spit at his feet.

Antonio could not yet meet her eye.

"So," she said, "you are not worthy to attend the funeral today or guard Bernardo Viscaya, either, no? Instead, you are sent for no other purpose but to accompany a mere woman to church."

Arturo did not flinch. "Not so, mademoiselle. The governor sees you as a most important charge for he fears you may come to harm without my assistance. The governor is just. If he sees you as such import, then, rest assured, so do I," he told her, pride evident in his voice. "The governor is very famous scientist and a very wise man and I am honored to do his bidding."

"Yes, he is that," Claire agreed, sharing his pride.

"Not just a commander but a man of science," Arturo continued, waxing in praise. "I myself have been permitted to attend scientific excursions with him and have seen him investigate all manner of things."

"You have?" she marveled, wishing she could have memories of voyages with Antonio. "What sort of things?"

"Why, the stars, creatures in the sea, strange plants, and precious stones. The governor, he asks questions like 'Why does the tide flow in and out?' and then seeks the answers. At first I thought only that since God makes the tide flow, why would he need to know more than that?"

Claire smiled, remembering her conversations with Antonio. The wonders he revealed were almost as exciting as the man. "Yes, but the governor, he sees the world differently, does he not? He shows patterns in God's universe, how the Lord connects each creature to each other as the moon is connected to the sea. It is most wondrous." And she, too, believed herself fortunate to have known him.

Her thoughts strayed to the drawing tucked safely in her pocket and all delight died on her tongue. "Well, I am certain attending me today will not be nearly so interesting for you."

"Not so, mademoiselle," he said with a bow, "for who would not enjoy such a fine day in the company of a beautiful lady?"

She studied him carefully, trying to assess his intelligence against her ability to control and deceive.

He could be no older than seventeen, a boy by the looks of the down skimming his chin. Yet she sensed a current of strength within. He must be among the youngest of the Spanish soldiers—a lesser soldier assigned to a lesser task—but one that Antonio would not take lightly. That he entrusted her care to this boy spoke of how high in Antonio's regard he stood. This young soldier would grow into a formidable man.

"Oh, very well." Turning on her heel, she strode quickly on. "But pray do not get in my way."

"Si, mademoiselle."

ROMY ARRIVED AT THE KOI POND BREATHLESS, SHAKING AWAY DRIFTS OF Claire from her brain. That last regression had slipped her back and forth in time with neither headache nor warning, as if the lines between their two lives were softening into a porous blur.

Oh, God. She wrapped her arms around one of Louisa's carved marble pillars and clung to the stone fiercely. This couldn't be good. Before, her regressions had been brutally defined, but now she simply strode into Claire's shoes without warning, taking the swift change in time and place in her stride, literally.

"Claire, I'm not you. You are not me!" She pressed her face into the cool stone and fought the urge to cry. Only then did she hear her name called out all over the garden. She lifted her head, listening.

"Romy! Where are you? Rae Dawn, try the Katrina garden!"

Romy stepped away from the pillar, calling: "I'm here by the koi pond."

In seconds, Rae Dawn and Louisa had reached her side. Louisa placed a hand above her substantial bosom near her heart. "Romy, you nearly gave me a coronary straying out of our sight like that. I thought for a minute you might be out there roaming the streets."

Romy wrapped her arms around herself. "It wasn't deliberate. One minute I was heading for the kitchen, the next strolling old New Orleans escorted by a Spanish soldier. Louisa, the events are getting more fluid now. I can barely feel the transition coming anymore."

"Stay calm," Louisa warned. "We'll find a way to make this stop. Tonight, it has to be tonight."

And then Joquita burst into the clearing. "Oh, thank God you're here. Adrian just arrived with Veronica. Hey, girl, you have to get dressed. It's getting late."

"Late? How long have you been gone?" she asked her friend.

"About two hours. Why?"

"So late? But Veronica?" Romy stiffened, staring straight at Jo. "Why is he here with Veronica?"

"I invited her to come," Louisa explained. "She plays a role in this."

But Joquita understood Romy's real question. "She's his sister-in-law. Yeah, she's visiting him while his brother's on one of the gulf rigs—staying at a hotel, just in case you wondered. Come on. We'll go in the side door and up the old servant's stairway so we can make a suitable dramatic, jaw-dropping entrance." She snatched Romy's hand, tugging her down the path. "Auntie, your toads and lizard tails are in the kitchen."

"There are no toads and lizard tails in those jars, Joquita Bonita," her aunt called after her.

The two women dashed down the gravel path, cutting cross the orchid garden and in through the side door.

"His sister-in-law?" Romy marveled. "I never liked her from the start but his sister-in-law? Why doesn't that make me feel any better?"

"Speak of the devil." Joquita braked by a small oval window set into the first-landing wall. "Look at her."

Romy squeezed beside Jo and peered down into the garden. Veronica strolled into the patio toward the fireplace wearing a black sheath with a plunging neckline, front and back. Adrian trailed behind her bearing a glass of wine in each hand like an attentive suitor. Veronica turned, flashing him a smile, and reached for a glass he carried, fingers lingering seconds too long on his.

"She's hitting on him," Romy whispered. "Hitting on her husband's brother."

"Yep. Woman's sure enough got her mandibles ready," Jo agreed. "If that dress got any lower, it would be tickling her adenoids."

"Adenoids are farther north and you're mangling your metaphors again."

"Oh, yeah, quibble at a time like this, why don't you. Look at him: the poor guy doesn't even realize she wants to eat him alive."

Romy pulled away. "Well, he's at the top of my food group, too. I'd better get down there and stake my claim. Where did you say you hung that dress?"

Twilight had softened the edges of the world by the time Romy and Joquita descended the grand staircase and strolled through the house toward the garden.

Silk swished against Romy's bare legs, every step a caress. The creamy lace bodice hugged her curves to within an inch below her hips before lace flared into chiffon above the knees.

What a complete and utter extravagance, a luxury dress more fitting a debutante than a poor doctoral student, but how she needed this dress this night. It enveloped her in confidence, made her feel beautiful and desirable, two things she desperately needed.

Louisa had set the stage with long-tapered candles and crystal bowls overflowing with flowers, every surface cradling something scented, brilliantly colored, or sparkling.

Romy paused to pick up a palm-sized sphere of glass nestled beside a bouquet of gardenias. "A paperweight?" She held the object with reverence, marveling at the spectrum sparking in its depths.

"A crystal," Jo sighed. "Oh, Lordy, Aunt Loo's brought out her crystals. That means she's sent invitations into the universe in some kind of mumbo-jumbo all-points bulletin, her woo-woo distribution list. Shit. You want to skip this and go catch a movie instead?"

Romy smiled despite the jangling nerves. "We're a bit overdressed, don't you think? Besides, the spirits will find me even without Aunt Loo's cosmic invitations so I may as well get it over with. Listen, the guests are here."

Clinking glasses and voices drifted in from beyond the open doors, deep male tones mingling with the lilt of female laughter. Jo gripped Romy's arm. "That's Telly and it sounds like Veronica the Vamp is wiggling her arsenal for more than one enrapt male."

"Right, then, let's enter the fray. The sooner this begins, the sooner it ends. Hopefully, just not permanently," she added.

"Don't even think that, let alone say it aloud."

With that, the two women swept into the twilight courtyard. All eyes turned in their direction. Though Romy registered Louisa, the detective, Veronica and Luke from O'Brien's, her attention fixed only on Adrian.

He filled her vision, swelled her heart, and nothing she did could wrestle her emotions in line. People talked around her; Louisa made introductions; someone asked her something—but nothing and no one else mattered.

He took a step toward her. "Romy, you look...beautiful."

Her name on his lips hit her bloodstream like a song but all she could do was stare into his eyes like a lovesick girl. His appreciation in those moments had nothing to do with scholarship or Claire, she knew that much.

He saw her. Seconds passed before she found her voice. "Adrian. Thanks for coming and for being here." Lame.

"Of course I'm here. How could I not be?"

Her body trembled in the heat. If only they were alone without so many people watching. "Ah, you mean because Aunt Loo demanded your presence?" she teased.

He laughed a low chuckle. "Though my knees quake every time she issues a decree, I'm here for you alone."

He was here for her alone. Oh my God. Her heart threatened to throb visibly beneath her finery. It took everything she had to speak her words with the strength they deserved.

"Thank you. I'm going to fight tonight for everything that matters. And I will return to my thesis; I will finish my degree. But, more importantly, I will end the chaos this night no matter what the cost. Before this night ends, you'll know the truth."

"Know what truth?" a voice interrupted. "Oh, how terribly melodramatic, Romy, dear. How are you feeling, by the way? You look a bit pale. Do you use blush?" Veronica stepped between them to stand directly in front of Romy, her back to Adrian.

Over the woman's shoulder, Romy held Adrian's eyes, saw his mouth quirk in annoyance at the woman's rudeness. "Just a moment, dear," Veronica was saying. "Your neckline needs a little adjustment." And with a flick of her manicured hand, she smoothed the lace around Romy's collar. "There."

Romy caught the woman's fingers in a firm grip, tearing her gaze from Adrian's long enough to fix a cool stare on Veronica. "How thoughtful to concern yourself with my appearance. I was surprised to hear you were coming tonight but Louisa says you play a role in my past life. Hmm, something about you does seem familiar but I can't just put my finger on it, but later tonight I'll finally know."

Veronica disengaged her hand and stepped back. "Oh, sure. Can't wait. I laughed when she told me I was involved in this little production but naturally curious. I had to come. How could I miss the performance? Could you stage me up as Marie Antoinette? I always liked that one, but I still think your best show was on your knees about to—"

"Veronica," Adrian warned, slipping to Romy's side and drawing her away. "Why don't you check on Susie? We hired a babysitter to stay with her here," he told Romy, "but I suspect she's in the kitchen sampling everything in sight. She's definitely my brother's daughter."

But as Veronica stepped away, pouting prettily, Louisa arrived, linking one arm in Adrian's and another in Romy's. "Are you two ready, my dears? It's time to begin."

"Ready? Of course." Romy's gaze flickered to Adrian, caught his gray-green eyes briefly, and then dropped to the paving stones. She didn't feel ready, couldn't imagine ever being ready, for what she sensed was about to begin. Or end.

"It's all right, child," Louisa told her softly. "You are among friends, very old friends. Come." She led them toward the Gothic fireplace where chairs sat in a semicircle before the hearth lit only by candles in myriad shapes and sizes. Plates of canapés sat on the low marble table beside a clear bowl of freesias.

Lucas, leaning against the mantel, popped a cracker into his mouth and waved at Romy while Detective Brown caught her eye and nodded, his expression grim. Jo lowered herself into a chair and made some attempt to position her legs in some vestige of demure while blowing her a kiss.

"Please, everyone, take a seat," Aunt Loo requested. The scrape of wrought-iron chairs against stone followed as all the guests positioned themselves around the fireplace.

A woman in a white apron circulated on the perimeter refreshing drinks from a clear pitcher. Romy, sitting beside Adrian, accepted a tall glass of what she knew to be Louisa's own julep iced tea and sat staring into its cool depths in an effort to stay fixed in the present.

Louisa, standing in the center of the semicircle with the fireplace at her back, silenced the hum of conversation with her presence. "Thank you all for coming tonight. It is not a small thing for us to gather in this fashion after so long a time, and I commend you for suspending belief long enough to be part of what will unfold this night."

She lifted her arms, sending the violet silken sleeves flowing downward. "For all of us are linked, interconnected, and enveloped by events long ago. Billions of such connections affect people every day only recognized in small flashes of déjà vu or perhaps a sense of knowing someone when you realize no such acquaintance is possible—in your lifetime. But, my friends, we all live many lifetimes, often in the company of the same souls."

Detective Thelonious Brown cleared his throat. "Ms. Dupré, with the deepest respect, you know I came tonight only as it may relate to an ongoing murder case. I don't believe this past life business for a minute."

Louisa only smiled. "Call me Louisa, Thelonious. Remember, I've known you since you were a tadpole and your mother and I go way back. Naturally, I would expect you to say exactly that being an officer of the law. I ask only that you keep your mind open and listen."

"And I'm here for the show," Veronica said as she entered the circle and sashayed slowly across the gathering as the men courteously got to their feet until she'd settled.

Choosing a seat on the opposite of Adrian, she hitched her skirt sufficiently to reveal a shapely leg, at which time all the men resumed their seats. "Pardon me if I don't believe this stuff, either. I will admit to being impressed by the performance, though." She flashed Romy a predatory smile.

"I don't expect each and every one of you to immediately accept what science and our culture has deemed impossible," Louisa continued. "Should this same gathering take place in another century or even another culture, the seemingly impossible would be viewed differently."

"We are defined by rational thought in this culture," Jo said.

"Indeed. We North Americans, like anyone brewed in the teachings of rational thought, quickly discard notions of past lives, ghosts, or regressions. Those same people may attend church, believe in God, or the miracles of both Old and New Testaments, the Koran, or even the teachings of Buddha, and yet not accept any miracles beyond those tomes. Faith is often a matter of upbringing and education. Others are scientists who have eliminated the concept of the soul because it can't be measured or weighted like a sack of potatoes."

"Hey," Lucas said, leaning forward. "Ms. Dupré, I don't mean to seem disrespectful but, like, this soul business confuses me some, too. Are you saying that all of us knew one another in another lifetime?"

"Exactly, Lucas. And I'm also saying that some of how we behave or feel in this lifetime is influenced by events in the past. Not always and not for everyone, though I suspect each of us occasionally has the sense of familiarity with a person or place they know they've never encountered."

"Déjà vu again," Joquita said.

"Paramnesia," Adrian added. "That's the medical term referring to a disorder of the memory where fantasy and objective experience are confused for reality."

Romy, who had been keeping her eyes focused on the mint leaves mingling with ice in her drink, glanced over at him now, startled to see his face shift to Antonio's as though through a transparent overlay. "No," she said aloud. She could not, must not, go back in time yet.

She stood up. Everyone turned to her. "I mean, that's not what's happening to me. Paramnesia is just a label applied to something science doesn't understand. If it's not understood, how can we categorize it, which little pigeonhole can we squeeze it into?"

"But—" the detective began.

"Wait, please, let me continue," she said. "Of course, those of us raised in the study of quantifiable proof must grasp at any label that makes sense within that framework. Anything else would create havoc in belief systems, and isn't science about organizing chaos?" She laughed at the thought. "I know because that was me trying to grapple with my experiences not so long ago. What's happening to me doesn't fit a scientific classification."

Louisa held out her hand and Romy crossed the space between them to grasp it gratefully. "But in other cultures, other belief systems, what's occurring to you is completely explainable. My child, how are you holding up?"

Romy smiled at her. "I'm still in this time and place, if that's what you mean."

"Hey." Joquita stood. "I was not a believer at first. I thought Rom had a psychotic break, but that was before I watched what she's been going through. Sometimes, just for an instant, I actually felt like I was another person in another time. You, too, Doc. Don't deny it. Remember standing in the hall kissing Romy and calling her Claire in Spanish?"

Veronica shot him a quick, venomous look while Adrian's mouth opened as if to speak but stopped himself.

"In any case, I have an analogy about this. I warn you that it's simplistic, suitable for children even. I kept it basic so anyone might understand." She shot Veronica a quick look. "Mind if I take it out for a test drive, Auntie?" Jo said, gazing from her aunt.

"Oh, my child, your analogies tend to be prosaic," Louisa said.

"And you always mangle your metaphors," Romy said fondly.

"Prosaic is just what our gents need. Let me give a try. Feel free to stop me if I'm making things sound too basic, girlfriend. Okay, then." Jo wiggled her skirt free from her legs, flashed Detective Brown a dazzling smile as she caught his appreciative glance, and began.

"Consider that we're all cars. Some are models from certain manufacturers—let's say Chrysler or Ford—and those manufacturers represent our racial heritage. So, Detective Brown, Lucas, Aunt Loo, and I are all from the same race/manufacturer. We have similar physical characteristics. We've driven up through time with our ancestral blood from mostly African roots, as an example." She held out her hands.

"Oh, dear," Aunt Loo sighed.

"Consider the blood in our veins as our genetic heritage, and the DNA that helps make us who we are as individuals, but that's only part of the story. As we drive along the road of our individual lives, we gather personal experiences from our particular voyage, which also helps make the persons we become. How am I doing?" She looked at Aunt Loo.

"Fine, child. I just can't wait to see where you're driving to next."

Joquita grinned. "So, we have this racial chassis plus a pile of personal experiences combining to make a pretty complex car. But—" she paused for effect "—every one of us has energy which drives our cars. It's the power that moves us, the spark of being that fires our engines. And this energy doesn't die, it only moves from one car to another as the equipment wears down. So in this lifetime, my spark is firing the engine of a Jeep Wrangler but eighty years from now I'll be in another chassis altogether."

"Interesting analogy, Miss Dupré." Thelonious Brown chuckled, gazing up at her with nothing short of admiration. "But I see your logic is about to break down."

"A breakdown, Detective? Maybe I can count on the police for roadside assistance?"

But before Thelonious could issue a suitable retort, Romy strode over to Lucas and began speaking in Spanish. "Excuse me but I must visit someone en route. You must wait outside."

Lucas shook his head and climbed to his feet.

Romy pressed a hand to her temple. "No, not now!"

29

"Stay well behind me," Claire scolded. "It will not do to be seen in the company of a Spanish soldier."

Arturo immediately fell back several carriage lengths.

Obedient at least. Claire dabbed her handkerchief on her forehead and carried on until she reached the two-story residence of Monsieur LeBlanc, stonemason to the town's wealthiest citizens. The building, newly constructed, still carried the scent of fresh cedar planking wafting from beyond its impressive stone wall.

Outside, a new carriage stood at the ready with two horses waiting to haul their owners away to church. Here, at least, was one of the more upstanding citizens. She spied the little Frenchman helping his rotund wife and three small children into the carriage.

"Monsieur!" She hailed him with a wave. "I beg your pardon, please. May I have a word?"

Monsieur watched her approach, surprise alight in his moon-shaped face, his ruddy cheeks ripening like fruit in the heat. Above the elaborate white periwig, he wore a plumed wide-brimmed hat that exactly matched the ivory brocade of his waistcoat. He looked too hot and too rich for the town, yet very self-content for all of that. "Mademoiselle?"

Dropping a curtsy to both Monsieur and his portly wife, who fanned herself from the open carriage, Claire checked over her shoulder to make certain Arturo remained a good distance behind. Satisfied, she began. "Monsieur, I come to pass a message to a man I believe is in your employ, a free man of color named Celestin. Do you know of him?"

"Celestin? But of course," the man said, his puzzled expression intensifying. "What would be your business with the freeman, mademoiselle?"

"It concerns his daughter, monsieur. She is part of my employer, the governor's, retinue. I must speak with him right away. Please show me where I might find him."

Monsieur LeBlanc's smile pushed the folds of his face into rosy mounds. "His daughter, eh? He speaks of her all the time. 'Monsieur LeBlanc,' says he, 'I will make that girl free someday.' And how he works! No rest for Celestin! Every day, sunrise to sunset, he shapes the stone and the quality of his work is beyond compare, mademoiselle."

"He is a mason?" she asked.

"*Mais non*, a sculptor, mademoiselle." He brought two fingers of his gloved hand to his lips and threw the kiss to the sky. "A sculptor beyond compare. He makes the angels appear from rock, true as I am standing here."

"An artist?"

"As fine as any stonemason in France, no matter the color of his skin. The Spaniards and French noblemen, they wish these grand edifices for their tombs and fountains, no? And does not the Order of Saint Ursula desire their grand monuments to God also? I take him to see these statues and he understands."

"Monsieur LeBlanc." Madame LeBlanc's shrill voice sliced the air. "Would you have your family roast here in this heat while you chatter?"

Monsieur blew her a kiss. "One moment, my precious."

Offering Claire his arm, he led her away from the street toward the rear of the house. "I say to him, 'Celestin, my man, the rich, they love your carvings. Let us not tell them it is a former slave who does such wonders in case they will not purchase, eh?' And he agrees—our little secret. In truth, it matters not what I say. The rich, they will not believe a black man does such masterpieces."

Enthralled, Claire took advantage of Monsieur's effusiveness to ask what might be otherwise considered an impertinent question. "But did you release him from slavery, monsieur?"

"I allowed him to buy his release, yes."

"But whatever for? Why not have him do this marvelous work as your slave? Would that not ensure his mastery remains with you?"

The man patted her hand. "Mademoiselle, I'll tell you something you may not understand, something most people do not understand. Celestin is an *artiste*, you see?" He slapped one hand over his heart. "One does not enslave art. Art is a gift from God."

Claire nodded.

"It is given to the world freely, in exchange for some trifle of money or food that enables the artist to eat and live, yet does not compare to the true value of his creation. To free the art, one must first free the man. Slavery, mademoiselle, is an abomination that kills the human spirit and all beauty with it."

"Henri LeBlanc, you get yourself right back to this carriage before I come over there and drag you back!" his wife called out, her shrill voice sending some little dog yelping down the street.

"I come, my sweet pea," Monsieur called out, mopping his forehead with a lace-edged handkerchief. Turning back to Claire, he grinned and shrugged. "Except for love, of course. For love a man is a willing slave always, yes? Proceed through those gates, mademoiselle, and you will find Celestin about his heart's desire—making stone speak. Good day to you, mademoiselle."

When Claire stepped into the yard moments later, pieces of white, gray, and black stone rose in pillars all around her with massive blocks, piles, and shards occupying every visible stretch of space.

Some blocks had human shapes twisting to life from the stone as if struggling for breath. To her right, a man's face seemed to press through a chunk of gray-veined marble. To her left, a collection of bricks carved with intertwining leaves sat stacked one on top of the other, as if waiting to grace a pediment or fancy doorstep.

All she could do was gaze and marvel. Though she had seen stonemasons at work around the convent, they merely chipped bricks or smoothed walls. Now she understood how the images of the Virgin and the other chapel statues had come to be. It amazed her that a human hand could bring forth life from such unyielding matter.

A clink-clink of metal on stone broke the stillness. Claire followed the glinting sound toward the far side of the yard. Picking her way around the great mounds of marble, her feet crunching beneath her, she carried on until she caught sight of an angel's outspread wings.

She stopped, amazed. The being, white and gleaming in the sun, stood with its back toward her, seeming about to lift its sandaled feet and leap for the sky.

She approached with reverence, running one hand along the hem of the smooth stone robe. So beautiful. She gazed upward, straining to see the angel's face.

"Mademoiselle?"

She swung around. A man stood glossed in sweat, a chisel in his hand and his bare chest like polished wood. For a moment, words did not come, so startled was she by the man's near nakedness and his commanding presence. Tall and lean, he stood, with eyes full on her face, not bowed in deference in the manner of most Negroes she had known.

How was she to address a free man of color? "Are you Celestin Picot?"

"I am."

"My name is Mademoiselle Comeau. I—I was just admiring the angel. This is your work?"

"Truly. Faces are my big trouble," he said, pointing to the angel. "I do wings and arms and feet, no problem. For faces I need a person. I need to see eyes, feel spirit, then I bring faces from the stone."

She nodded, understanding. "You need a model."

"Yes, a model. For Gabriel there, I use a Frenchman named Jacques, see? He work here cutting stone but he no angel." He laughed, his white teeth flashing in the sun. He nodded toward the angel's sly smile. "I draw Jacques, then chisel stone, but when I finish, angel look like Jacques—a man who likes wine too much."

Recognizing the indolent play of pleasure about Gabriel's marble lips, Claire laughed with delight. "Oh, he does look as if he enjoys himself. You are a very, very good artist," she told him, warming to the man. "I'm sure this Jacques will be most pleased to be immortalized in stone."

"You make good model also," the man said, as if an idea fired in his eyes. "I do this angel now and her face blank. I need a model. Come, I show you."

Intrigued, she followed after him, her reason for coming forgotten. Soon, she stood by another amazing creature, this one kneeling with one knee on the ground with the other supporting an upraised arm that, as of yet, held only an unformed chunk of marble. The wings, folded behind the angel's back, were so lovely and richly detailed Claire believed the feathers might quiver beneath her stroking fingers.

"Oh, my," she marveled as she circled the angel. "And what do you use to model these wings? Surely not Jacques?"

"No, not Jacques," Celestin acknowledged with a grin. "Birds, mademoiselle. I feed birds and make them my friends."

She nodded, noting for the first time how a little flurry of bird life did seem to be swooping and alighting with unusual abundance about the yard. She returned her attention to the angel, a young woman with breasts discretely mounding beneath the folds of the marble robe.

Her eyes traveled upward until they saw the raw stone where the face should be. The blank marble seemed to hold a spirit struggling to breathe. Claire's hand unconsciously went to her throat.

"A banker, he wants angel for daughter's grave," the sculptor explained. "Girl, she die of fever. No likeness for me to follow, only painting destroyed in fire. Monsieur LeBlanc, he say father want guardian to hold love safe against death and time."

Claire swallowed hard. "A guardian to hold love safe against death and time. Yes, yes." Who would not crave such a one to hold love safe for parents, brothers, lost villages, oneself, against death and time? Everything lost, every face missing, would rest safe with such defense. "You must finish her face soon. It is as if the angel suffocates within the stone."

"Yes, yes! Come, mademoiselle, you help her breathe, please. You sit and I sketch. You be my face."

"Oh, not me!" she exclaimed, swinging toward him. "I am like Jacques —no angel—and this girl, she deserves a proper guardian, no?"

But Celestin had already picked up a board he found lying on the stony ground. "Please. You be model," he begged. "I need model. Hold still. I am very quick, see?"

He rooted about in a rubbish pile until he found a piece of charcoal and deftly began to sketch on the back of the planking. Claire marveled at the speed in which he worked, his hand darting across the rough surface with surety and confidence. Undeniably hers, a face burst into life despite the crude tools.

She turned to the unfinished statue. Gazing at the marble surface, she ached for the being struggling to emerge. How that angel must long to seize its noble calling, to grasp a sword still trapped in stone and brandish it against time itself. In a moment, she fell to one knee, oblivious to the dirt, and held one arm upraised.

"Look," she said, "I warn death: 'Death,' I say, 'nothing you do will ever vanquish me! I am love remembered. I am the love that lives in those we leave behind. Love stands forever on guard. Love does not remember pain. Love remembers only the tenderness between parent and child, the sweet affection between child and grandparent, the deep love between man and woman. Love,'" she cried, tears rolling down her cheeks, "'love is all there is worth defending. Love obeys no master but the heart. Death and oblivion, stay back! Love will survive your darkness!'"

The man had stopped sketching, his eyes fixed on her face. "Amen," he whispered softly.

Claire collapsed into sobs, great racking heaves that she feared would never stop. For a moment, it seemed as if another woman, deep within her heart, cried also, keeping her company in sorrow, the two of them burdened down by remorse and the endless ache of love and loss.

"Mademoiselle," Celestin said, holding out his hand to help her to her feet.

Huddled and rocking herself, she gazed up to him through her streaming tears. "I am such a sinner," she sobbed. "I am a soldier sent to war only to learn I am on the wrong side. I crave an angel's heart and dignity, yet have nothing to offer but something wicked and diseased."

"An angel may be soldier, too, mademoiselle," he said.

She turned to him and their eyes locked, a profound current of understanding passing between them. "Please call me Claire."

"Claire, the difference is the weapon," he said.

She shook her head. "But I have chosen my weapon and can never go back."

Then, in a flash, she pictured herself kneeling in the dust like this and realized with a start how she neglected her mission. "I forget myself." She accepted his hand, got to her feet, dusted off her skirt.

"Maybe it is only now you remember?" Celestin said.

She gazed at him, struggling to grasp the meaning at the edge of his words. "Do you see the ghost of a murdered woman hovering about me?" she asked on impulse.

"No, Claire," he said, his deep voice holding such volume and substance it made her ache to hear it, "but I feel much sorrow and confusion."

"Monsieur—"

"Call me Celestin, Claire. No title fits a man but his name."

"Monsieur Celestin," she said, "your carvings move me so I forget who I am and why I have come." She pulled out her handkerchief, found it too balled and damp to use, so stuffed it back into her pocket.

Wiping her eyes with her sleeve, she continued. "I must tell you something I should have said earlier had I not lost my thought. Your daughter, she sees the ghost that haunts me and it is for her I come to see you."

"Odette?" Celestin said in alarm. "Odette is sick?"

"No, well, yes." In a torrent of words, she described the activities that led to his daughter's beating, ending up with Bernardo's loss of status and his resulting incarceration. She did not mention the murder of Señora Viscaya but sensed he knew all the same. "Odette asked for me to tell you to meet her tonight at Congo Plains but would not say why. She said you had to make a choice."

His expression changed, the glow in his eyes shifting to a fierce burn. A tremor of apprehension shivered through her.

"I have made my choice and well she knows it. She must not do this," he said.

"I am certain you are right, whatever it is she means to do. What is it?"

"My daughter, she practice the old ways, the African ways."

"The voodoo?"

"Yes, the voodoo."

"But you do not? No," she said, answering her own question.

"I follow angels but Odette does not."

"You can stop her, yes? But now I must go. I have spent far too much time away from my task. Good day to you, Monsieur Celestin, and thank you. Perhaps one day I will come by to see your angel, yes?"

He nodded, lost in thought.

Turning her back on him, she hitched her skirts and scrambled from the yard. Only when she reached the gates did she turn back to see Celestin picking up his chisel, the sketch in his hand.

30

Why had she behaved so in the stonemason's yard? She had dropped onto one knee like Monsieur Celestin's stone angel as if overcome by some strange emotion. The incident had almost undone her resolve. She checked the sun's position in the sky. So much time wasted.

"Mademoiselle? Wait up, if you please!"

She glanced over her shoulder to see Arturo approach, reddened from the heat.

"Are you well?" he asked, panting slightly.

"Yes, of course. Why would I not be?"

"Wake up! Come to, Romy," a strange voice commanded. Claire swung around, scanning the dusty street for the source of the voice but saw nothing. Somebody else spoke within her head, a sound both immediate yet far away. Pressing her hands to her head, she doubled over. "Cease this!"

Arturo touched her shoulder. "Mademoiselle? You were gone so long a time inside the yard, I mean, and in the presence of a black man. I grew worried," he said. "If this is an act, it's a damned impressive one," he added.

"Romy, speak English!"

Who were these voices? Claire shook her head, baffled. "Pardon? What is it you say? Do stop tormenting me. Do you not hear those other voices? Why do you say these things?"

She squeezed her eyes shut. The heat, it must be the heat. "Come, we must go. I am late and fear unwell. Besides, your safety is at risk. Haven't I heard people calling out threats to you from the windows and doors?" That must be what she heard, the citizens calling insults to the Spanish soldier. In strange accents. Inside her skull.

"I have heard those insults, yes. It matters not to me. They do not understand," Arturo assured her. "They believe we Spanish mean them harm when our intent is nothing of the kind. Governor Ulloa will convince them in time."

"For God's sake, Romy, come back!" A woman's voice this time so loud its owner could be right by her side.

Claire faltered. How could she make them stop?

Then a man's voice cried out: "Return to Spain, you blue-coated infidel! Spain will never rule here!"

Claire grasped Arturo's arm. "Do you hear that woman? She could be standing right here." But even as she spoke, she saw nothing but signs of the citizens' rancor as they hurled insults from the safety of their homes. "Come, let us go."

Catcalls and threatening whispers dogged their heels all the way down the street but Claire did not worry much for the Spaniard. Had he not his sword and musket? Let him see how the townsfolk felt about Spanish rule. She worried more for the strange voices inside her head and those crying into her ear as if from invisible beings. More ghosts? Was she besieged by demons?

She must think of something good but something not of angels and demons. Longing for the cool respite of the convent walls, she picked up her pace, passing cottages and houses where the scent of cooking stroked her nostrils—spices and garlic, baking bread and simmering sugar.

She hoped the convent cooks had made that sticky candy she and the other girls loved so well—sugar boiled into thick syrup, poured over bread dough, and baked until all had massed into a sweet, gooey chew. Maybe she should try such a recipe on Antonio and lure him away from his endless tomatoes and rice?

Reaching the convent gates, she rapped twice on the gray wooden door and waited for the gateman, Monsieur Loutrin, to let her pass.

"Mademoiselle," he cried, delight beaming in his wrinkled face. "Welcome back. The Holy Mother, she said you would come today, but all the sisters are at prayer."

"Never mind." She smiled at the old man. "I will wait."

The gateman nodded and let her pass, catching sight of the Spanish soldier as he did so. "And what of him, mademoiselle?"

"My escort. He is to remain outside, of course," Claire said, without turning around.

"You, you wait down at the end of the wall," the gatekeeper called out to Arturo. "Out of my sight! No Spaniard is wanted here!"

Claire fought guilt at leaving the poor young man outside to parch. Maybe he'd find a shady spot to sit and she'd even bring him something to eat and drink before the day ended.

Inside the thick white walls, the air felt as cool as the hand of God pressing absolution onto a fevered brow. The fever of sin, Claire thought, but she'd find no absolution here. How could she even beg for forgiveness with all she had done and had yet to do?

She dared not so much as glance at the statues of Jesus in case she saw reproach. She no longer belonged here—or anywhere—but at least the ghost of Señora Viscaya would not dare shadow her inside.

The high clear lilt of singing echoed through the corridors as one hymn ended and another began. Claire made her way to the first-floor receiving room where she had been instructed to meet Mother Superior; the sweet music gilded her way. Like angel song, she thought. Perhaps every soul yearned to become an angel as it teetered on the verge of either heaven or hell. Had she any doubt which direction she would head?

The receiving room lay close to the sacristy and chapel but apart from the living quarters, thus removing her from opportunity to speak privately with her former convent mates. She had been sullied, made unfit for the company of young ladies, and so Mother Superior had forbidden her to make contact.

She did not squander much emotion on her former companions, in any case, for she had made few friends. Most had been spoiled rich girls fallen down on their fortunes who held her in contempt—a mere peasant girl only slightly above the status of slave. Her time spent in the kitchens learning housekeeping had not dispelled this notion any more than her eagerness to read books no lady should touch.

It suddenly struck her that she would never be permitted to rejoin convent life. How could they let her mingle with the others now? Perhaps an agreement had been forged between Madame Letourneau and Mother Superior, a pact based on the idea that, once one behaves as a whore, it must follow that one becomes such. She'd accept her fate. Life had been nothing but trauma and loss, proof that she did not deserve otherwise.

Claire proceeded to the meeting room unseen. She had been there a few times previously, usually to clean the silver and dust the tables. On coming to the convent, it had been her first experience with tangible wealth and she had lingered there, spending treasured moments stunned by the luxuries the Order of Saint Ursula had appointed for God's glory.

The room had been designed to accommodate outside guests and, as such, had an exterior door as well as the one leading from the corridor.

Easing open the interior entrance, she slipped inside the large whitewashed space with its reliquaries, crucifixes, and woven hangings. The velvet and gilded richness had once held her wonder. Even now, familiar as she had become with the room's painted ceiling of the Madonna limned in gold and backed by a deep cerulean blue, the urge to stand in awe almost overcame her.

Until she caught sight of a lone woman standing in the far corner, a woman whose very presence leeched piety from the air.

"There you are, *chérie*!" Madame Letourneau said, her voluminous black silk gown rustling like ravens' wings as she walked toward Claire. "Mother Marie has not yet come but we wait together, yes?"

"Will Monsieur Campeneau and the others not join us?"

"Later, perhaps. They must not flaunt their relationship so openly, no? Bad enough a woman like me comes here in daylight. But, of course—" her lovely smile glowed with deceptive sweetness "—in my case, Mother Marie pretends to convert me to the true church, our little ruse. I go to mass and bow my head and look oh-so-contrite for my wicked, wicked ways." Her laughter trilled out across the painted chamber. "But we know how this life has its rewards."

"We do?" Claire asked.

"Do we not?" Madame stopped within inches of Claire, her eyes flickering. Taking Claire's chin in one gloved hand, she studied her face, turning it first in one direction, then the other. "So, our governor has moved you with his skills in lovemaking, yes? For all your impertinence and brave words, you allow lust to woo your heart. Don't deny it. I can see it in your face, the flush of passion. Be careful, *ma chérie*. Love turns women into fools and strips us of the only tools we possess."

Claire stepped back, jerking her face free. "I have seduced him as required but, in so doing, find he is no monster."

"How little you know, *ma petite*," the older woman tsk-tsked, her painted beauty mark twitching above her lip. "We do not condemn Monsieur Governor because he is a bad man, we condemn him because he is a Spaniard in a land that desires to remain French. He could be a saint and it would make no difference. Enjoy his bed, *chérie*, but do not forget why you are there."

Claire took another step back. "I did not think this would be so painful. I thought revenge would cause me to feel strong but it does not."

"You are wallowing in desire, that is what plagues you. Allow it to penetrate your body but never your heart. Love makes women weak. Have you learned nothing from me?"

Claire choked back a laugh. "I have learned much from you, Madame. I have learned that a woman should wield her body like a weapon and freeze her heart until it is dead."

"No more than a fortnight from Mother Marie and myself and already you think yourself wise."

At that moment, the door clicked open and Mother Superior entered the room, nodding to Madame. "Hello, Claire, my child. I trust you are well?" Her tone seemed weary and worry-born.

But Madame did not wait for Claire's reply. "You can see she is well enough, Mother, and well-pleasured by Spanish treats."

Mother Superior's usually calm demeanor cracked. "Cease such talk. Remember you stand in a house of God." She turned to search Claire's face with her bright blue eyes. "So, my child, how do you fare?"

"I do not know, Mother, for I am so confused."

"What information have you brought us?" Madame interrupted. "I have promised to pass our friends something this very night for the city stirs against the Spanish."

Claire lowered her eyes. "Nothing."

"Nothing?" Madame swept up to her, standing only steps away from Claire, one hand flicking a silk fan. "What do you mean, 'nothing'? Have you not been with the governor for many days with time enough to find something of interest? I have educated you in how to loosen a man's lips and trained you over these last months for just such a task. Have we been mistaken in trusting this mission to you?"

Claire sighed. "No."

"We need something now," she insisted. "My customers, they speak of how their fortunes wane because this Spaniard dares block our trade. Your good sisters starve and must sell their silver. Still, our people hesitate to support a rebellion but they will not wait while these Spanish bring us to ruin! We must have something that will prove Ulloa's devious intent. Now, we ask you again, what have you found?"

"Nothing," Claire repeated, stepping back another step, the torn page in her sleeve seeming to burn her skin. "Only he does not seem the bloodthirsty scoundrel I expected. He seems just and concerned for the well-being of the people."

"Phaw! You are so easily fooled by a fine manner or is it how he makes love to you that dissuades? Sorry, Mother," she quickly added. "Have you forgotten he is our enemy?"

"When I asked you to take on this task," Mother Marie said, stepping between Claire and Madame, "I did so with a heavy heart. I saw how your soul burned with anger, an anger that I could not help ease or you would not permit God to cleanse. I had hoped you would yet serve Him in other ways."

"By stealing information, lying, and betraying?" Claire cried. *By murder?* the voice in her head screamed.

"By sacrificing yourself for the sisters of the Ursulines and the girls I keep safe within these walls, child. We all sacrifice for others. That is the burden we carry in His name. If I can provide Monsieur Campeneau and others some scrap of valuable information through you, the convent will be his beneficiary. That is how you are to serve God."

Claire chewed her lip as the voice in her head whispered: *Hold fast to your beliefs, Claire. Think what she's really saying: that you're worth less than the other girls. Why? Because you're poor? Acadian? What?*

The voice had grown so loud she was amazed Madame and Mother Superior couldn't hear yet it and yet it was this strange sense of otherness that caused her to falter. She tapped the side of her head with one hand as if to dislodge the intruder.

"What are you doing?" Madame asked, annoyed. "Pay attention."

Claire continued to hold her skull. "My head...hurts."

"We need this money, Claire," Mother Marie said, her voice soft. "Without Campeneau's support, we will surely starve. The king has forsaken us and the Spaniards hardly acknowledge we exist. A French ship has not entered this port for weeks. The governor forbids it. Without tithes, we suffer. Would you have the convent and all its charges starve?"

Claire swallowed and shook her head, letting her hands fall to her sides.

"Good. Remember, only you can help us. We need something, anything, for Campeneau to incite a rebellion and secure his support. I do not believe you tell the truth when you say you have found nothing," Mother Superior added. "I see much conflict in your face, child."

"And yet I have become such a good liar," Claire moaned, "but it is true, Mother. I have found nothing incriminating, just odd drawings that make no sense."

"What drawings? Let us see." Madame Letourneau held out her ringed hand, the lace foaming around her sleeve.

Don't show them. Keep the drawing safe, her inner voice told her.

Claire fingered the page through her sleeve. "They are not important."

"Show me."

Don't!

But Claire reluctantly pulled out the folded paper and passed it over.

Mother Marie studied the page for a few moments with Madame gazing over her shoulder. "What matter of thing is this?" she asked.

"Very strange indeed," Madame remarked as Mother Superior turned the page this way and that.

"I thought it something to do with war, at first," Claire said, trembling, "but now I think it speaks of light and circles and the moon. The governor is a very clever man who studies all manner of things, like the sun and stars."

"War," Madame Letourneau said with a nod. "What else can it be? The Spanish king plans some hideous fate for the French colonists. This must be how he plans to block further trade from France and keep our people in check, with this...thing."

"No, I don't believe so. I think—" Claire began.

"Think? You have not been instructed to think, only to listen and report," Madame said. "Campeneau will decide the import of this, is that not so, Mother Superior?"

Mother nodded but seemed deeply troubled. "Certainly. Let us hope he finds this drawing useful. Now, Madame Letourneau, please take it and be on your way. I must speak to Claire in private."

Claire broke down, her body quaking with sobs.

Madame Letourneau curtsied. "As you wish, Mother Marie." She tucked the page into her sleeve.

On her way past Claire, she paused. "*Ma chérie*, do not cry so, for it does make a woman less becoming in certain circumstances. When all this is done and the governor dispatched, I shall see you at my establishment where your charms will better serve Frenchmen." With that, she flicked her fan closed and swept from the room, the door clicking behind her.

Mother Marie gathered Claire in her arms. "I am so sorry, my child. Forgive me for using you so but know that you have been a good soldier and will be rewarded in heaven."

"No, I will not," Claire cried, inconsolable in her grief, her face pressed against the nun's scratchy white cowl. "How...can I be rewarded for treachery, lying, whoring, deceiving and...murder?"

"Murder?" Mother Marie gripped her by the shoulders and held her at arm's length. "What is this you say?"

"I pushed the old housekeeper down the stairs when she caught me stealing the page. Had I not done so she would have called the alarm and all would be lost."

"Oh, dear God, what have I done?" Mother Marie crossed herself while murmuring a quick and fervent prayer. "Claire," she said, tears welling in her own eyes. "Many die in war, far too many of them innocent. Soldiers kill. It is the way of war, though I confess I had not thought you to be quite such a one. Still, it is done. Now you must confess and ask to be forgiven your sins."

Just then, a young novice knocked on the door and entered, dropping a quick curtsy to Mother Superior. "Mother, forgive me but Sister Claudette bid me give you this." The girl passed Mother Marie a letter, curtsied again, and left.

Mother broke the wax seal and read the letter, Claire watching the woman's eyes dart back and forth. "The council has voted to oust Governor Ulloa. The insurrection has begun. You must stay within the safety of the convent, child. I will order the gates closed as the streets will soon turn dangerous. Wait here where's it is safe and pray for your sins."

Claire watched as Mother Superior left the room. Alone and torn by misery, she paced the floor and cried for too long afterward while inside another tried to possess her body and soul.

"Leave me be!" she cried aloud, but her inner self seemed to be in torment also and neither could help the other.

An hour, maybe two, passed, with every inch of her being aching as she circled the room again and again. She felt trapped inside a cage of her own making, hemmed in by remorse and fear. She hardly felt the passing time.

What had she done? What had she become? She had murdered an old woman for no other reason than she had got in her way. Equally damming, she had betrayed a good man, a man she loved, and maybe all for nothing if, in truth, the insurrection had begun without her help. And then a sudden pain shot through her temples. She pressed her eyes closed, hands on either side of her head.

Romy, come back! a voice demanded.

A STRANGE BLACK WOMAN WAS ATTEMPTING TO SHAKE CLAIRE AWAKE. "Romy? Can you hear me? You must return now! I know what will happen next and you can't remain with Claire." The woman spoke a strange language, not quite English but similar.

"Who are you?" Claire struggled to free herself but the woman held her fast. Had the slaves revolted, too?

The woman gripped her shoulders tighter. "Oh my God, it's Claire. Adrian, Joquita, it's Claire."

"It can't be," a man said in that same tongue, English but not English.

He stepped within Claire's line of vision as her eyes began to focus. Tall, very tall, with such short hair and plain clothes—no breeches, no boots, nothing, just long tight pants in some rough blue hopsacking and a black shirt completely without lace or jabot—a pauper, then. But, oh my, he was a very good-looking pauper, despite the oddities.

My God, she must be dreaming. For one instant she thought she saw Antonio.

And then the man spoke French in a manner she could understand. "Please state your name and the year."

"My name is Claire Comeau and of course it is the year of our Lord 1768, is it not? Who are you and why do you dress in such a fashion?"

But before he could answer, a lean black woman poked her face in hers speaking more gibberish. "Romy, are you in there? Come back this minute. You're freaking me out!"

"Romy? I do not understand you. Wait, is that Odette? What is a Romy? Where am I? Is this a dream?" Claire looked around at a place that didn't exist, couldn't exist. A garden, perhaps, lit by candles and glowing orbs. Other people stood about in odd clothes looking at once concerned and bemused. Turning back to the girl, she said, "I know you, no?"

"Yeah, you know me but I know Romy better. You share the soul of my friend and I want her back."

And the man translated in a language Claire could understand, adding, "Joquita, this isn't helping. Step back, please. Louisa?"

And the large black woman returned to touch Claire with gentle hands. "My child, this is very hard for you to understand, I know, but please try. That voice inside your head is real. She's your soul remembering your life over two centuries into the future. Her name is Romy. Try to let her go. Try to find your way to the light."

"Let her go? Find the light? There is no light for me!" Claire tried to back away but the woman held her fast. "You must be demons all. I am punished for my sins and hell is here on earth."

"You must not think that. Such thoughts will drag you under and keep you chained and Romy, too. We are not demons nor angels and you are no better or no worse than most of God's children. We are all souls striving for the light and all humans stumbling along the way," the woman said while the handsome man translated her words. "Forgive all who have harmed you but forgive yourself first."

"No!" She pushed herself away. They would drive her mad. She had frozen her heart in the name of duty and for what? She had allowed herself to be driven by others' ambitions, been used to fuel the very violence she so hated. What difference did it make if the Spanish ruled the French? Were the French so superior? Black, white, French, Spanish—maybe even English—all the same! She cursed her blindness, her wickedness.

Around her, the mysterious garden began to fade and in its place the convent reemerged. Every painting, statue, and reliquary leaned forward in silent reproach. Even the walls washed baleful shadows as, minute by minute, daylight bled from the room. No one came to light the candles so she remained in the dark.

She paused, trembling. Voices could be heard just beyond the walls. Slipping across the room, she pressed her ear to the exterior door, an area that led to an alcove at the rear of the building. Men's voices rose, very agitated. She recognized that of d'Entremont and a few others.

"It happens! The citizen's revolt! Unrest is everywhere," one man said. "The council ruled and it is done. Tonight will be the night we move. No more waiting."

"We have added fuel. The governor has devised a plan for a war machine to further block our trade," Claire heard Madame Letourneau add. "Surely such a thing would help to convince the last holdouts?"

"You have it there, yes? Let us see it, then." That from Jean d'Entremont.

A brief silence followed. "This looks like no war machine I have seen," one man remarked.

"And how many wars have you fought, monsieur?" Madame challenged. "Are you not but a farmer, after all? Ulloa, he is a general who invents more deadly ways to ensure our subjugation."

"I do not understand. It is but a sketch."

"It is a drawing proving his intent, even though it is too advanced for us to understand," Madame continued. "Claire has overheard him describing the huge firing implement he plans to hurl at French ships and all boats not authorized by Spain. Explain its meaning to the others."

"No war machine," Jean d'Entremont insisted. "More like big plan of evil. I see it there—Satan in the sky! The governor, he means to kill us in our beds!"

Claire almost choked. She slapped both hands over her mouth to stifle her rage. Fools! And she allowed herself to be misled by these people, the devious and the ignorant?

She could not stand it a moment longer. She would find Antonio and warn him, tell him of her hideous mistakes, and throw herself on his mercy. If he should hang her, it was all she deserved, but at least she would spend the last hours of her waking life trying to undo the wrong she had done.

By the time she made her way to the room's vestibule and slipped along the corridors to the convent's main entrance, darkness had thickened the shadows below a dying sunset.

Another gatekeeper stood watch, a younger man she did not know, who doffed his cap to her as she went past. "Beware, mademoiselle," he warned. "There is violence in the streets tonight."

She nodded, slipping from the convent's enclosure through the gate and glancing in all directions. "Corporal Arturo?" she called out. Half expecting him to scramble out from somewhere puppy-like, it puzzled her when he did not reply.

She took a few tentative steps forward, reluctant to leave the relative safety of the convent alone. "Corporal Arturo? I am ready. We must proceed home at once. I must find the governor."

No response, though she heard the sound of shouting from the streets closest to the river. Usually the town remained still this time of night, caught in dusk's deepening hush. A flush of unrest seemed to enflame the air.

Perhaps the soldier had found himself a shady spot and dozed the day away? Shoving her hands deep into her pockets, she headed down the length of the convent's exterior wall looking this way and that, and continued calling. He must be around the corner. Yet, when she reached the corner and looked, no Arturo.

Claire stood uncertain of what to do next. She had not expected to be so late leaving the convent and, though the way home was not long—perhaps a half of a mile at most—she needed an escort after dark, especially if the streets were full of angry citizens.

Then, just on the edge of her senses, she heard a tap-tap on the path behind her. Slowly she turned, peering into the gathering shadows of early evening. Even as the thought crossed her mind that she must be imagining it, the sound grew more distinct, increasing in volume and heading toward her with a steady and relentless tap-tap-whack.

Her blood froze in her veins. She turned and bolted headlong down the street.

31

Claire ran without thinking, driven to get as far away from that hideous tapping as possible, hoping to bury the sound under the noise of her own footfall.

She hurled herself in the direction of the governor's house as the streets around her had exploded into activity. People shouted while others called from the windows and the bitter scent of burning wood permeated the air.

She heard the cries: "Kill the Spanish!" "Long Live France!" and "To hell with France and Spain!" from all directions as the town's citizens swarmed the streets. Thoughts of her ghostly pursuer vanished in the flesh-and-blood reality of revolt.

As she stumbled on, she saw people throwing rocks at Spanish homes and two men attempting to batter down a door with a tree trunk. Four men dragged an old Spanish gentleman from his carriage and carried him away screaming for mercy while an angry mob surged in behind them. They headed toward the river, waving bottles of wine while torching every Spanish-owned cottage or carriage along the way.

Claire leaned against a wall, pressing her handkerchief to her mouth. How bitter the taste of smoke and desperation. They clawed the throat and gouged the heart. Though the British destroyed her village in a more methodical way, the results had been no less horrific.

She heard a child crying, "Mama, Mama," a child who could have been herself long ago had the words not been in Spanish instead of French. Her heart broke again. Another innocent victim. They were all innocent victims, the French and the Spanish. She hated herself for having anything to do with this travesty, no matter that it would have occurred without her help.

Where was Antonio in all this? Would his soldiers keep him safe? She had to find him.

"Come on, *chérie*, come with us!"

Claire turned to stare straight into the reddened face of Susanna LeForte, a prostitute at Madame Letourneau's establishment. The woman's companions, four men and a girl Claire did not recognize, beckoned her into their company.

"No, no," Claire said, shaking her head. A swelling crowd swept past.

"Come!" the woman cried, grabbing Claire by the hand. "We are going to hang the governor!"

"No, you cannot!" Claire cried.

"Why not?" one of the men asked, pressing his filthy face closer to hers as if trying to suck every secret from her soul. His eyes flickered with a murderous intent.

"Because he goes missing," Claire said quickly. "No one can find him."

"Well, we will hunt down the bastard, no?" Susanna laughed, pulling the man back from Claire by his shirt. "Come, join the fun. At last we will have our revenge."

Despite Claire's protests, she was swept into the throng, her hand released only long enough for Susanna and one of the men to pin her between two of them, arm in arm, until Claire was hurled forward, helpless to slow her progress.

"Wait!" Claire cried. "Stop this!" But no one listened.

Ahead, a mob threw stones at something or someone caught in its midst. Claire glimpsed the flash of blue-and-white Spanish uniforms between the crowd's shifting force. One of Susanna's companions cried out: "Louis, what have you there?"

One man turned a smoke-blackened face in their direction while displaying a fist-sized rock in his hand. "We've got ourselves a pair of Spanish dogs, Yves," he said with a feral grin. "We stone the curs to death! No sword can beat the likes of this, eh?" The man returned to his task, bringing his arm back to hurl the rock at the target as he did so.

The vicious knot of citizens parted long enough to reveal two bleeding soldiers standing back to back, each with their swords drawn in a desperate attempt to stave off their attackers.

Claire recognized the man who often guarded the governor's compound, shocked at the sight of the oozing dark wound on his skull, at the way one arm hung useless at his side. He looked so young, so desperate.

A stone hit the soldier just above his right eye, a blow that dropped him to one knee. As the mob surged forward, cheering and calling for death, their bodies shrouded the men's final moments from view.

"Come!" cried Susanna. "We find ourselves a bigger quarry!"

Claire's captors pushed forward toward the river while she stumbled among them, sickened and appalled. She prayed to God she could escape this vicious clutch to find Antonio before the crowd caught him. For all she knew, it might already be too late.

A man ran against the throng calling out: "Look ahead, the Spanish are with muskets! Get out of the line of fire!"

A blast exploded from somewhere close at hand. As a river breeze blew wisps of smoke away, seven soldiers could be seen advancing in a horizontal line down the street, muskets firing into the crowd and peppering the streets with flays of lead.

Her captors scurried for cover, leaving Claire free to run toward the soldiers, crying out and waving her arms: "Hold your fire! It is me, Claire Comeau, the governor's housekeeper! I am not the enemy!"

Why did she say such a thing? Of course she was the enemy, had been from the very moment she stepped foot in Antonio's house, whether they knew it or not. A musket shot pinged against a rock at her feet and she stood trembling, recognizing the steely resolve in the soldiers' faces.

Turning, she sprinted for the bushes fringing the street and plowed through the thicket. She did not see the body sprawled on the ground until she tripped over it and fell to her knees. She barely had time to feel for a heartbeat on the fallen woman when a voice said nearby: "Do not waste your time, señorita, for she will not breathe again."

Claire peered through the smoky murk at a crouching soldier busy pouring gunpowder from a leather bag into his musket's gullet. "You killed her?"

"*Sí*, it was either her or me," the soldier said without looking at her. "She tried to whack me with a bottle. Should you should try that, too, I will be forced to do the same to you, señorita."

"I am unarmed and no enemy of the Spanish. Do you not recognize me? I am Señorita Comeau, the governor's housekeeper. I know you from the governor's guard under Comandante Angelo." She crouched on her hands and knees toward him. "I've been at the convent all day and, when I left, found myself swept up in this revolt. Where is the governor? Is he safe?"

The soldier glanced at her before returning his attention to his weapon. "*Sí*, I recognize you, señorita. I recognize also that you speak Spanish very well. Why had I not noticed this before?"

She hadn't realized she'd been speaking in Spanish. "I—I have learned much of the language while in the governor's services," she stammered. "It has always been easy for me to learn new tongues. I am on the Spanish side, I swear. Where is governor? Is he safe?"

"I know not." The soldier poked the tip of his musket through the brambles. "He left with three other men directly following the funeral services today and we have not seen him since. His brother, Señor Juan, said he was about one of his scientific investigations. Myself and the others have responded to the revolt under Comandante Angelo's direction while Señor Juan de Ulloa hastened the Spanish staff to our ship upriver where it will wait until the governor is located."

So, Antonio might still be safe. "You will not leave without him, no?"

"A handful of guards await the governor's return at the house. We will make for the ship the moment he is found. Too few of us to hold out against this rabble for long. As for you, señorita, I suggest you not remind the citizens that you have been in service with the Spanish. Tonight is a night when it is far safer to be French."

He had positioned himself to guard the backs of the advancing soldiers. Others would be hidden elsewhere along the street.

"They are stoning two soldiers farther up toward the market. I pray to God you can save them but I fear it is already too late."

229

With that, she hitched up her skirts and leapt to her feet, plunging through the bushes, still on course for the governor's house. Where else could she go? Perhaps Antonio would make his way there or the house staff would know his whereabouts, though she doubted that. The governor never felt obliged to inform his servants of his plans.

The streets farther from the river were quieter, less snarled by rabid townsfolk hunting for blood. Over her shoulder, she saw the sky suffused with smoky orange as if the heavens themselves smoldered. Half the town burned. Fools. Did they think fire destroyed only Spanish buildings and would spare French cottages nearby?

Though she could hear the tapping far behind her, Claire barely paid it any mind. Her thoughts remained centered on the living, on Antonio, on what she had done or tried to do, on the destruction raging through the streets. The ghost of Señora Viscaya seemed a nuisance in the face of all that. Let her do her worst. After she'd found Antonio and made her confession, what difference would it make?

The voice inside her head tortured her more. That endless pleading and demanding. She tried desperately to shut it all out.

She avoided the main streets; taking to the side paths though the dark made the going difficult. Some townsfolk barricaded themselves inside their cottages, keeping their lanterns unlit and refusing to partake in the revolt.

Several times she tripped over empty ale kegs, perhaps looted from Spanish owners, and once fell over a drunk passed out in the lane. He grunted and she stared, peering down at the face in the shadows as she passed. A slave? Had the slaves abandoned the houses once the revolt erupted? No time to think of that now. She had reached the governor's street.

Ahead, the governor's property appeared like an inky mass against the evening sky. She slowed her pace before stepping closer. No torches or lanterns burned along the fence and the building itself hunched over the street like a giant huddled against the night. At first she hoped the staff and guards, like other citizens, had barricaded themselves behind the doors but the sight of the gates ripped from their hinges doused that thought.

She swallowed hard. Where were the soldiers left behind? She thought of calling out Antonio's name but something stopped her. Inside her head, she felt a fear that was both hers and not her own, as if both she and her newly strident conscience trembled together. She took another step forward, desperately wanting to run in the opposite direction.

Had Antonio been slaughtered inside his residence? Would she find his body stoned to death, her beloved bleeding but still alive? She could not bear the thought. She would nurse him; she would stay by his side forever.

Heart in her throat, she resolved to go through those gates with courage. Seeing a broken lantern on its side with a half-burned candle still flickering within, she took it in hand, righted the candle, and carried it high as she passed into the courtyard.

The bodies of three soldiers lay sprawled just inside the gates. Steadying herself, she glanced down at their corpses, noting how at least one had been bludgeoned to death by the pulp of tissue and blood smearing the dust.

Fighting the urge to be sick, she realized the deaths had been recent— no more than an hour or two judging by the freshness of the blood. Massacre, she thought. The mob must have burst in and slaughtered the guards. Had they found Antonio, too?

Nothing moved inside the courtyard besides a mewing cat that quickly skittered away. The only thing she heard besides the faraway roar of musket fire and shouting was the ghostly tapping at her heels. The cane followed her deeper into the courtyard and, when she stopped, it stopped, too.

Claire swung around, holding out the lantern toward her stalker. As she expected, the yard lay empty to the eye despite the distinct enveloping chill that had begun to crawl toward her.

"I don't care that you follow me," she said aloud. "I don't care if you follow me for all the days of my life right into my grave and beyond because nothing you do to me can match what I've done to myself."

Turning her back on the ghost, she carried on and ran into the house calling out for Antonio. The interior, like the yard, stood deathly silent as she traveled from room to room searching for life. Everywhere she met signs of looting—chairs upended, drawers hanging open, and silver pieces gone but, thankfully, no more bodies.

The door to Antonio's room hung half-torn from its hinges. Inside, piles of books and papers smoldered as if someone had attempted to set fire to them but the documents had no will to burn. She stood for a moment, hand over her mouth, staring. Every memory they'd shared together seared her heart. *Antonio, where are you?*

Where else could she look? And then she remembered Odette and the girl's claim to magic. Perhaps the slave girl could locate Antonio through other means, perhaps help free him in some impossible way? An uncanny miracle might be the only thing that would work and Claire was desperate enough to try anything.

But Odette said she would be going to the Congo Plains that night. With a rebellion waging all about, would she have thought better of that plan? If not, maybe one of the others would know the direction to head. Surely not every slave abandoned the premises when the mob crashed down the gates? They, at least, would be in no danger from the French.

As she turned and headed for the slave quarters, her footsteps sounding too loud against the silence of the house, she noticed for the first time that the tapping had stopped. Not a good sign. She knew the old woman's spirit followed her still. The strange cold thickened the air, weighing down the shadows and causing her neck hairs to stiffen. It was as if the spirit knew something she did not, something horrid.

A foolish thought.

As she crossed the courtyard heading toward the slave quarters, she tried to calm herself. A ghost couldn't do more than torment the living, surely?

She fixed her mind on unimportant details in an effort to distract herself. The chickens had gone. The marauders had stolen the governor's chickens! And look, they had looted the bakery and granary and probably taken all of Antonio's fine wine, besides. He so loved his wine, shipping it in by crate loads from Spain to savor over his meals.

And to think she had meant to cook him something delicious and very French yet had never had the opportunity. There would be no more opportunities now. Those precious moments had been shattered forever.

The tapping resumed but in a different manner. Instead of the sound of an old woman making her way across the ground by cane, this seemed more like a harsh punishing whack on the earth accompanied by heavy footsteps marching along beside.

Claire's steps faltered, though she carried on, determined to ignore the torment. Halfway to the slave quarters, she stopped, aghast. Ahead to her right, the door to the stocks hung open. Open. The prisoners were gone!

With her stomach seizing and a scream building in her throat, she turned slowly around. There, at her back, stood a man, a man she recognized immediately without seeing his face.

Bernardo.

32

"**D**id you think you would escape me, French bitch?"

"I—we must find the governor," she pleaded, hating the sound of her desperation. "The French will slay him if he is caught unawares. No one knows where he has gone. Help me find him and I swear you can do anything to me afterward."

Her words trailed away. He had begun to laugh, a noise as foul as the unearthly whack that moved around them as if the man's ghost mother cordoned off an invisible cage.

"Do you think I care?" he said, stepping into the light. "Let Antonio de Ulloa fry. Let him roast in hell until his very heart is seared from his chest. I would help do the deed myself, had I the chance, but you, bitch, I will enjoy killing more. The governor I leave to the French."

As Claire took a step backward, a cold object prodded her spine. The cane, she didn't have to see it to know. Shivers flooded her body as if the old crow's stick poured icy water straight into her veins.

She tried to step away only to have the ghostly wood deliver a vicious crack straight across her wrist. Snatching her hand back, she stared into the shadows, searching for a way to escape but seeing none.

"Stop this!" she cried, trying to ward the cane away with hands too numb to function. Flinging the lantern toward the spirit did nothing but douse her only light.

The lantern fell to the ground and shattered, leaving the candle sputtering in the dark. "If you must kill me, then for God's sake just do it!"

Bernardo laughed. "What enjoyment would that bring? My mother wants her revenge. It is her due after all you have done to her, but enough. Mama, now it is my turn. You can have her beyond the grave where she will soon join you."

And he lunged forward, snaring Claire's wrists in his hands and shoving her to the ground. She fell hard on her back, the breath going out of her body as Bernardo threw his weight on top of her. All she could do was lay winded, her legs too numb to feel the blows still raining down from the old crow's cane.

"As much as I would enjoy taking you now, wench, I will be content to only kill you. Some things a man can't do in front of his mother." He laughed as his hands wrapped around her throat. "I will squeeze, Mother will beat. Together we will make you pay for what you have done."

The hands circling her throat tightened. Red spots flared before her eyes. Her lungs fought for air; her throat burned as he squeezed and squeezed and, all the while, the ugly whack-whack hurled down on her outstretched limbs.

And then another voice sounded overhead—a death angel, perhaps, something coming to ferry her to hell. She could barely make out the creature's words as she sunk deeper and deeper into the darkness. She heard Bernardo grunt, felt his limp weight collapse on top of her, and a sticky warmth seep onto her skin.

"Go, you wicked, wicked thing!" a man cried out—familiar but Claire's befuddled mind couldn't identify its owner. "Your son is gone and now so must you! Be gone, I say! Go back to whatever hell spawned you! There is nothing left for you here!"

An unearthly shriek followed a hiss and then the battering cane disappeared along with its hideous chill. Claire lay gasping for breath as Bernardo's body was heaved to one side, leaving her blinking up at a lantern held over her face.

"Señorita? Señorita."

Someone cradled her head. Claire coughed and wheezed as she forced breath back into starving lungs.

"Señorita, are you harmed? Forgive me for leaving you at the convent, but when I spied revolt brewing in the streets, I had to warn the others. I thought for certain you would never leave the convent's safety."

Some sweet-tasting liquid dribbled down her throat. She coughed and forced down more mouthfuls. The burning sensation proved at least she still lived, whether she deserved to or not.

"Brandy," he said.

She nodded. Understanding seeped into her brain. "Arturo, thank... you," she gasped.

"Try not to speak. I fear he bruised your throat."

Claire shot a look at Bernardo's body. "Dead?"

"Completely, and should his mother find some way to haunt you along with that useless oaf, I will curse them both to eternal damnation. Can you stand?"

He helped her onto feet that felt as though a thousand pins pricked her soles. "So cold," she mumbled, reaching for her legs. Her limbs ached. "She...froze...me."

"The witch is gone now."

Claire gazed into the young man's face, seeing his bruised and bloody cheek and understanding that he, too, fought many trials since they last saw one another. "I am sorry...for leaving you...in the sun."

Arturo shook his head and smiled a grim smile. "The sun, señorita? What is a little sun to a soldier? Can you stand by yourself for a moment?"

She nodded as he left her leaning against the wall and retrieved the knife from Bernardo's back. He wiped the thing on his breeches, returning the weapon to his belt in one swift movement. "My orders were to guard you. I care not for my own comfort. I regret only that I left my post to warn the others before I could escort you to safety. By the time I reached the house, the damage was done. Later, I located the comandante, who ordered me to return here to await the governor's return. I have been hiding in the slave area ever since."

"Are the slaves gone, too?" Claire managed to ask, her voice more rasp.

"Yes. The place was deserted until Bernardo appeared."

"The French seek the governor," she told him. "They will kill him."

"Thank the good Lord they have not found him yet. I was told the governor has gone off to observe some secret rite, though of what nature I know not. No one knows where he has gone."

"Secret rite?" Claire's hand reached for her throat.

"The governor is a man who is fascinated by how people behave—"

"Yes, yes, I know that. What else have you heard?"

"The comandante learned that he went off alone to observe something of the like earlier this evening but had no idea where. At first he was to take a few men with him but changed his mind."

"I know where he's gone!" she said excitedly. "I know!"

"You do?" Arturo asked.

"Come with me." She had only to take one step for her legs to buckle beneath her.

33

The Congo Plains burned that night, not with fire, though cook fires enough blazed in the dark, but with a strange ferocious energy. Claire could sense it the moment she and Arturo pushed their way through the thicket into the clearing. Smoke and fire, angry crowds, and, far in the distance, the sound of frenzied drums.

"Be still, señorita," Arturo warned. "What is this?"

"Over there in the distance must be the voodoo," she whispered. "The old magic from Africa. Very powerful. Wild magic. Odette is yonder and... maybe her father, Celestin, too. The governor would have—" she heaved air into her bruised throat "—interest in such a ritual."

But how could they find him amid so much smoke and frenzy? He would surely hide to better observe but where?

She could see the slave dancers in the far distance moving around their fires while, near at hand, others gathered—Frenchmen, she realized by the voices. She peered into the smoky darkness, trying to make out shapes and faces until a gust of wind blew away enough smoke to bring clarity to the scene. She gasped. "Look, Arturo! Over there."

No more than fifty feet away, a crowd clustered in a rough circle between two large oaks. High on an overhanging branch silhouetted against the rising moon, a body slowly twisted in the breeze.

Fear clutched her. Antonio? But no, Claire realized with relief, the corpse's blue uniform pinned him as a Spanish soldier.

Angry citizens shouted, "Hang him! Hang him!" in French while waving bottles and staves about. An unseen man called for silence— Campeneau. Claire knew his voice immediately. Panic struck again.

"Hide, señorita! You must not be seen."

Shaking her arm free, Claire stumbled forward. When she heard Antonio's voice cracked and gruff, trying to pitch above the rabble, she nearly fell to her knees. They held him captive in that tight, vicious knot. Their bloodlust would see him hang.

"No! Let him go! He is innocent!" Pushing through the crowd, she struggled through to the center where the ragged knot of conspirators held a man bound hand and foot, propped up on either side by a man who wrenched his body to make him wince.

At first she didn't recognize him, this bloodied man trying to retain dignity among brutes. A wicked gash lashed his face from forehead to cheek, leaving one eye swollen shut. Blood seeped through his linen shirt as though he had been sliced through the shoulder, yet the face that turned toward her could only be Antonio's.

Claire slapped her hand over her mouth. Antonio's one good eye fixed on her an expression that did not yet hold the contempt she deserved. "Claire? My God, Claire?" he rasped. "Why are you here? Save yourself, for God knows this mob knows no reason."

"Release him!" she rasped, spinning around to Campeneau and then, spying d'Entremont, added, "He is innocent. You all know this to be true. You are drunk! Do not do this thing. Do not carry the weight of the governor's murder on your hands."

The rabble muttered in angry dissent. Someone threw a rock, hitting her painfully on the leg. Another cried out: "Is this wench French or Spanish?"

"Wait!" Campeneau held up his hand. "What is this you are about, Claire Comeau?" He held up the journal page for all to see. "Here is proof that Governor Ulloa means us harm, a drawing of a cruel contraption designed to sink French ships at our very port! Mademoiselle Comeau stole it from the governor's journal to prove his guilt to all."

All eyes turned to Claire but only Antonio's mattered. "Claire," he whispered. "This cannot be true. Are you a spy, is that it? Speak, why don't you? I trusted you!"

"I thought myself a soldier," she said at last, dropping her head. "A soldier does what must be done."

"You betrayed me."

"I believed a soldier should not mix love and war. Forgive me."

But whether he would forgive her or not, Claire was not to know, for at that moment Arturo leapt into the fray, brandishing his sword. "Unhand him or be prepared to fight!"

Hopeless—one man against a vicious crowd. Claire knew it and Arturo would know it also, but he would die defending the governor or his life would not be worth living.

When the rabble descended on him, whacking viciously, tearing the sword from his hand and trampling the soldier to the ground with their boots, she could not bear to watch. Shoved away by men eager to participate in the kill, Claire stumbled backward, losing sight of Antonio in the press of bodies.

The air reeked with the stench of blood, smoke, and fury. Hate blazed in the faces of the men surging forward. Claire wailed in misery, her cries sounding like howls to her own ears. Nobody heard, nobody cared.

Someone clutched her arm. "Claire, come! I find safe place!"

She turned, finding Odette pulling her away. "I hide you."

"No." She tore her arm from the girl's grip. "They will kill Antonio. If he dies, I die."

"They will kill you, too," the girl said, pitching her voice over the mob. "Come. My people over there, they help. Come, hide!"

But Claire refused to leave even though the crowd shoved her farther away until she could see neither poor Arturo, her gallant protector, nor Antonio. Antonio! Everything and everybody she loved was lost.

Odette screamed into her ear. "They come for you next! You must hide!"

Claire wrenched her arm away. "Save him, not me. I am nothing!"

Odette stared at her. "You are mad!"

"Perhaps, but save him, Odette. Do it for me, if you can. He is innocent of all the crimes against him. I am not!"

And then the girl dove into the crowd and disappeared. Claire backed farther away as the heated press of bodies pushed toward the knot of men holding Antonio.

She stumbled backward until the rough trunk of a huge oak barred her progress. Bottles and swill jars littered the exposed roots beneath her feet. Rumpled clothes lay strewn and tangled everywhere as if some woman had met a gruesome end—rape or murder or both.

She sunk into a crouch onto the heap of skirts and petticoat. A fine place to die, then. Let them find her here.

The voice inside her head screamed, *Claire, no. Get away from here! Antonio will live and so must you!*

Claire laughed bitterly. "Be gone, you. I am doomed. Let me be."

Her back pressed against the tree half-shrouded in shadows, she did not at first discern the subtle shift in the crowd before her.

She stared with unseeing eyes as dark faces dressed in white clothing encircled the masses of angry French. They remained silent at first while the far-off drumming intensified like the thud of some massive beating heart.

The slaves encompassed the French, thickening to ten or twelve people deep. Then the chanting began, a wild howling that swerved in volume to meet the drums until all fused into a deep, powerful chant of spirit meeting magic.

The slaves on the outer edge of the circle began dancing, arms swaying overhead, casting strange elongated shadows across the trees. Someone screamed.

A man called out in alarm. Frightened, the French turned to face the frenzied dancers, calling to one another to attack but they did not seem to know how. One raised a stick to beat at the dancers but saw something in their faces that terrified him. He dropped the stick and ran, pushing through the ring, and dashing off into the night.

Squeezing her eyes shut, Claire quickly opened them to confirm the swell of slave men barreling their way into the throng to wrestle Antonio free. Pandemonium exploded. Two bonfires ignited at once, hurling oiling plumes of smoke and sparks far into the night sky. Women screamed; men yelled. An animal howled as if being slaughtered.

Power coursed through the clearing. Whatever had been unleashed dissolved the crowd into splinters of terrified people hurling away from the Congo Plains, mad with fear.

Claire remained riveted to the spot. Unable to see through the smoke, she could only hear the crying, feel the crowd disperse, yet one voice rose above it all, a voice that brought such a crazy jolt of joy into her heart she almost cried aloud:

"*Sacre bleu*, but the governor escaped! Those slaves have taken him away!" Campeneau had lost his quarry.

Relief trembled through Claire. She laughed, she cried, she hugged herself in blessed thanks. Odette and the slaves saved Antonio! Clutching the rough bark for support, she climbed unsteadily to her feet and stood trembling, gazing out into the clearing.

"Odette, thank you!" she called out with her heart.

34

Dawn clawed streaks of orange light into the sky, sending blue-black shadows scuttling for the undergrowth. The bonfires burned low, spewing coiling wisps of smoke. Most of the crowd had gone, leaving a grim and muddied clearing where bodies lay twisted in a shamble of violence and destruction.

Claire stumbled forward, half-numb with anguish and some strange distorted joy. Antonio lived. Nothing else mattered. Weaving around fallen men, she tried not to look too closely at the bloodied bodies until she reached the trampled spot where Antonio once stood. Above her head, the Spanish soldier swayed in the wind while at her feet another sprawled, beaten beyond recognition.

"Arturo," she whispered, crouching and gazing at his battered face. "I am so sorry. You were the true soldier, not me. With all my heart, I thank you. Rest in peace."

"There she is! There's the scheming Spanish wench!"

Claire spun around. A handful of men trudged through the clearing, one stooping long enough to loot a fallen comrade as the other four lumbered toward her.

She would not plead for her life by claiming French heritage. What did it matter? She belonged to no country now. But to die at their hands without a fight? Let them work for that satisfaction. Picking up her skirts, she ran.

But exhaustion made running impossible. She broke into a stumbling trot. Which way to go? With no home, no friends, no family, all she could do was force her feet to move somewhere, hauling her numbed heart along for the ride.

The men still dogged her, jeering and hurling insults when they weren't busy pawing through heaps of charred remains or looting a corpse by the road.

Claire snorted in grim mirth. So they'd rather loot than rape her, eh? *Mon Dieu*, how she had lessened in importance. But they had not finished with her yet, she knew. Why rush when your quarry can barely hold herself upright? No, they were content to follow until her legs gave out.

Which would be soon.

Dawn continued to drag the sun higher into the bloodshot sky as if the orb had no will to bring in the day. Hazy amber light born of smoldering fires poured into the town like poison, thick and bitter, the best the sun could do.

This ragged town could be her village long ago; her family torn asunder, her parents dead. British soldiers led that travesty with more discipline but with equal heartlessness.

A man lay facedown in the road with his bloodied nightshirt half-torn from his body. The door of his house wide open as people carried out chairs, trunks, and silver plate, stepping over his corpse like so much rubbish. A baby cried from somewhere upstairs, probably wailing beside its dead mother.

Was life all one long wail of despair?

French soldiers marched past Claire, muskets in hand, boots crunching on the road, but they paid no mind to the looters or to her. Where they headed, she neither knew nor cared.

Why should they bother with another despairing woman rambling dazed down the streets of New Orleans when hundreds like her sprawled drunk in the doorways or slept where they'd fallen?

She stumbled, sagging to her knees only to struggle to her feet again.

The men still trailed behind her, only two remaining now. The others must have found new victims or richer plunder. Make the last two hounds walk with her to the end, then.

She pitched herself forward, quickening her step for another ten paces before tripping again. For an instant she lay facedown in the mire, thinking how easy it would be to just remain there. No more struggle, no more fight. But no. Up on her feet again, she stumbled on.

Not for her the convent life, nor would she ever offer herself to Madame Letourneau's employ. Claire sealed her fate long ago and, before the day was done, she would die. Her heart strangled long ago so why not her body?

She had once dreamed of another life but Claire had chosen a different path with a different end. The only question remaining was where to die. Not here in these mean streets, surely?

The decision swept down upon her like a bright promise. True, she'd need every dram of what strength remained to get there, yet once the destination fixed in her heart, she fortified her resolve.

Her pursuers called out. "Hey, wench! Why such a pace? Come back, we mean you no harm."

"No," hooted the other. "Pierre and I, we give you good time, yes? Come share our wine."

Claire broke into a half-stumbling run, pitching herself down the street in a desperate hurl. Only two more house-lengths before she reached her sanctuary. Footsteps pounded the ground at her back, determined now to catch their prey.

Like all good citizens, Monsieur LeBlanc's house sat shuttered against the violent night. Boards had been nailed across the door with more barricading the lower windows in case the shutters could not hold.

Signs of violent intrusion were strewn in broken boards about the yard, the upended carriage in the streets. Monsieur's home had been looted and she could not bear to think what became of the family.

She had strength only to stumble toward the stone yard, whose gates, thank God, yawned open.

"Celestin? Celestin Picot?" she called out, hoping against hope to see the angel maker's face one more time.

The freeman did not respond and for a terrible instant Claire feared he may be harmed. But no, she realized, the yard lay empty but for the sculptures, each of which remained untouched. Surely he'd be safe with Odette somewhere.

She stepped into the world of stone angels. Dawn gilded the marble wings in a wash of old gold as Claire stepped into the sanctum, as close to heaven as she would ever come.

Her angel awaited solitary as always in the center of the yard, a beautiful creature perched high on a pedestal, white wings folded at rest with Claire's own face staring off into the distance, her expression profoundly sad and watchful.

"Oh, Celestin!" Claire said aloud. "Why have you bequeathed such ever-lasting sorrow to my face?" But how fitting to be frozen forever with such a burden.

Footsteps pounded into the yard. "Come here, *chérie*! Let Jacques and Pierre give to you what a wench really wants, eh? Do not hide. We know you are here!"

Pulling off her shoes, Claire climbed up the stone pedestal, positioning herself so that she crouched awkwardly beside her angel, balancing on her toes. With one arm flung around the creature's shoulders and the other gripping the edge of her wing, Claire waited, embracing her angel as if clinging to eternity.

Inside her head, the inner voice spoke softly now.

It is all right, mon amie. It will be all over soon. You are forgiven by me and I am you.

Claire turned her head in the direction of her angel's gaze, fixing her expression in the same profound watchfulness. Together they waited, identical angels, one flesh and one stone.

The two men loped into the yard. "*Mon Dieu*," one muttered, crossing himself, "but look how she clings to the angel who shares her face."

"*Oui*," one said at last, his voice deceptively gentle as he stepped forward. "Come down, *chérie*, or we must drag you down, no?"

But she did not move, the girl, like the angel, stone still.

"Ah, *mon Dieu*, do not make us do this thing. Make it easy for yourself."

But the girl did not see to hear or even turn her head in his direction.

"Ah, *sacre bleu*," he cursed under his breath. "Jacques, the knife. Let us do this in the name of France and be done. We will be merciful and quick."

Claire clung fiercely to her angel.

I will be with you in the end, the voice said inside her heart. *You will never be alone.*

"Consider me gone," Claire whispered as a hand clutched her leg.

35

Romy drifted untethered in a murky place as deep and profound as a bottomless sea. Sharing Claire's last moments—the torment, the pain and anguish—had been far worse than she could ever have imagined.

Together they had screamed and sobbed, raging against the brutality of life, the terror of death. Finally, one man had enough pity to slit Claire's throat, after which they slipped into this deep peace.

Romy enveloped Claire's spirit in love, holding her wounded soul together like filaments of shredded mist. They were one yet not whole, fractured pieces of the same being. One could not find peace without the other.

Claire, she spoke with her heart for they were far beyond words now. *Love is all that matters. Not death, not pain, not myriad slights, real or imagined, that burdens the soul inside a living body. Forget everything but love. Don't relive anything, let it all go. Become one with me. I love you, I understand you, and we have many lives to travel together. Don't let me go on wounded.*

But Claire did not respond. And Romy would not let go.

Could she return to life? Romy wondered. Was that even an option? This strange in-between state had no physical pain yet still stirred with torment and confusion.

Would they float like this forever? Where was she, anyway, in some kind of comatose limbo? Or had her body died with Claire so that she, too, was dead? All she knew was that she had been locked inside Claire's life right up until the moment of her death and then...this nothingness.

Now that she floated in this bodiless state, a deep sense of knowing occurred to her with a strange clarity as if life had been a distraction all along. That made sense.

The Claire part of her soul had frozen in shock and agony, and now limply floated in this limbo protected only by some essence of her. They were somehow one yet separated. If she let go, Claire would drift someplace deeper, darker, or worse, and remain there forever, leaving Romy to float incomplete.

She couldn't let that happen.

Was this it, then, floating in this womb of nothingness for infinity?

Time had no meaning here but gradually Romy began to feel and hear, though not with eyes and ears. Currents buffeted them as they floated, some darker than dark and doused in horrible cold, while others slipped by in light-suffused warmth.

Romy embraced one lovely, bright current wanting to remain enveloped there forever. *No,* Romy told her gently, *you do not belong here yet. You must go back.* But Romy didn't know how to find back and sensed she'd need to release Claire in order to find it, which she'd never do.

Once, a rigid black shadow whipped beneath them like a soul-shark, tugging and clawing as if to separate Romy from Claire. *No!* Romy sent forth her heart-cry. *Go!* But the thing would not let them be.

Romy struggled to hold on to Claire while focusing every part of her being in imagining a bright white light brimming in prism shards to push the entity away.

Goodness is light. We don't belong to you, Darkness! she cried. And with that, it released them. Gone.

Well, that felt powerful. How did she even know how to do that? Maybe she wasn't as helpless as she thought? And, if she wasn't helpless, she couldn't be hopeless, either.

And then she saw a light far above as if viewing the surface of the ocean from many leagues below. She heard voices calling her. Aunt Loo, Joquita, Adrian, all calling her.

Adrian. Her body must still live, she realized with a jolt. She missed everybody so much! How hard would it be to get up there? She must go back but how?

She tried kicking until she realized she had no legs. Instead, she needed to propel herself forward with her intent, her need and desire, the way she'd bested the soul-shark.

With tremendous effort and imagination, she finally began to float upward, drifting toward the light, using her will as the engine, keeping Claire with her all the way.

The world became lighter and warmer as she neared the surface. Oh my God! She could hear them, almost see their faces, through that translucent surface. Like glass, she thought.

"Romy, can you hear me?" Adrian's voice. "Come back, please."

She tried to speak but couldn't and she couldn't see anything more than indistinct blurs. She may as well be wrapped in cellophane.

"Louisa, we must get her to the hospital immediately. She's been under too long." A voice she didn't recognize.

"No," Aunt Loo said. "If we move her, we take her away from everyone she's connected to and that could lose her for sure. We can't risk it."

"I'm advising you as a physician that you could lose her regardless. A coma isn't something to play with."

"You don't understand what's happening here, Richard. This is no ordinary coma. She has to find her own way home, and moving her body far from this spot and us won't help. Help me get her into the shade."

"You hear that, everyone?" Adrian's voice. "Romy stays, we stay. Veronica, get back here and wait with the rest of us and, Detective Brown, don't you dare leave. If there's one thing I've learned through all this it's that there's more than one kind of law in this universe."

Romy wanted to laugh and cry all at once. Adrian, she knew he was special—her soul mate all along—and her incredible friend, Joquita, was the same soul who'd watched her back through time! She sent a fervent thank-you for true souls everywhere, for all those that bonded across time and place.

And then suddenly she stilled as she felt Claire stirring inside her.

Antonio?

Claire, listen, they are all up there waiting for us. Odette, Sister Marie, and Antonio. They are with us still.

Antonio?

Antonio is Adrian in this lifetime, Claire. He waits for us up there. He forgives you—us.

The voices continued, Aunt Loo holding court. "All of you, you saw what happened here tonight. It all played out and every one of us had a part. Don't you go shaking your head, Veronica. This isn't live theater. This is simply a reality you have yet to understand. Open your mind."

"Ms. Dupré, I'm not being disrespectful. This was all fascinating and I'm delighted to have witnessed it. Hypnotism, right? Very impressive, but I have a little girl here and should return to the hotel."

"Susie's had a good night sleep and is in the kitchen devouring pancakes. Why not join her? You could stand to gain a few pounds," Aunt Loo said.

Men spoke off to one side, perhaps out of earshot of Aunt Loo, yet Romy caught every word.

"Hell, man. Do you expect me to believe I murdered someone because I was a Spanish soldier in 1768?" Lucas's voice choked with disbelief.

"No, frankly, I don't expect you to believe that any more than I expect to believe I was some damn stonemason carving funerary monuments back in 1700-something!" Detective Brown's usually honeyed drawl strangled with emotion. "I only know what I saw and felt, damn it, and what I apparently did in this garden last night. Louisa has us on video, remember? Do you think I could believe what I saw myself doing and saying otherwise?"

"Nor I, believe me." That was Adrian. "But trust me when I say that I now realize that I was Governor Antonio de Ulloa and that I loved—love —that woman lying there."

"Well, Professor, admit it's hard to swallow," Detective Brown muttered.

"But am I going to stand trial for murder?" Lucas again. "It was that soldier who killed that tourist, not me!"

"Calm down, man. You will not be convicted, I guarantee that." Brown's voice. "We'll get this dropped before it ever makes it to trial. You intervened to save a woman's life against a drunken predator. You'll be viewed as more hero than offender. That he died was more accident than anything else. I probably shouldn't say this but the coroner's report states that the man had some kind of cardiac event during the attack. The knife missed his heart but his heart got him, anyway. Bernardo was doomed one way or the other. Besides, he would have killed her if you hadn't intervened."

"Excuse me, guys," Joquita interrupted. "I hate to break this up but Aunt Loo wishes to inform you that breakfast is served in the dining room. Food for the soul, so to speak. Lucas, why don't you go on in and feed yours?"

"I'll go with you," said Detective Brown.

"No, wait. I'd like to speak with you alone, Detective," Joquita said. "Just step over here with me for a moment. I promise not to frisk you for concealed weapons."

"I don't think that's such a good idea, Joquita, even if you don't make a grab for my gun."

"And why's that?"

"You know why. Being alone with you has never been a good idea."

"Look, Telly, you've got to see how all this plays out—you, me, in the space-time continuum stuff. I've always, you know, felt something for you. Oh, hell, I've felt lots of things for you—strongly, I mean. I was just confused, soul-boggled, see? I kept reliving the battered slave role, mad as hell, and I couldn't let myself love."

"Don't go there, Jo. It was over between you and me a long time ago."

"That's just it, it wasn't. It will never be over between you and me, Telly. You know it, I know it. I understand that now the way I never have before and you must, too. You heard Aunt Loo say how some souls reconnect with one another over and over again for many lifetimes but not always in the same physical circumstance? Sometimes we come back as mother and son, or sister and brother, or...father and daughter."

"Stop." His voice softer now but no less gruff. "I got enough on my plate to analyze without grappling with the possibility of having made out with my former daughter from another life."

"Just for the record, Detective, you ain't my daddy now and I swear I've never had one paternal feeling for you in this lifetime. All my thoughts for you have been strictly of the carnal kind but my heart really lives in a higher place. I'm just ready to call it home now. Give me a second chance and, I swear, I'll be yours alone."

And then Romy heard, felt, knew, that her friend had just stood on her tiptoes to bring that tall, lean man's head down to kiss and that he wasn't fighting it.

And with a soaring sweep, Romy rose through the barrier into her world, overwhelmed with fluttering joy to be sailing into sunshine witnessing their love. Only, she instantly smacked into the shocked realization that only her soul had broken through, her body remained elsewhere.

Below, Joquita and Telly stood locked in a kiss so deep it looked like time itself couldn't pry them apart, while, all around, the garden bloomed gold in the rising sun.

Voices floated to her from inside the mansion, sounds Romy followed through to the dining room where she hovered in panic, gazing down at Lucas, Veronica, and little Susie as they scooped food onto their plates and made awkward conversation. No Adrian, no Aunt Loo, no her. Was she a...ghost?

Claire stirred in confusion. *That makes two of us confused,* Romy told her soul. She had to find her body now. And Adrian.

Back into the garden she sailed, spinning in frenzy, thinking that maybe this is how hauntings happen: a bewildered spirit chasing a lost life in this strange, disembodied world.

Stop, think! A soul can find its body, surely? Romy tried to settle, to regain that deeper hearing and sight she'd experienced in the limbo zone. *Better. Easy, take it easy. Just breathe,* she reminded herself before realizing she couldn't, tried to laugh, couldn't do that, either, but managed to steady herself, anyway, calming down into an even sense of awareness. Only then did she feel something tugging as though an invisible cord urged her away from the courtyard.

Relaxing into the flow, she floated through the palms—right through the fronds, past the koi pond, through a stone pillar, into the Katrina garden, and deep into the meditation room hushed in flowers and birdlife. There, at last, she found three people sitting beside a pale young woman stretched out on a stone bench framed in jasmine branches.

"Listen, her pulse is weakening. You must get her to the hospital now." Dr. Wilkins held the limp woman's wrist and glared sternly at Adrian, who sat cradling Romy's head in his lap. "If we wait too long it will be too late." The doctor got to his feet. "I'm calling an ambulance." He tapped his phone and made an urgent call, firing off details into the phone

"No, don't!" Aunt Loo said. "If her body leaves this spot, the cord will be broken."

"What cord, damn it! The girl is dying!" the doctor exclaimed.

"No, she isn't. I won't let her. Put the phone away," Adrian ordered. "In this, Louisa is the expert, not us."

"You called me here for my medical advice and I'm giving it, Adrian," Dr. Wilkins insisted. "Minutes longer may kill her."

Romy hovered over her body, stricken by the sight of that pale young woman in torn finery. Her bare feet peeked out from under the light sheet they'd thrown over her. The rose in her cheeks had flown and a blue bruised her lips as if she'd been kissed by death. Yet the man who gently held her head did so with such love it was as if that force alone would bring her to.

She was dying!

Tears rolled down Aunt Loo's cheeks. She had never seen her cry before. "Do what you must, Richard. By the time the ambulance comes, it will be too late, anyway. Only Romy can save herself."

Save herself? She was vapor. How could she save herself? And why couldn't she go home since home lay stretched out on that marble slab below? Stretched out like a…corpse…in a morgue. Her panic twisted her in despair. Why couldn't she reconnect, just slip down into her corporeal self? She couldn't really be dying!

And Claire seemed to be evaporating. Up here in the almost-world, Claire grew wispier while Romy lay dying, dying! How could this be? Everything, everything, leeching away!

Adrian leaned forward, his lips nearly touching Romy's cheek. "I found her, Romy," he said breathless, "not in the St. Louis Cemetery as I first thought, not in any cemetery but—" he halted as if choked with emotion "—but I found her still—your stone angel wearing your face. Dear Romy, come back to me. Now that we've found one another, let's heal our souls in this timeline."

Romy swirled and dove and twisted and sailed around him, so needing to touch him, so craving to be in her own body so she could feel him touching her. To be this close and feel nothing! To know he could only see her dormant shell not her, that every sense that mattered stayed trapped except her heart, her real heart, the one that loved.

Adrian, I'm here, I'm here!

"She's stopped breathing. Stand back," the doctor announced, "I'm administering CPR."

"Come on, Romy, child. You can return to us and you must!" Aunt Loo said.

An ambulance screeched from somewhere down the street. Joquita ran into the clearing. "Holy shit, what's wrong? She's not dying, is she? She can't die! You hear me, Rom, don't you dare leave me!" Then she bent over at her waist wailing and clutching her stomach while Thelonious Brown braced her shoulders from behind.

"Goddamn it, Romy," Adrian choked. "Get back here. You were right about everything! You have a thesis to finish and a life to live and a man to love right here waiting!"

Suddenly Adrian turned his gaze toward the sky and spoke in French: "And I love you, too, Claire! I am Antonio, do you hear me? I am Antonio de Ulloa and God knows how many lifetimes we've loved each other and never been together. Now we must. This is our chance. I know nothing about the universe, absolutely nothing, but I know I love you, and I don't want to go through another lifetime without you by my side."

Claire stirred, a wisp becoming a breeze flowing around Romy's spirit in fluttering joy. *Antonio?*

The doctor pushed down on Romy's chest before tilting her neck back to open her breathing passages.

"Step aside, Wilkins," Adrian commanded. "Do you think she needs your lips on her at a time like this?"

He pushed Dr. Wilkins aside and pressed his lips to Romy's. Then it was his breath flowing into her lungs, her breathing deeply in as a flurry of jasmine petals rained down on their heads.

The scene flashed in Romy's spirit-self for only an instant before a prism-lit vortex spun her down into darkness, pain, love, tears, and straight into everything worth living for.

36

Everything streamed into Romy in a dizzying vortex of love mingled with the trauma of a life lost and regained. She awoke reborn, whole and alive, yet reeling with vivid images of all that she'd been and seen. Her body ached, the very act of breathing now a conscious effort.

She sat up on the bench, soaking in every sight and sound—the birds, the wind, the color, the light. Adrian sat beside her, one arm over her shoulders, gazing at her with such intense emotion that her heart swelled. She smiled deeply into his eyes before turning to each of her companions, one by one.

On her other side, Aunt Loo held her hand while Jo crouched in front of her, sobbing and laughing simultaneously. Dr. Wilkins stood several feet back, looking perplexed, while Detective Thelonious Brown stood, hands plunged in his pockets, shaking his head with his lips tugged into a wry smile. Lucas stood beside him, gazing at her in total wonder. The world around Romy sang with birdsong and heightened color, everything brilliantly alive and limned with light.

At first, everyone seemed too amazed and overwhelmed to speak. Romy gazed back at them and smiled. "Thank you for calling me home, my friends. And for loving me. I've never appreciated caring as much as I do now. For a few seconds, or however time is measured wherever we were, Claire and I almost didn't return," she said.

Then the comments and exclamations erupted.

"Oh my God, I thought never you'd come back! You were all over this garden being Claire and you had us worried shitless!"

"Joquita." Aunt Loo smiled wearily. "What my beloved niece is trying to say with her usual eloquence, my dear, is that we were very worried. You had much help last night, not all of it from the living. Adrian and I were running out of ideas to bring you back. Finally, he had the brainstorm to find your angel."

"I know," Romy said quietly.

"Were you watching it all? Did you see how we all played out parts of our past lives right here in the garden?" Joquita asked with a little laugh. "Telly was so powerful defending you as Celestin Picot. You should have seen him staving away the throng for the right to use his stone angel as your grave marker. I mean Claire's grave marker," she caught herself, looking briefly stricken. "I meant Claire's," she repeated.

Romy gently released the arms and hands that held her, and leaned over to envelope Jo in a big hug. "Thank you, my friend. Thank you from us all."

"All?" Jo asked, her face buried in Romy's neck.

"Antonio, Claire, and me."

Then, releasing Jo, Romy got to her feet. Adrian helped steady her as she took tentative steps toward Thelonious Brown. "Celestin, thank you. You were a man with such spirit you cut through all the noise right to the truth of both human and stone. You are the same person still, whether you know it or not."

Telly pulled his hands from his pockets as if to protest but Romy caught them in her own and squeezed tight, gazing into his eyes. "Our true spirits can be awakened in each of our lives to enact the people we truly are. You may not be an artist in this lifetime but you'll defend those who need you most just as Celestin did."

She turned next to Lucas and threw her arms around him. "Oh, my dear Arturo, thank you, thank you, thank you. You are so amazing! You were then and you are now. You saved my life many, many times, and I swear you won't suffer in this lifetime for it."

Lucas squeezed her back. "I'm honored—confused as hell, but honored."

And then Romy returned to Aunt Loo, who stood up as she approached. The two embraced in a hug as deep and tight as love itself. "And you, my dear Mother Marie, you know more than anyone how being human is about making mistakes, inevitably and often. We can't help ourselves, though we try so hard. We crave to be angels but first we must deal with being flesh and blood. That's why we must forgive over and over again so we don't end up wallowing in poison. Claire forgives you."

Aunt Loo nodded, dabbing her eyes with the corner of one floaty sleeve. "I know, my dear. I can see that shining all around you."

Romy turned to the man by her side. "And, Antonio, it wasn't our time back then but it is now as Romy and Adrian. You know that, don't you, my love?"

And Adrian smiled, framing her face in his hands. "I know that and, now that I've found you, I'm never letting you go, should all the scud missiles of academia come raining down on my head." And he leaned over to whisper in her ear in archaic Spanish, rolling his *r*'s seductively. "Once we're alone, we'll relive that first night Antonio and Claire shared together, rolling around the floor in his office. I recall every detail."

Romy laughed. "And will you perform all this rolling while the god Ulla looks on?"

"And why not? What are fertility gods for?"

"I have one request," Romy said, touching one finger to his lips, suddenly serious. "Take me to see her today, now. I know you found her and thank you for that."

"Whatever you want, my love. Louisa and I thought taking you there would deliver you and it turns out Thelonious knew the place—always knew it. We'll take you now."

"Bravo!" The sound of clapping interrupted as Veronica strode into the garden. "So, the curtain falls at last. And, Romy, what a big surprise. You've risen from the dead."

"Oh, Veronica, shut up before I do something I might regret." Joquita glanced up while busy tracing Telly's lifeline with her fingernail.

"Jo, that's okay." Romy left Adrian's side and stepped over to Veronica.

"And were you the only one not to have encountered your past life in this garden last night?"

"Oh, she encountered it, all right. She just chooses not to believe or even look at my videos," Aunt Loo explained, standing up again and shaking the wrinkles loose from her robe.

"All this drama is a little rich for me, that's all. I prefer lighter fare." Veronica smiled, turning to Adrian. "I just can't believe you're falling for this stuff."

Adrian grinned. "I'm not falling for anything, Veronica. I've simply allowed myself to think and feel with an organ other than my brain. You could try that yourself."

"You were Madame Letourneau, a courtesan in the court of France who later relocated to New Orleans," Romy told her. "You offered Claire an education in how to seduce a man—a very good one, I might add. Seduction remains your specialty."

Veronica held up her hand. "Oh, please. Enough. I've just come to say that I'm leaving now. Adrian, will you drive me back to the hotel?"

Romy touched Veronica's arm. "Listen. Your soul will play out these inclinations again and again, damaging your relationships with men, maybe irrevocably. You can change all that if you just try."

Veronica locked eyes with Romy. "Listen to you? What are you, a counselor now? My soul is my business."

"We can't win them all," Aunt Loo remarked. "Some just have to go their own way, no matter what."

Veronica rolled her eyes and pulled away, calling out: "Susie, over here. Hurry, sweetheart. We're leaving."

Susie. Romy brushed past Veronica into the path to watch the bright blond curls bopping up and down through the ferns like a tangle of living sunshine.

As the little girl broke through the tall grass into the clearing, Romy went to meet her. The child paused briefly to watch a dragonfly catching emerald light on its wings before hopping along toward the adults. Catching sight of Romy, she stopped. "Angel Lady? You okay?"

Romy crouched, holding her arms wide. "I'm fine and, Susie, you were right all along: I can fly."

The little girl ran into her arms laughing. "Cool! Show me!"

Romy laughed and hugged her. "Some kinds of flight are invisible. Come." They walked back into the meditation garden together, hand in hand.

Aunt Loo watched them approach. "Romy, tell me how this child plays out in all this. That's one thing I couldn't figure out. Who was she?"

Romy released Susie's hand, fighting pangs of remorse as the child ran to her mother. "Claire was pregnant the night she died."

EPILOGUE

Joquita, Thelonious, Adrian, Louisa, and Romy stood together on the sidewalk before a blue two-story cottage on Decatur Street. The sun hung midsky, blanketing the city in thick, humid heat.

"The original burned down in 1876 and this house was constructed in its place. It managed to survive the hurricanes admirably well," Adrian commented, squeezing Romy's hand.

She looked up at him and smiled, thinking that the moment had come at last.

"They couldn't explain why the funerary angel remained when no other statuary existed on the property but she's always been there apparently," he continued. "However, the history of the land indicates that a stone yard once stood on this spot in 1759."

Thelonious cleared his throat. "Celestin beseeched his employer to let the angel stay where he created her and to bury young Claire on that very spot. His former master was a kind man and agreed."

"Dear Monsieur LeBlanc. He survived?" Romy asked.

"He hid his family in a false wall and survived the uprising."

"Still, it doesn't look anything like what I remembered. Everything's changed. Telly, how did you ever find it?" Romy asked.

The detective stood linking Louisa's hand on one arm and Joquita's the other. "Don't be asking me that now. I just know. My mind's become a jumble of mixed memories since last night. Some moments I'm not even sure whose skin I'm in but I always knew about this house."

"Don't worry, Telly," Aunt Loo told him. "This will pass and soon enough all your past life memories will fade until they feel more like a dream."

"Good news, Aunt Loo, good news. I must admit, I look forward to dealing with this life's memories alone." And he gazed at Jo.

"In the meantime, just remember you're not my daddy now," Jo said with a sly smile.

"We'll see about that." Thelonious grinned back. "Now, let's get this done. I have a job to get back to. Adrian, did you call ahead?"

"I did. The owner has left his gate open and just asked that we pull it shut when we leave."

"Are you sure you want to do this, Rom?" Jo asked. "Are you sure seeing that statue won't send you hurling back into Claire?"

"Jo." Romy turned to her. "Claire is safe now. She's with me. We're one. There's no her and me anymore."

"Really?" Jo said in wonder. "You've assimilated her, then?"

"In a way."

"Do you feel differently? I mean, besides living somebody else's life in another century, dying their death, and then coming back to this century, which is all pretty mundane stuff. May as well watch TV for the same effect."

Romy laughed, shielding her eyes against the sun with one hand. "I do, I feel very differently but still very much myself. You might say I feel very pulled together."

"Look, ladies, as fascinating as this is, can we move along?" Thelonious urged. "Your aunt is getting fried out here and daddy here has work to do."

"Yes, let's go," Romy agreed, heading up the walkway. In truth, she wasn't sure how ready she was to see her stone angel after all these centuries when the true face remained so vivid in her mind. But she had to do this and do it now.

The garden opened up around them in neatly trimmed hedges marching around a close-clipped lawn with a classic fountain tinkling in its center. Pots of topiary roses marched like pink sentries along the flagstone path.

Romy knew then exactly where Claire's remains lay as if the garden had superimposed on top of a mason's yard long ago. Dropping Adrian's hand she slipped past the others and ran along the path into the shade garden beyond.

There on her pedestal surrounded by lush undergrowth, her stone angel perched, face time-worn, moss greening her wings and coating her pedestal, but still absolutely her.

Romy stifled a sob, born more from joy than sorrow, and reached up to touch the angel's feet. "We're home now, Claire, and we'll never be alone again."

JOIN MY NEWSLETTER

Join my newsletter on my web page at janethornley.com to stay up to date on all the creative things I get up to as well as my latest books.

ABOUT THE AUTHOR

JANE THORNLEY is an author of mystery and suspense. Though both a writer and a designer, Jane has lived many lives including teacher, school principal, superintendent of schools, travel host, ghost-watcher, and librarian. Today she loves nothing better than to travel the world seeking exotic settings and researching art and history.

Otherwise, Jane lives a very dull life in Nova Scotia, Canada, but luckily her imagination makes up for it.

This is the first book in JANE's *Time Shadows Series* and book 2, *The Spirit in the Fold*, will arrive in early 2021.

AFTERWORD

Like many works of fiction, this novel names real historical personages but takes creative license with many of the individuals that bring the story alive. The uprising described did occur and Antonio de Ulloa was the first Spanish governor of Louisiana until ousted by the French Creoles in 1768. He was by all accounts an amazing explorer and scientist and is cited for the discovery of platinum. Odette and Claire, on the other hand, plus many others are entirely from my imagination.

And yet, perhaps the struggles of these ordinary folk may be the truest tales of all…it's just that no one hears them.

As for reincarnation, no matter what you believe, it's always interesting to ponder the possibilities.

ALSO BY JANE THORNLEY

Crime by Design Series:
Crime by Design Boxed Set Books 1-3
Crime by Design Book 1: *Rogue Wave*
Crime by Design Book 2: *Warp in the Weave*
Crime by Design Book 3: *Beautiful Survivor*
Crime by Design Book 4: *The Greater of Two Evils*
Crime by Design Book 5: *The Plunge*

None of the Above Series:
None of the Above Book 1: *Downside Up*
None of the Above Book 2: *DownPlay*—COMING SOON

The Agency of the Ancient Lost and Found Series:
The Agency of the Ancient Lost and Found Book 1: *The Carpet Cipher*

Made in the USA
Coppell, TX
15 September 2023